# IANTHE
## LET H

Ianthe Jerrold was born in 1898, the daughter of the well-known author and journalist Walter Jerrold, and granddaughter of the Victorian playwright Douglas Jerrold. She was the eldest of five sisters.

She published her first book, a work of verse, at the age of fifteen. This was the start of a long and prolific writing career characterized by numerous stylistic shifts. In 1929 she published the first of two classic and influential whodunits. *The Studio Crime* gained her immediate acceptance into the recently formed but highly prestigious Detection Club, and was followed a year later by *Dead Man's Quarry*.

Ianthe Jerrold subsequently moved on from pure whodunits to write novels ranging from romantic fiction to psychological thrillers. She continued writing and publishing her fiction into the 1970's. She died in 1977, twelve years after her husband George Menges. Their Elizabethan farmhouse Cwmmau was left to the National Trust.

## Also by Ianthe Jerrold

The Studio Crime

Dead Man's Quarry

There May Be Danger

# IANTHE JERROLD

# LET HIM LIE

With an introduction
by Curtis Evans

DEAN STREET PRESS

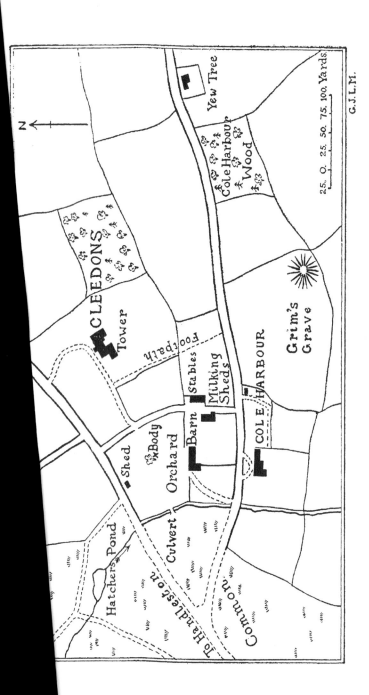

INTRODUCTION

A full decade after the publication of Ianthe Jerrold's *The Studio Crime* (1929) and *Dead Man's Quarry* (1930), both of which titles have been republished by Dean Street Press, another Jerrold detective novel, penned by the author under the pseudonym "Geraldine Bridgman," finally appeared in print. *Let Him Lie*, Jerrold's evocatively titled third detective novel, was issued in 1940 by William Heinemann, the prestigious English publisher of both Margery Allingham's critically applauded mystery novels and John Dickson Carr's ingenious Sir Henry Merrivale detective series (the latter published under Carr's "Carter Dickson" pseudonym). During the ten-year interval between the publication of *Dead Man's Quarry* and *Let Him Lie*, Ianthe Jerrold had produced five mainstream novels; and presumably her adoption for her new mystery of the Geraldine Bridgman pen name--a transposition of the middle and last parts of her full name, Ianthe Bridgman Jerrold--was a move on her part to distinguish her more "serious" writing from any future fictional mystery mongering that she might perform.

John Christmas, Jerrold's brilliant amateur sleuth in *The Studio Crime* and *Dead Man's Quarry*, is nowhere to be found in *Let Him Lie*, his place having been taken by a young woman whom the author likely never viewed as a potential series character. The decade of the 1930s increasingly saw a movement in mystery fiction away from the improbable Great Detective figure of romance to more naturalistic depictions of characters impacted by crime, in the style of the realistic mainstream novel. Saddled in their mysteries with the popular Golden Age investigators Hercule Poirot, Lord Peter Wimsey, Albert Campion and Roderick Alleyn, the British Crime Queens Agatha Christie, Dorothy L. Sayers, Margery Allingham and Ngaio Marsh never could bring themselves to banish the figure of the male Great Detective from their books (though after the Second World War Margery Allingham came close with Campion and Christie would write fewer books about Poirot). However, by 1940 Ianthe Jerrold obviously felt sufficiently empowered with her new detective novel to send John Christmas, already inactive for ten years, to the sleuthing sidelines. While readers of *The Studio Crime* and *Dead Man's Quarry* may miss Christmas, they nevertheless should derive much enjoyment from *Let Him Lie*, a superb vintage English country mystery.

In *Let Him Lie* the amateur detective figure is not some colorful and eccentric investigative genius but rather a young former art student named Jeanie Halliday, recently settled "in proud and lonely independence" at Yew Tree Cottage, the rustic Gloucestershire residence she purchased from her idolized ex-schoolmistress, Agnes Molyneux (formerly Agnes Drake) and her new husband, Robert Molyneux, owners of Cleedons, "that most comfortable of small Elizabethan manor-houses tacked on to the remains of a medieval castle." Currently Jeanie Halliday is disturbed not merely by the round of dreary repairs that her new domicile requires ("Who would have thought that making oneself the owner of a small, a very small, cottage could involve one in such fearful, and such dull, expenditure? Jeanie had looked forward to buying a grandfather clock, a carved coffer, a four-post bed; and here she was spending all her substance on things like step-ladders and gum-boots and smoking chimneys and loose roof-tiles."), but also by her friend Agnes's disillusioning transformation into a capricious and supremely self-centered lady of the manor. When the seemingly inoffensive Robert Molyneux is discovered shot dead in the orchard on the grounds of Cleedons, Jeanie discovers to her mortification that there is no shortage of suspects in his murder, including Agnes herself. Superstitious

local villagers avidly speculate that Robert Molyneux wa down by unearthly forces on account of his plan to open Grave, an ancient local tumulus enshrouded in mists of but the rational Jeanie is a believer in more material e: Jeanie eventually will discover the truth behind the cr her in peril of her life. Would she have been wiser to l lie?

*Let Him Lie* is an impressive detective novel witl sense of character and place penned by an author m use of her knowledge of period domestic architectu and art. Ianthe Jerrold's twin sisters Daphne and I flower painters who had once resided together in studio, and in the 1930s Ianthe Jerrold and her h Menges, a brother of the celebrated concert violi Menges, acquired Cwmmau (pronounced "Coon rambling seventeenth-century timbered resider Herefordshire (adjoining Gloucestershire, the s *Lie*), spending much of their time there—all of Jerrold with ample material on which to draw accomplished third mystery. Comparing favo naturalistic detective novels produced in the Forties by Christie, Allingham and Marsh, a talented newcomers to British mystery ficti Brand, Elizabeth Ferrars, Dorothy Bowers *Let Him Lie*, happily disinterred after seve enterprising Dean Street Press, should fir audience today among devotees of classic

# INTRODUCTION

A full decade after the publication of Ianthe Jerrold's *The Studio Crime* (1929) and *Dead Man's Quarry* (1930), both of which titles have been republished by Dean Street Press, another Jerrold detective novel, penned by the author under the pseudonym "Geraldine Bridgman," finally appeared in print. *Let Him Lie*, Jerrold's evocatively titled third detective novel, was issued in 1940 by William Heinemann, the prestigious English publisher of both Margery Allingham's critically applauded mystery novels and John Dickson Carr's ingenious Sir Henry Merrivale detective series (the latter published under Carr's "Carter Dickson" pseudonym). During the ten-year interval between the publication of *Dead Man's Quarry* and *Let Him Lie*, Ianthe Jerrold had produced five mainstream novels; and presumably her adoption for her new mystery of the Geraldine Bridgman pen name--a transposition of the middle and last parts of her full name, Ianthe Bridgman Jerrold--was a move on her part to distinguish her more "serious" writing from any future fictional mystery mongering that she might perform.

John Christmas, Jerrold's brilliant amateur sleuth in *The Studio Crime* and *Dead Man's Quarry*, is nowhere to be found in *Let Him Lie*, his place having been taken by a young woman whom the author likely never viewed as a potential series character. The decade of the 1930s increasingly saw a movement in mystery fiction away from the improbable Great Detective figure of romance to more naturalistic depictions of characters impacted by crime, in the style of the realistic mainstream novel. Saddled in their mysteries with the popular Golden Age investigators Hercule Poirot, Lord Peter Wimsey, Albert Campion and Roderick Alleyn, the British Crime Queens Agatha Christie, Dorothy L. Sayers, Margery Allingham and Ngaio Marsh never could bring

themselves to banish the figure of the male Great Detective from
their books (though after the Second World War Margery
Allingham came close with Campion and Christie would write
fewer books about Poirot). However, by 1940 Ianthe Jerrold
obviously felt sufficiently empowered with her new detective novel
to send John Christmas, already inactive for ten years, to the
sleuthing sidelines. While readers of *The Studio Crime* and *Dead
Man's Quarry* may miss Christmas, they nevertheless should
derive much enjoyment from *Let Him Lie*, a superb vintage
English country mystery.

In *Let Him Lie* the amateur detective figure is not some
colorful and eccentric investigative genius but rather a young
former art student named Jeanie Halliday, recently settled "in
proud and lonely independence" at Yew Tree Cottage, the rustic
Gloucestershire residence she purchased from her idolized ex-
schoolmistress, Agnes Molyneux (formerly Agnes Drake) and her
new husband, Robert Molyneux, owners of Cleedons, "that most
comfortable of small Elizabethan manor-houses tacked on to the
remains of a medieval castle." Currently Jeanie Halliday is
disturbed not merely by the round of dreary repairs that her new
domicile requires ("Who would have thought that making oneself
the owner of a small, a very small, cottage could involve one in
such fearful, and such dull, expenditure? Jeanie had looked
forward to buying a grandfather clock, a carved coffer, a four-post
bed; and here she was spending all her substance on things like
step-ladders and gum-boots and smoking chimneys and loose
roof-tiles."), but also by her friend Agnes's disillusioning
transformation into a capricious and supremely self-centered lady
of the manor. When the seemingly inoffensive Robert Molyneux is
discovered shot dead in the orchard on the grounds of Cleedons,
Jeanie discovers to her mortification that there is no shortage of
suspects in his murder, including Agnes herself. Superstitious

local villagers avidly speculate that Robert Molyneux was struck down by unearthly forces on account of his plan to open Grim's Grave, an ancient local tumulus enshrouded in mists of legend, but the rational Jeanie is a believer in more material explanations. Jeanie eventually will discover the truth behind the crime, putting her in peril of her life. Would she have been wiser to have let truth lie?

*Let Him Lie* is an impressive detective novel with a strong sense of character and place penned by an author making effective use of her knowledge of period domestic architecture, archaeology and art. Ianthe Jerrold's twin sisters Daphne and Phyllis were flower painters who had once resided together in a London art studio, and in the 1930s Ianthe Jerrold and her husband, George Menges, a brother of the celebrated concert violinist Isolde Menges, acquired Cwmmau (pronounced "Cooma") Farmhouse, a rambling seventeenth-century timbered residence in Herefordshire (adjoining Gloucestershire, the setting of *Let Him Lie*), spending much of their time there—all of which provided Jerrold with ample material on which to draw when she wrote her accomplished third mystery. Comparing favorably with other naturalistic detective novels produced in the late Thirties and early Forties by Christie, Allingham and Marsh, as well as by such talented newcomers to British mystery fiction as Christianna Brand, Elizabeth Ferrars, Dorothy Bowers and Harriet Rutland, *Let Him Lie*, happily disinterred after seventy-five years by the enterprising Dean Street Press, should find an appreciative audience today among devotees of classic English mystery.

Curtis Evans

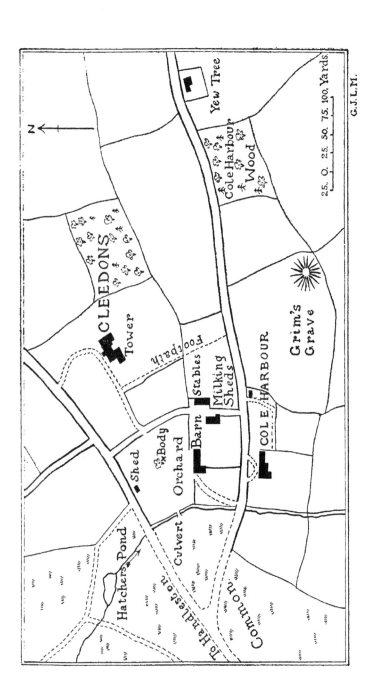

N

Yew Tree

Cole Harbour Wood

CLEEDONS

Tower

Grim's Grave

Footpath

Stables

Milking Sheds

COLE HARBOUR

×Body

Barn

Shed

Orchard

Culvert

To Handleston

Hatcher's Pond

Common

25. O. 25. 50. 75. 100. Yards.

G.J.L.M.

## Chapter One
## DEATH OF A KITTEN

"Oh dear, oh dear!" said Jeanie Halliday sadly, picking her way over cart-ruts which one night's downpour seemed to have turned from iron to butter-icing. "I shall have to buy some gum-boots!"

She sighed deeply, for she saw no end to the things she would have to buy before she could settle down at Yew Tree Cottage in proud and lonely independence. A pair of steps, two more buckets, an oil-stove, a saw, a screw-driver—the list was endless. Worse, a builder's bill long as a medieval court-roll unwound itself every night on the darkness before she dropped off to sleep. Who would have thought that making oneself the owner of a small, a very small, cottage could involve one in such fearful, and such dull, expenditure? Jeanie had looked forward to buying a grandfather clock, a carved coffer, a four-post bed; and here she was spending all her substance on things like step-ladders and gum-boots and smoking chimneys and loose roof-tiles.

She ought to have employed a surveyor, of course. She saw that now. But Agnes Molyneux had seemed in such a hurry to sell the cottage. And Jeanie had loved it so at first sight, and had feared to be discouraged by the prosaic criticisms of a surveyor. Her old lawyer's remarks had been quite discouraging enough! She loved it still, but with more reproach than rapture in her love, like a lover continuing in thrall to a mistress fair without and false within.

At the gate which opened upon the footpath to Cleedons Manor she paused, with some idea of going up to the house and telling Agnes about the smoking parlour chimney at Yew Tree Cottage. But what was the use? At this hour, Agnes was probably resting, or trying on clothes. And Agnes seemed to see no reason, anyway, why she should be held responsible for the dilapidated condition of Yew Tree Cottage. She was perfectly within her rights, of course. Jeanie had rashly bought the cottage, and must make the best of it, smoke and all. She decided to walk on along the road and find little Sarah Molyneux at the stables and inspect the kittens, as they had arranged between them; for it seemed that Jeanie as a householder was doomed to add a kitten to her other responsibilities.

As she walked along, she thought about Agnes and tried hard not to be both sad and resentful. Miss Agnes Drake had been very kind to Jeanie Halliday some years ago, when Jeanie Halliday had been a lonely, impulsive schoolgirl and Miss Drake a mistress on the staff of a large private school. And Jeanie had formed for the aloof, gentle Miss Drake one of those fond, unreasoning, lasting attachments which parentless children so readily and sometimes so incomprehensibly bestow. They had both been lonely people, for Miss Drake also was parentless and had recently been bereaved of a much-loved younger sister. Jeanie had transferred to the elder woman some of her feeling for her dead mother, and Miss Drake had seen in Jeanie, and often commented on, a resemblance to the young sister she had lost. No one had rejoiced more than Jeanie when, in her last year at school, Miss Drake had left to marry Robert Molyneux, an elderly Gloucestershire land-owner she had met on a holiday abroad. Jeanie herself, leaving school soon afterwards to study painting in Paris, had not seen her friend for some years, but had fitfully bombarded her with long affectionate letters, and had accepted with joy an invitation to visit Cleedons and renew this affection of her school-days. She had fallen in love with Cleedons, that most comfortable of small Elizabethan manor-houses tacked on to the remains of a medieval castle. She had fallen in love with the grey stones and golden field-flowers and wide skies of the Gloucestershire countryside, and with the charming grey stone cottages that stand modestly along the quiet lanes. Finally, she had fallen very violently in love with little, empty Yew Tree Cottage and finding Agnes anxious to sell it, had bought it all in an afternoon for three hundred pounds and disregarded the ensuing groans and wordy remonstrances of her old family lawyer. She told herself, and him, that she had done a very practical, sensible thing. She wanted to settle down somewhere in the country and paint. And why not here, near darling Agnes?

It was only recently, since she had come to take up her residence at Yew Tree Cottage, that she had begun to wonder whether she had really been so practical and sensible, whether a studio in London would not have been a wiser investment, and finally and most searchingly, whether she really wanted to live near Agnes and whether darling Agnes were darling Agnes any longer?

For Agnes was altered. Or Jeanie was altered. Or both of them. And poor Jeanie was beginning to perceive that Mrs. Molyneux had no wish nor intention at all of playing a motherly part towards the old pupil she had once been so kind to. She was kind but distant. Friendly, but casual. No longer, it seemed, did Jeanie remind her of her lost sister. She seemed quite to have forgotten her sister, and her former loneliness, and Jeanie's affection for her, in the satisfactions of being Mrs. Robert Molyneux, mistress of a spacious country household.

"It's horrible when people change," thought Jeanie, with quite a lump in her throat, kicking a stone down the lane and badly grazing the toe of her shoe. Agnes in prosperity seemed to have shrunk and withered instead of expanding and blooming. The cool reserve which had characterised her in her teaching days seemed to have grown into a positive secretiveness, as though she feared continually, and wished to forestall, demands on her generosity. The fastidious care she used to bestow upon her clothes seemed to have become an insatiable vanity for ever occupied with dress and beauty treatments. It was horrible when people changed. And horrible when one changed oneself and found only the workings of a critical cool judgment where once had operated the warm impulses of the heart.

Foolish Jeanie found quite a haze in front of her eyes. She firmly reminded herself that Yew Tree Cottage was an adorable little cottage, that the Cotswold country was just what she had always wanted to paint, and that there were plenty of other people in the world she could be friends with, besides Agnes Molyneux.

In Cole Harbour Wood, that lay off the road to Jeanie's left, a man was cutting down trees. She heard the sharp thudding of the axe strokes, and paused at a gate to see if she could catch a glimpse of the woodman. All country labours had a charm for her. She stood a moment or two watching the labourer at his work on the edge of the wood some distance away, enjoying the rhythmic swing of the axe, the powerful easy lift of arms and shoulders, watching the white chips fly out, noting how late the hard thud of impact came to her ears, as if it were the echo of the impact-sound, and not the sound itself. Down came the axe, and an instant later, almost as it rose again, thud! came the sound. Jeanie hoped that Cole Harbour Wood was not going to be entirely cut down, for she was looking forward to exploring in the spring under its tall larches and silvery oaks.

The sudden stir and gallop of a pony at grass the other side of the hedge took Jeanie's enchanted eye as she walked on, and she watched the endearing rough-maned creature kick up his hoofs and gallop off towards Grim's Grave, that great bell-barrow crowned with firs which stood up so steep and round among the irregular contours of the fields.

"Suppose Agnes had lived when that tumulus was made," thought Jeanie, "what would she have done then, with only a bit of fur and a string of clay beads to make herself lovely with?"

Jeanie was, she was aware, shockingly ignorant of archaeology, as that queer Mr. Fone, who lived at Cole Harbour House, had informed her at dinner at Cleedons not very long ago. She had horrified him by supposing that the men of the Neolithic Age were skin-clad savages who spent their time lurking in caves and cracking one another's skulls. He had informed her sternly that they were as civilised as herself and in some ways more so. A queer, rather alarming man, Neighbour Fone. But Jeanie liked him. And she liked his house, Cole Harbour House, whose roof she saw above the surrounding trees ahead of her. A comfortable house, a light, pleasant house, made to take a painter's eye, with its plum-coloured bricks and lavish creepers and the arch-shaped windows of its low, built-out library.

"And here's the great Neolith himself," said Jeanie, as a man emerged from a shed near Cole Harbour gate, carrying a sheet of heavy lead. But she was mistaken, for this man walked upright without the sticks that helped poor William Fone along. It was Hugh Barchard, Mr. Fone's secretary, nurse, companion, general factotum. Jeanie called to him as she approached the gate.

"Good afternoon, Mr. Barchard."

He propped his piece of sheet lead against the gate.

"Afternoon, Miss Halliday. Nasty wet night it was."

"Yes, outdoors and in," agreed Jeanie. "The rain's been coming down my parlour chimney, and the smoke's simply awful. The builder's there to-day, bricking the ingle-nook in. Pity to brick in an ingle-nook, but I'm not a haddock. I'm having a new hob-grate. Very Adamy and recherché."

"It's the chimney wants a new cowl on it. I wouldn't go spending a lot of money till you've had that seen to."

"The builder says the chimney's incurable, except by putting in a high grate and bricking it round."

Barchard stuck out a dubious under-lip. He was a wiry colonial with an agreeable lack of the English countryman's usual self-consciousness.

"Well, Miss Halliday, if you put a high grate and have a coal fire in it just under the cross-beam of the chimney-breast you may be having the place burnt down one of these days."

"Oh Heaven, don't say that! The builder's going to put asbestos sheeting over the beam."

"I wouldn't risk it, even so."

"But what am I to do?" cried Jeanie in despair. "Is there anything in life worse than a smoking chimney?"

Barchard grinned faintly, as though he could think of many worse things.

"It used to smoke a bit in my day, I admit. We used to sit in the kitchen, mostly. I used to live at Yew Tree myself, I dare say you've heard."

"I know," said Jeanie, as casually as possible, for she had also heard that Hugh Barchard had lived at Yew Tree Cottage to the great scandal of the countryside, with a lady to whom he had not been married. "Did the roof leak in your day?"

"Only after snow. I expect one or two of the tiles had slid off."

"One or two! Great Heavens, the roof of Yew Tree Cottage has the secret of perpetual motion!"

"Ah, those old roofs can't be depended on. We've got the same trouble here, only ours is rotted leads—worse in a way. This flat roof here's always giving trouble. I've been up there most of the morning laying new lead, but there's no end to the repairing once the leads start going."

"You could have a roof-garden up there," said Jeanie, glancing at the long room built out by some early nineteenth-century owner from the side of the square Queen Anne house, and admiring the pleasant "gothick" glazing bars of its tall windows and the swelling balusters of the stone parapet that ran round the flat roof.

"Mr. Fone does spend quite a lot of his time up there, though there isn't anything in the garden line," said Barchard. "You get a splendid view down over the hills from up there. You see a lot of burial mounds."

Jeanie laughed.

"Burial mounds! Is that Mr. Fone's idea of a splendid view?"

Hugh Barchard smiled, taking up his heavy sheet of lead. He had a pleasant smile that wrinkled the skin about his eyes.

"Mr. Fone's interested in the lay-out of the mounds. He thinks there used to be roadways in Neolithic times running from one to another of them all over the country."

"Rather third-class roads by now, I should imagine," said Jeanie cheerfully. "Mr. Fone ought to go up in a balloon. They say you can see all sorts of extraordinary things buried under the earth if you only go high enough up in the air."

They parted, and Jeanie turned towards the farmyard, where thirteen-year-old Sarah Molyneux came running to meet her.

"Oh Jeanie!" cried the child tragically as they met. "Your kitten!"

"Oh darling, don't say you've discovered it isn't house-trained!"

"Worse than that!" Sarah's rather pale narrow little face which made so piquant a contrast with the living springing gold of her hair, wore quite a tragic expression. "He's dead!"

"Dead! What, the kitten you've been saving up for me? Oh dear! Oh well," said Jeanie hastily, as she saw that there were tears in Sarah's eyes, "never mind, my pet! Poor little chap! I expect it ate something."

"It didn't. It got shot."

"Shot! Oh, poor wee thing!"

Sarah's full underlip stuck out and trembled.

"I'd like to know who did it. The beast. The brute. The foul damned cad."

"Langwidge! Langwidge!" said Jeanie in half-affected horror. Sarah had had a queer upbringing before her Uncle Robert took charge of her, Jeanie knew. Her father, Robert Molyneux's younger brother, had died, leaving her in the charge of a queer, neurotic, unhappy mother who had dragged the child with her round Europe in the course of two more ill-starred marriages and one or two less regular alliances. Three years ago, Robert had at last persuaded his sister-in-law to hand over to him the responsibility of his brothers little daughter. She had been well pleased, then, to be rid of her child. But Jeanie had heard from Agnes that she had latterly altered her mind, and now nourished a maternal sentiment in her bosom, and wrote every week or so passionate but ill-spelt letters to her brother-in-law demanding the immediate return of her child, and had even threatened to swoop down on Cleedons and abduct the unwilling Sarah, "who, after all, is the only creature in the world I have to love!"

"Whoever did it," said Jeanie reasonably, stroking the child's damp cheek, "probably thought the poor kit was a rabbit."

"A *white* rabbit, how could they? You could see him from miles away, my darling little white kitten! He used to go hunting beetles in the orchard! He used to jump up after butterflies! And now he's dead! Oh, Jeanie!"

"Don't cry, my pet, but tell me all about it. I'll have one of the tabby ones. I don't mind."

"There isn't anything to tell," said the child dejectedly, raising red eyes from Jeanie's chest and allowing herself to be led towards the gate. "I couldn't find him anywhere this morning. And I went to look for him in the orchard. And I found him, shot."

She searched around her knees for the handkerchief that was absent from the legs of her knickers. Jeanie proffered her own and they went in through the barnyard gate. Jeanie paused a moment as Sarah led the way towards the stables, forgetting both the poor dead kitten and Sarah's sorrow in the scene before her. In the damp air of this sunny November afternoon, the grey mossy roofs of the barns and milking sheds, the cooler grey of their stone walls, the watery ground that reflected here and there in puddles the wistful blue of the autumn sky, the pale gold of the ricks in the yard to her left, the dark gold of the lingering leaves on the tall trees, made a picture in low muted tender tones sweet as a scene by Corot. Men were carting litter into the barn. Through the tall barn doors she saw the wagon piled high with rusty bracken. A man in a bright blue shirt wielded a pitch-fork upon that rusty brown, and the orchard behind supplied a note of rich damp green. The westering sun made that wagon framed in the dark doorway, that blue, that green, the centre of a picture.

"What are you looking at?" asked Sarah curiously.

"Oh—just things," uttered Jeanie vaguely. "The bracken. The green grass. Things."

"You look at things like that, and then you paint them?"

"Sometimes."

"There's so much stuff in the world I don't see how you ever know what to paint."

"Ah well!"

"There was an artist staying at the White Lion the summer before last. He was thin, and rather old, and had a beard."

"Hubert Southey. I know him. He used to teach at an art school I went to."

"I suppose you know all the artists in the world," uttered Sarah, climbing like a spider up the worn silvery steps of the loft-ladder.

"Not quite all. Have I to go up there?"

"Aye, aye, me hearty!"

"Heave ho, then, mates!"

The loft, with its dry, warm, enticing scent of hay, its pale rafters heavily hung with cobwebs, its grey boards strewn with old faded wisps and empty husks of grain, enchanted her. She went to the large window at the end, and cleaned the smeared glass with a sack that hung beside it.

"This'd make a splendid studio, if you put a skylight in. You get a good view from here, don't you? There's your Uncle Robert going into the orchard."

"Pruning his apple-trees. He was at it all the morning." A sleepy tabby kitten emerged from its nest in a dark corner, exposed the elegant pink ribbings of the roof of its mouth in a yawn and then, sitting down and neatly bringing its tail around its fore-paws, made gleaming crescents of its eyes and silently mewed.

"That's a sweet one!"

Sarah swallowed.

"Timkins was the sweetest!"

"Never mind, my pet. One casualty out of four kittens isn't too bad."

"Yes, but he was the only white one! He was rare!"

"It can't be helped now."

"That's what Uncle Robert said," muttered Sarah. "People seem to think a kitten doesn't want its life. How'd Uncle Robert like it if somebody went shooting at him while he was catching beetles and butterflies and playing in the sun?"

Jeanie stifled an ill-timed giggle, and Sarah looked at her with cold reproach over her lapful of assorted kittens. Jeanie said hastily:

"May I have this one? What's his name?"

The vivid image which her picture-forming mind had presented to her of the burly, tweed-clad Molyneux pouncing on beetles and leaping after butterflies among the orchard grasses, amused Jeanie a good deal.

*"Her name is Petronella," said Sarah pointedly.

"Her! Oh dear!"

"They make the best mousers."

"I know, but—"

"She might not have kittens more than once a year."

"All right. I'll risk it. But Petronella! Must I call her that?"

"She was called after Peter, you see. Peter Johnson." Jeanie recalled to mind the dark-eyed youth who had been Molyneux's secretary when she was staying at Cleedons in the summer.

"What's happened to him?"

"He left," said Sarah rather grimly. "About three weeks ago, all of a sudden. There was some row; I don't know what. Miss Wills said he was never coming back, and I wasn't to write to him. But I *did* write to him," added she, flushing defiantly, "because I knew he'd want to know about the Field Club outing this afternoon, and I didn't see why he shouldn't come if he liked."

"Oh, is the Handleston Field Club outing this afternoon?"

"Yes. I shall have to go in and wash soon. I've got to help with tea. I didn't want to, but Aunt Agnes said I must. She was cross because Uncle Robert said he must prune his trees while it was fine, and couldn't meet the Field Club at the tumulus. Sir Henry Blundell is coming," said the child.

"I see," said Jeanie. Sir Henry Blundell, Chief Constable of the county, a landowner in whose mansion Cleedons might be swallowed almost unnoticed, was certainly a personage of some importance. Agnes, a snob of the more simple and whole-hearted kind, as Jeanie was reluctantly coming to realise, would certainly make a special occasion of the Field Club's visit to Cleedons if Sir Henry Blundell were of the company.

"She *was* cross," pursued the child. "And so was Miss Wills."

"Miss Wills? Why on earth should she be cross?"

"She's always cross when Aunt Agnes is cross."

"Dear me, how awkward!"

"She adores Aunt Agnes. When Aunt Agnes said she might call her Agnes, her nose went all pink."

"Is that a sign of adoration?"

"I don't think she's staying much longer," said the little girl with satisfaction. "I hope not, anyway. Uncle Robert says I'm beyond her and must go to school."

"Little wretch! I wouldn't be your governess for a million a year! What are the Field Club looking at this afternoon?"

"Oh, the usual things, I expect," replied the blasé dweller in a historic house. "Black Ellen's tower, and the medieval kitchen where the wine-cellar is now, and Grim's Grave."

"I thought your Uncle Robert was talking of opening Grim's Grave."

"He is. Aunt Agnes is cross about that too. She says it's a waste of money and there's nothing in it but a few nasty bones and a bit of broken crockery."

Jeanie smiled.

"Probably, but then how thrilling nasty bones are to those that like nasty bones! Mr. Fone, for instance. He'd be delighted."

Sarah opened her greenish eyes very wide.

"No!" she said with bated breath. "He's *furious*! He says if Uncle Robert opens Grim's Grave there'll be a curse on everyone for miles! He says Grim's Grave is sacred ground. He says if we open it Awful Forces'll come out and destroy us!"

"Oh dear, how you make my flesh creep!"

"Well, he's a poet, you see," explained Sarah. "But Uncle Robert says *he's* no confounded poet and he's going ahead, and old Funnybone can put his poetic frenzies in a book if he likes, but he won't have him going round upsetting all the local people."

"Why, does he?"

Sarah looked vague. Her quotation from Uncle Robert stopped there.

"Quite a lot of people wouldn't like Grim's Grave opened," she admitted. A slight uneasiness came into her young eyes. "After all, Jeanie, people don't usually go digging up people's graves. And it's just as much a grave, even if it's a very old grave. What's that?"

She sat up suddenly, and the kitten, grasped too tightly, gave a plaintive mew. Jeanie listened. Somebody was talking in the yard below, and she heard the clump of heavy boots on cobbles, but there was nothing in this to bring that look of apprehension into the child's eyes. With a gesture Sarah silenced her. Listening, with her eyes curiously on the little girl's face, Jeanie heard a drawling female voice.

"Well, thank you, but I know my way to the house, when I want to go!"

The cowman's boots clumped heavily away.

Sarah stood up softly, putting the kitten down on the floor. She tiptoed to the doorway which overlooked the yard, and of which the half-door stood open. Jeanie rose and went softly to look out beside her at the woman who was standing irresolutely in the yard, as if undetermined where to look next for something she was seeking.

"Surely this isn't a member of the Handleston Field Club!" remarked Jeanie.

The woman below had pulled off her little velvet cap and her thick, mechanically-waved hair, strangely bleached to an unnatural gold for half its length, looked like a head-piece of some coarse woven fabric. Her cheeks were brightly pink, her lips crudely red. The cool November sunlight smiled at the youthful pretensions of her lined and weary face. Her mackintosh coat hung gracefully on her slim figure, but her neck stooped, her hands were thrust stiffly into her pockets, she stood heavily with bent knees on the high heels of her thin town shoes.

"That's a very lively bit of painting," murmured Jeanie to herself, "but not much technique about it. Ought we to go down and offer to help her, I wonder?"

"No," said Sarah in the queerest little hard voice. Glancing at her in surprise, Jeanie saw that her eyes were dark, her upper lip drawn to a straight line. She added: "That's my mother."

"Your *mother*!" echoed Jeanie, with an involuntary unflattering surprise.

So this was the much-talked-of Mrs. Peel, Robert's sister-in-law, Agnes's *bête noire*!

"Did your aunt know she was coming?"

"I shouldn't think so."

"Don't you think we ought to do something?"

"No!"

"Not go down and speak to her?"

"No!"

"But she *is* your mother, my kid!"

"It isn't my fault I was born, is it?"

Jeanie, about to combat this somewhat elementary view of filial duty, suddenly caught her breath. The woman in the yard below had taken her right hand out of her pocket, and glancing furtively around the yard, had taken a long look at that right hand and what it held. What it held gleamed darkly in the November sunlight. It was a heavy service revolver.

## Chapter Two
### A SHOT IS FIRED

The stranger started at Jeanie's exclamation, and thrust the weapon back into her pocket. She looked up. Her eyes, darkly lashed like a china doll's, narrowed in an anxious, uncertain look. She seemed to hesitate whether to explain that revolver or to assume that Jeanie had not seen it.

"So there you are, Sally!"

She had a clear, rather intense voice, and Jeanie remembered hearing that she had been an actress before her marriage to Franklin Molyneux.

"Mrs. Peel?" asked Jeanie. "Do you want Sarah?" To Sarah, who had withdrawn herself from the doorway and stood frowning, she murmured: "Why not go down and speak to your mother? I won't desert you."

"No," said Sarah, tight-lipped.

"Sally! Sally!" called the clear voice coaxingly from the courtyard below. "Don't be silly, dear! Mr. Agatos has driven me all the way from London specially to see my little girl! I thought we might go for a picnic!"

The child, standing against the wall, out of sight of her mother, pressed her hands together and compressed her lips. Her eyes were dark and frowning. Looking at her, Jeanie could make a guess at the past relations of these two, and her guess hardened her heart against Myfanwy Peel. Looking cautiously out, she saw the angry, thwarted look upon Myfanwy's face, the tight, dragged line of the mouth. Yes, said Jeanie to herself, I think you could be cruel, like most sick neurotic people!

When the other woman spoke again it was with the sort of factitious brightness with which nervous people seek to win the confidence of children.

"I say, Sally! Give you three guesses what I've got in the playroom at home! It begins with a D! Two words! A D and an H! And it's for you to play with when you come back to stay with me!"

To hear the artificially lilting, foolish brightness of that voice and at the same time to see the stony, experienced look upon the little girl's face, was not a pleasant thing. Jeanie felt suddenly absurdly sorry for Myfanwy, who thought she could win with dolls'-houses the confidence of a child who could wear this look.

"The fact is, Mrs. Peel, Sarah's a bit nervous of firearms. She saw that revolver you've got in your pocket."

"Revolver?" echoed Myfanwy. "Oh, that!" She hesitated. No guilty blood could stain her cheeks a brighter colour, but a patchy red appeared upon her neck.

"I—I—oh, how silly, darling! It's not loaded!"

She took the weapon from her pocket and pointing it at the ground, dramatically pulled the trigger. There was a click, nothing more.

"Why carry such a thing around?" asked Jeanie.

Something in her friendly tone seemed to touch a chord in the other woman's unstable spirit. With a gesture too clumsy to be studied, she put her hand to her eyes, she gave a little sob.

"Oh, I don't know! I'm a fool! I was—I was going to see Robert! I thought I'd—"

"Sarah'll come down and speak to you, if you want her to."

"I shan't!" uttered Sarah. "I shan't!" she whimpered. "Jeanie, no!"

Looking at Sarah, Jeanie's common-sense view of the situation wavered again. What, after all, did she know of Myfanwy Peel? What was the woman doing here? Why, if she wanted to see Robert Molyneux, had she not driven to the house? Was it possible that she contemplated the forcible abduction of her daughter?

"Oh!" cried Myfanwy, with a melancholy sound, half-sob, half-laugh. "Don't trouble her! I see she's swallowed everything Robert and Saint Agnes have said about me! She's forgotten what fun she used to have with her mother! I shall have to see what my lawyer's got to say about this! You can't stay away from me for ever, you know, Sally, just because your Uncle Robert's got a big place for you to play in and plenty of money to give you! It won't be very nice for you, you know, being made to come back to me by the law! And I dare say by the time the lawsuit's over I shan't like you quite as much as I do now!"

Myfanwy's voice, which had started on a low emotional note, had grown harder and shriller through this recital until she was speaking like a very virago. Her hands nervously clenched and unclenched, the stiffness of anger made her look old and ill.

"Why don't you go and see Mr. Molyneux? He's in the orchard," suggested Jeanie. "I'm sure he'd let you take Sarah for a picnic, if you want to!"

She was not sure of any such thing. But at her level friendly tone Myfanwy's hands unclenched, she stood helplessly, her whipped-up rage seemed to break and fall away from her. She cried in a strangled voice:

"Don't keep calling her that! Her name's *Sally*!" and stamping her foot less like a virago than like a child, she burst into tears and ran across the yard out of sight.

"Oh dear!" said Jeanie disconsolately. "Sarah, I do think you're a little beast."

Myfanwy's sob, her final pathetic cry, so fraught with maternal jealousy, had touched Jeanie's heart, and her ready sympathies were at the moment not with this cold child but with Mrs. Peel, a silly woman, a light woman, no doubt, but, after all, the child's mother and perhaps too rigidly barred from her child by Robert's well-meaning powerful arm.

There were birds chirping under the eaves of the farm buildings and singing in the trees. There was the sound of heavy wheels in the lane, and the clop of horses' hoofs and the sound of men's voices. Farther away, a motorcar hummed along the road, and farther still a threshing-machine was busy. Yet so quiet was it in the hay-loft that Jeanie, conscious of none of these other sounds, heard a gun-shot as though it came shattering a perfect midnight silence. That sudden crack woke Jeanie's startled ears, and as its echoes died away in her mind she became aware of the wheels, the men's voices, the threshing-machine. She stared at Sarah. Sarah's eyes, wide and dark with apprehension, stared back at her.

"What was that?" asked Jeanie in a bated tone. "It sounded like—"

"It was a shot, wasn't it?" said Sarah, with a nervous tremble in her voice.

"But of course in the country one's always hearing shots!" said Jeanie.

"I thought it didn't sound much like a sporting-gun," said Sarah nervously.

"What then?"

"Well—" said Sarah, licking her lip. "Perhaps a rook-rifle. Miss Dasent has a rook-rifle. It might have been her."

"Miss Dasent?"

"You know, Jeanie. She lives in Handleston. Old Dr. Dasent's her father. She goes riding with Uncle Robert. And she comes shooting about here quite a lot. Uncle Robert lets her."

"Oh, Marjorie!" murmured Jeanie, who had not recognised under the title "Miss Dasent" the plain, pleasant, sport-crazy girl she had met once or twice at Cleedons.

"She's our guide-mistress, you see," said Sarah, as if apologising for her use of the surname. Her lip trembled. The kitten clasped too tightly to her bosom mewed indignantly. "Oh, Jeanie! You don't think—"

"My dear, we're two sillies to listen at all to a gun being let off at a rabbit. The country's full of guns and rabbits, isn't it, worse luck!"

As she spoke, Jeanie glanced out of the smeared window in the crutch of the roof, half hoping to see a man with a gun crossing the lane to lull their foolish fears. She saw no man, but what she did see made her approach nearer to the window and rub it quickly clean.

Two women were standing in the lane some twenty yards down. One was Myfanwy Peel, the other Agnes Molyneux. Jeanie noted the pleasant plum-colour of Agnes's dress before she noticed her face, but when she saw her face she became oblivious of everything else. Agnes's face was a clayey white upon which the delicate touches of make-up showed hard-edged and strange, like paint on the face of a grotesque doll. She was clutching at Myfanwy's arm. Her lips parted stiffly, writhingly, but whether she spoke or not Jeanie could not tell. She saw Myfanwy with a crude, cruel gesture shake off that clinging hand and pass on quickly up the lane. Agnes looked wildly round, and at the same time Jeanie, taking up an old horseshoe that lay among the hay on the floor, broke the glass in the window. Smashing the jagged edges away, she leant cautiously out and cried:

"Agnes! Agnes!"

Agnes looked up at her. Jeanie had never in her life seen a look so sick, so despairing on a woman's face. Agnes's eyes seemed scarcely to recognise Jeanie, but glanced up and then wandered round her. She tried to speak, and could not.

"All right, Agnes! I'll come down!"

"Oh, what is it?" cried Sarah at her back, in a voice panicky with fright. "Jeanie! What is it?"

Agnes put out a vague hand as if to feel the air, and then, with a queer, limp motion as though she were indeed the doll her make-up made her look, let her head drop forward, her shoulders, her waist, her knees, and soundlessly fell, and lay face downwards in her plum-coloured gown in the mud of the lane.

## Chapter Three
### DEATH IN THE ORCHARD

Slithering down the loft-ladder, running out into the sunlight, stumbling along the rutty lane, Jeanie had a dreadful prevision of herself lifting Mrs. Molyneux from the mud and seeing her face clayey and dead, mud-streaked, with half-opened eyes and blood oozing through and darkening the cloth of her gown. One could be

a long time about one's dying, shot in a part not vital. And here, so
soon after the shot, lay Agnes still as the dead in the muddy lane.

Agnes's face was pale enough, and splashed with mud, but the
long fair lashes lay quietly on the cheeks, the lips, so strangely out
of tone with the rosy cosmetic upon them, were quietly half
parted. Briskly chafing the cold hands, Jeanie heard a squeaky
voice utter uncertainly:

"You ought to undo her stays."

It was Sarah, almost as white in the face as Agnes herself.

"I don't think she wears any," said Jeanie helplessly, "but you
could go and get some water from the pump in the yard. There's
bound to be a pail or something."

However, almost as soon as Sarah had sped away, Agnes
sighed and moved. Her eyes opened slowly. Her lips looked dry
and cracked. She looked too tired, too sick, having made the effort
to lift her eyelids, to move another muscle. But after a moment
memory came back into her blank eyes. Her face contorted. A
restless movement passed over her body. She gasped:

"Jeanie! Jeanie!"

"What is it, Agnes?"

"Robert's dead, Jeanie. Somebody shot him. Robert's *dead*,
Jeanie. I saw him. Oh, Jeanie, I feel so *sick*! I feel so awful!"

Kneeling in the wet lane, supported against Jeanie's shoulder,
she fell to trembling violently, like a frightened animal or a patient
in a fever.

"Where is he?" asked Jeanie. "Agnes, do you know what you're
saying?"

"Yes. In the orchard. Oh God! Oh God! Jeanie! Oh, Jeanie!"

She struggled with Jeanie's help to her feet. Standing, wildly
dishevelled, covered in mud, she pushed her hair away from her
eyes, she moaned distractedly:

"Oh, *look* at my dress! Oh, Jeanie!"

Jeanie, supporting her, looked towards the yard for Sarah, and saw her coming slowly and carefully along carrying an enamel basin full of water between her hands.

"Oh ducky, you have been a long time!"

"I couldn't find a bucket! I had to get the chickens' basin from the orchard!" explained Sarah, whose face looked, poor child, whiter and clammier even than Agnes's own.

"Well, we don't need it now. Will you take your aunt up to the house as quickly as possible? I must go to the orchard at once. Don't look so scared, darling. It's just an accident, you know—somebody shooting rabbits and—and just winged your uncle, perhaps. I don't suppose he's badly hurt. Go along now. And find Sir Henry Blundell or Dr. Hall or both of them, and quietly, without making a fuss, ask them to come to the orchard. Got that?"

"Yes, Jeanie," said the child obediently, licking her pale lips. She glanced with a sort of stony horror towards the orchard gate, and did as she was told.

When Jeanie, with a dreadful feeling of unwillingness, entered the orchard there seemed to be no one there but a speckled hen strayed from the barn-yard and pecking about for grubs, giving the orchard, even in its wintry gauntness, a homely, peaceful quality quite at variance with Jeanie's feelings. A ladder stood up against one of the tall old trees which still remained among the more recently planted ones. There was no one on the ladder. But someone lay at its foot, and lay very still.

Jeanie's heart gave two great thuds, and she found herself walking slowly, slowly across the grass. She heard, not far away, a car start up and drive off, humming on an ever-rising note into silence.

Could a man lie as still as this, and not be dead? Perhaps, but he could not stare up at one so blankly from a face so queerly pale around the patchy, weatherbeaten cheeks. He would have to blink. He could not stare in such a long surprise. His hand lying upon the turf, might be as cold, but not his cheek. He might bleed, but not from a small black hole in the temple.

Jeanie rose quickly from her knees and turned away. There was a sort of blankness upon her inner lids. Raising her eyes from the grass, she saw two men coming in at the orchard gate. One, she knew, was brisk little Dr. Hall, the other, tall and loose-limbed, she supposed, Sir Henry Blundell. They wore, both of them, that slightly abstracted, slightly self-important air with which men try to express their sense of the gravity of events.

"I think Mr. Molyneux's dead," said Jeanie baldly, as they came up.

"Oh, don't say that!" responded Dr. Hall, dropping upon his knee. There was a certain lack of conviction in his voice.

Sir Henry, who had been looking at the still body at his feet with that remote, inexpressive stare which is often used to cover a good deal of nervous distress, turned and looked suddenly at Jeanie. He had that kind of blue, well-focused, direct eye for which the word "piercing" scarcely seems exaggerated. He was a good-looking, long, elderly man of the grey-faced soldier type.

"Did you say you saw this happen, Miss Halliday?"

"No. But I heard the shot. At least, I suppose it was the shot."

"What direction did it seem to come from?"

"I don't know! We were in the hay-loft, you see, Sarah and I. We heard a shot. It might have been from anywhere. It sounded fairly close."

Dr. Hall rose stiffly and brushed at the knees of his trousers.

"I'm afraid there's nothing I can do. He died instantly, I should say. A bullet in the brain. See here."

He pointed to the small black hole in the left temple round which the blood was already clotting.

"The cause of death's pretty obvious. The only thing that puzzles me is the way he's lying. On his back like that. I should have expected a man hit like that to fall on his face."

"But suppose he fell out of the tree," said Jeanie.

Both men looked at the tall old tree with the ladder leaning against it.

"I should say there's very little doubt he did," said Sir Henry. "And, in that case, it may be very difficult to fix the direction of the shot. I suppose it couldn't possibly have been suicide?"

Dr. Hall briskly shook his head, looking down at the body of Robert Molyneux, smiling faintly as a specialist smiles at the absurdities of the layman.

"Absolutely not. That shot was fired from quite a distance. I'll be able to tell you more after the autopsy. But you can put the idea of suicide out of your head right away. Some careless ass after birds, perhaps, down in the meadows—"

"'Careless,'" said Sir Henry gravely, "would scarcely be the word, I think. How could such an accident have happened?"

Dr. Hall shrugged slightly. Man's carelessness, he seemed to imply, was equal to anything.

"There's nothing more I can do here. I'd better go in and have a look at Mrs. Molyneux."

"Would you ring up the police station at Handleston? Say that I want Superintendent Finister to come out here at once and bring a couple of men with him. I shall wait here till they come. Oh, and Doctor! Ask Denham if he'd mind coming to me out here and bringing his camera and gear with him. Some photographs may be useful later. This tree, for instance."

A branch almost sawn through hung limply, swinging a little, towards the grass. It was a long slender branch, about a couple of inches through, and had been sawn through almost to the bark about two feet from the fork of the tree against which the ladder stood. A small pruning-saw lay in the grass below. The stub from which the bough dangled pointed roughly towards the northwest hedge of the orchard, near which stood a little rickety wooden shed known as the lambing-shed.

"That ought to give us some idea of how the poor chap was standing, anyway. He was in the act of sawing through that bough when the shot took him, that's pretty clear."

Sir Henry Blundell picked up the pruning-saw and climbed up the ladder, the foot of which pointed towards the orchard entrance gate. When he had gone up about half a dozen rungs he placed the saw at right angles to the half-sawn bough and settled himself comfortably as though to continue the work Robert Molyneux had begun.

"How's that?" he called down to Jeanie. His left profile was towards the hay-barn.

"It looks as if the shot must have come from there," she said, pointing towards the barns.

"Yes," he agreed, descending. "From almost due south."

"Unless," said Jeanie slowly, "he turned his head."

"You mean, somebody may have called him, made him turn?"

"Perhaps. Or he might have turned his head or altered his position just because he was tired. Sawing's a tiring job. One looks around one and takes little rests sometimes."

Sir Henry smiled politely, looking with narrowed eyes around the orchard as if he half expected to see the murderer still lurking there. Suddenly with an exclamation he strode towards the lambing-shed, leaving Jeanie to contemplate the apple-tree, the ladder and the bough. A sound broke on her ears as she stood there which she might have taken for distant thunder had it not coincided with a man's voice uttering adjurations to his horses. It was the hay-wagon rumbling back down the farm-track from the common. In a moment it came into view, piled high with bracken, led by the man whose blue shirt Jeanie had admired a thousand hours ago. Another man rode on the shaft. The wagon turned into the barn with a great clatter.

"Who are those?" asked Sir Henry, returning to Jeanie's side, looking down the slope towards the wagon turning in at the great hay-barn door.

"Two of the men carting litter from the common. I saw them before. And I remember now that just before we heard the shot I heard that thundery noise—that noise the wheels of a wagon make. It was the wagon going off empty towards the common, I suppose."

"Look at this, Miss Halliday. It was lying on the ground just inside the shed there. It's perfectly dry, in spite of the damp ground and the damp air, and I am certain it hasn't been there long."

He held out on an envelope the stub of a cigarette.

"A 'Honeybine,' " said Sir Henry. "Somebody's been inside that shed to-day."

"Then—" Jeanie looked up from the fag-end and met Sir Henry's eyes fixed grimly on her face. "It wasn't an accident."

"I never thought it was," said Sir Henry. "Carelessness has its limits."

Suddenly the orchard grass seemed to Jeanie to whisper with the stalking, tiptoeing footsteps of evil, death dodged in a horrible game of hide-and-seek from apple-tree to apple-tree. She shivered. She said, to disperse these horrors:

"Perhaps Mr. Molyneux left it there himself."

"I thought he was a non-smoker."

"Oh yes. He was."

Poor Robert Molyneux! He had prided himself on his abstemious habits, held that a man's health of mind and body is his own to make or mar, lived the simplest strenuous life and never been ill. He had immoderately disliked both doctors and doctoring. Now here he lay, helpless under the hands of little Dr. Hall, at whose cocksure assumptions he had so often smiled.

"Well," said Jeanie indistinctly, "if I can't be any more use here, I think I'll go in."

At the orchard gate she encountered a tall young man in horn-rimmed spectacles, carrying a camera and tripod. He wore a half-scared, half-avid look. He spoke in a solemn whisper.

"Is Sir Henry here?"

"Over there."

"Oh yes! I say! What a—what a—"

The young man could not, all in a moment, transfix the right adjective. Nodding, hurrying on towards the house, Jeanie thought she heard the word "shocking" dropped softly on the air behind her. But she really could not, at this moment and in this state of mind, linger and listen to young Mr. Denham pursuing adjectives.

## Chapter Four
### LADY'S CHAIN

Dr. Hall was coming out of Agnes's bedroom as Jeanie arrived at the door. He wore a tiptoeing, sad, sympathetic look.

"Mrs. Molyneux is quieter now. I've given her a little sedative. After she's seen Sir Henry, I'll give her something stronger. Sleep is a great boon at such times." He looked at Jeanie with a professional gleam in his eye. "You look a little shaken yourself, Miss Halliday, if I may say so."

"Oh, I'm all right," said Jeanie somewhat brusquely.

But entering Agnes's bedroom, and meeting her own reflection in one of the many mirrors, she was not surprised that Dr. Hall had looked on her as a possible patient. 'Shaken' was, she thought, a polite word to use of so ghastly an aspect. Hastily she seized a comb from the dressing-table and ran it through her disordered locks.

Somebody moved in the big dim-lit room, and Jeanie, turning, saw Miss Wills standing on the hearth-rug in front of the electric fire. She had not realised that there was anyone in the room besides Agnes lying on the bed, and was absurdly irritated to see Miss Wills. Jeanie pitied, but did not much like, Sarah's tutor Tamsin Wills, one of those queer unhappy people who mask a profound self-dissatisfaction under an appearance of cold conceit.

"How are you now, Agnes?"

It was Miss Wills who answered, as though she were Agnes's nurse:

"She's quieter now. We're trying to get her to sleep."

"I think Sir Henry wants to see her first."

"Let him wait!" said Tamsin Wills with a short pugnacious laugh. It was evident that she would be only too glad to have the chance of defending Agnes from the inquisitions of the police, with her body, if necessary. Jeanie remembered Sarah's irreverent remarks about her tutor. Agnes, charming, selfish creature, had always had this capacity for arousing devotion. As Jeanie looked down at her old friend's soft hair, of that shade of ash-gold which does not for a very long time show the encroachments of ash-grey, Agnes looked up suddenly with swimming eyes.

"Oh, Jeanie! Don't leave me!"

"I won't, my dear!"

No doubt Agnes had uttered the same plea to Tamsin Wills and would to everybody who came near her. She must always be the centre of her little stage, poor Agnes; she must always have her audience.

"Agnes, I think Sir Henry Blundell would like to see you before you go to sleep."

"Sleep! I shan't sleep!"

Miss Wills interposed eagerly:

"You needn't see him if you don't want to, Agnes."

"Oh, of course I must see him," said Mrs. Molyneux, more pettishly than tragically. "If *only* you wouldn't talk so loud, Tamsin! It goes right through my head!" Tamsin flushed a deep dull red, and said nothing. Jeanie fancied she saw her lids redden behind her horn-rimmed glasses. Tamsin Wills was a heavily-built tall girl of about Jeanie's age, which was twenty-six, with a self-conscious taste in picturesque clothes that did not suit her. She was wearing a pair of green cord gardening breeches and hand-knitted stockings, with a shirt of tomato-coloured silk, its sleeves rolled up her thick strong forearms. She had the stiff, inelastic pose of the athlete who has taken to a sedentary life. Five years ago she had been a first-class hockey-player, but one would not think it now, to look at her. She had grown heavy for her age, and stooped. She wore her hair, which was thick and black and might, with more attention, have looked beautiful, knotted in great coils that bristled with hair-pins over her ears.

"I don't know why it is," pursued Agnes, "but your voice seems just to be pitched on a note I can't bear. I—I twang all over. Where's the eau-de-Cologne? My head aches horribly!"

Eyes averted, standing rigid, Miss Wills put the scent spray in Agnes's feebly stretched-forth hand. She could be sulky, then. Jeanie looked across the bed at the girl's exaggeratedly cold expression and stubborn posture. Couldn't she, at a time like this, take Agnes's pin-pricks with a smile? But, of course, they were not pin-pricks to her, but dagger-blows. A female Malvolio—that was her type. *To be generous, guiltless, and of free disposition, is to take those things for bird-bolts that you deem cannon-bullets...*

"Oh, don't stand there and stare at one another!" uttered Agnes peevishly. "Say something, Tamsin, for Heaven's sake! You get on my nerves! What are you thinking about?"

"I was wondering where Mr. Fone was," said Tamsin frigidly.

"Mr. Fone!"

"Yes. He wasn't with the other members of the Field Club downstairs. He was in the top Tower room when—it—happened. I saw him. He was by himself."

"What about it?"

"I was only thinking it was funny that he should have been sitting there by himself, and that he should have gone home now."

"Why? What are you talking about?" Agnes's head rolled fretfully on the pillow.

"You asked me what I was thinking about. I've told you."

Jeanie visualised the higher Tower room, a little octagonal chamber with a large mullioned window overlooking from on high the green lawn sloping down towards the orchard. It and the room below it in the Tower were used as—gun-rooms. Jeanie looked searchingly at Tamsin. Was it possible that the girl intended to convey—? yes, apparently she did.

"You can see the orchard from the Tower-room window," pursued Tamsin coolly. "When I looked out, I could see Mr. Molyneux quite plainly. It's only about a hundred yards away. Of course, it was an accident, just someone shooting rooks, but still, it's funny, there doesn't seem to have been anybody out shooting at the time. I just happened to go into the Tower room—"

"What for?" asked Jeanie, hoping to disconcert the odious girl. She succeeded. Miss Wills blinked and hesitated.

"Oh, I just happened to! And Mr. Fone was there, sitting on the window-seat. I suppose I looked surprised, because all the other Field Club people were down in the old kitchens. He was looking out of the window. He said he was tired, and was sitting down to rest his legs. I thought it was a funny place to choose for a rest, up at the top of that staircase! I went away. A few moments afterwards I heard a shot. That's all. You asked me what I was thinking about, and I've told you."

"Where were you when you heard the shot, then, Miss Wills?"

Once again the girl blinked, as if the question took her by surprise. Jeanie had an instant impression that she was wondering whether to tell the truth or not. Almost at once, she answered:

"In the lower Tower room. I was—I was looking for Sarah."

"I see. Then you must have seen the thing happen?"

"No, I didn't. When the shot went off, I'd turned away from the window and was going out of the room. I saw *you*," she added coldly to Agnes, "going across the lane. *You* must have seen it happen. You asked me what I was thinking about and I've told you."

Agnes struggled up on to her elbow and looked with eyes wide and wild from Tamsin to Jeanie, from Jeanie to Tamsin. She had gone extraordinarily pale.

"But do you mean," she uttered brokenly, "that— that—?"

"What, Agnes?"

"Jeanie! Does she mean that—that Robert's death— *wasn't an accident?*"

Jeanie realised that this notion, which, thanks to Myfanwy's antics, had never been quite absent from her own mind, was new, new and horrible, to Robert's widow.

"Don't think of it before you need," said Jeanie pitifully. "She doesn't know! No one does!"

"But it was an accident! Tamsin, how can you? You've never liked Mr. Fone since you asked him to marry you and he refused!"

"I didn't!" cried Tamsin, trembling, with suffused eyes.

"You did! How you can *bring* yourself to suggest—! Mr. Fone is a *friend* of Robert's!"

"That's all you know! I've been seeing to the letters since Peter went, and I know better!"

"What do you mean?"

"Mr. Molyneux had a threatening letter only yesterday from Mr. Fone!"

"Threatening! What about? What *are* you talking about?"

"About opening the tumulus. *You* know."

"Oh, that! Really, Tamsin, you are an idiot! You'll be saying next that Mr. Fone that Robert—that Mr. Fone—"

Suddenly Agnes's face, to which spite had lent a flush and a spirit, grew woeful again. She turned helplessly to Jeanie, in tears.

"But, Jeanie! It was an accident, wasn't it?"

"My dear, I don't know," uttered Jeanie helplessly.

"Well, you *asked* me what I was thinking about and I've *told* you," reiterated the odious Tamsin stubbornly.

## Chapter Five
### POLICE INQUIRY

"May I stay? Mrs. Molyneux would like it."

"Certainly, Miss Halliday. We'll take you next." Agnes, who had five minutes ago implored Jeanie not to leave her, now dropped her eyelids and looked weary, as at the fussing of a too-solicitous friend. They were in the little panelled room that lay next to the hall and was usually called the parlour. There was a big flat-topped desk in the room, but nobody sat at it. Superintendent Finister sat at a small side-table, and another policeman, a note-book open in front of him, sat sideways at its end. Some feeling of delicacy, Jeanie supposed, had prevented Sir Henry from bringing poor Molyneux's desk into use. Sir Henry stood with his back to the window.

"This is Superintendent Finister," he added. "We won't keep you longer than we can help, Mrs. Molyneux."

"I'm very sorry to have to trouble you at all, madam," added the superintendent. Jeanie had seen him in Handleston. He was very tall, spare and saturnine, with deep lines in his cheeks and a bristling dark moustache. Without his cap he looked very human and intelligent. The other policeman, burly, red-faced and bald, conformed to a more usual type.

"You can't help it," murmured Agnes.

She looked at Sir Henry, who responded with a melancholy, sympathetic smile. Finister made a respectful pause, fiddling with his pencil and looking at Agnes with dark lively eyes more adapted to express a sardonic than a sympathetic humour.

"May we have your account/' he asked gently, "of what happened this afternoon?"

"What happened?" echoed Agnes, looking frightened. "But I don't know what happened!'

"I mean," the superintendent corrected himself, "the course of events from your own point of view. I understand you first made the discovery?"

"Yes."

"What took you to the orchard?"

"I went to remind my husband to come in and receive the guests. The Handleston Field Club—our guests—had arrived. My husband was working in the orchard and wanted to go on as long as possible. But of course when our guests came in—"

"I see. When did the Field Club actually arrive?" Agnes looked vague.

"I don't know. I was in my room, dressing. They were in the old kitchen when I came down at a quarter-past three. At least, Bates said so."

"It was ten minutes to three when we came in to Cleedons and went to the old kitchens," said Sir Henry Blundell.

"Oh, had you been there all that time, Sir Henry? I do hope Tamsin or somebody looked after you properly! Robert was very anxious to get his fruit-trees done, or he would have been with you."

She began to cry helplessly. There was a pause, while Sir Henry looked out of the window, Finister gazed with grave attention at the fire-place, and Jeanie strove to console Agnes and stem her tears. The burly policeman with the notebook looked with rosy concern at the two ladies.

"I'm sorry!" said Agnes at last. "Only, it seems so dreadful now to think, if he had come in earlier, he would have been—this wouldn't have happened."

Superintendent Finister made the smallest sympathetic sad grimace. Many things were dreadful, it seemed to say, in this dreadful world: dreadfulness was almost the order of nature.

"What time was it when you went out, Mrs. Molyneux?"

"Oh, what time did I say I left my room? At a quarter-past three. And I just—I just spoke to a few people—I mean, to one or two of the servants—I mean, to Bates, to ask if the Field Club had come, and—and he said they had, and I went out to tell my husband."

"At twenty-past three, then, at latest?"

Agnes looked dubious and frightened, as though time were a spectre and haunted her. She had been punctual enough in the old days at school. But life at Cleedons, reflected Jeanie, revolved so much around her will and her convenience that she had grown out of the habit of watching the clock.

"Well, perhaps. I suppose so! Or a little later..."

"*About* twenty-past three," murmured the burly policeman, writing.

"And then?"

"I—I went to the orchard."

Agnes's voice faltered, and her eyes widened and seemed to grow dark, approaching horror.

"Yes. What way did you go?"

Finister's steady voice had a bracing effect.

"I went out of the Tower door and across the lawn and out through the gate by the garage. Across the lane. The orchard gate's just there. I—I saw a kind of movement in the orchard. I can't explain! A sort of movement, something falling. I didn't know what it was. You know how you see things sometimes without realising what you've seen. It was like that. There was a shot and at the same time something falling in the grass. I wondered what on earth Robert had let drop out of the tree. I thought the shot had startled him and he'd dropped his coat or—or something. I thought it was funny the thing he'd dropped should have a *boot* on it!"

A giggle escaped Agnes, and as if that hysterical giggle rather than her recital horrified her, she gave a sob and turned blindly towards Jeanie. After a moment she went on:

"You see, I *saw* it was Robert who'd fallen out of the tree, but I didn't *know* it was! I just thought it was something he'd dropped. Everything was just the same. There was a cart rattling about. And a bird singing. And then I suddenly sort of knew it was Robert. I ran towards him. I ran. I *ran*!" she iterated piteously, and Jeanie had to suppress a mental picture of her friend creeping unwillingly, slowly, in horror across the grass. "I thought at first perhaps he'd fainted or had a stroke or something."

She spoke fast now, on short sobbing breaths, holding Jeanie's hand in a hot dry clasp.

"But he hadn't!" she wailed suddenly, and her tears came. "Oh, please! I saw—I saw he'd been shot. Blood, I saw blood," said she, mastering herself and speaking in a matter-of-fact level voice, the sharp nails of her fingers digging into Jeanie's palm. "I saw blood and I knew he'd been shot. Rabbit-shooting always makes me sick. Only this wasn't as bad as rabbit-shooting, really. Because I simply didn't believe it. Not for ages. I ran all round the orchard, kind of gasping to myself. And I went out of the orchard. And—and I thought I was going to faint or something. And Jeanie came. Oh. And there was Myfanwy Peel. Or did I imagine it? What was she doing there, I wonder?"

"Myfanwy Peel?" murmured Finister, prompting her.

"Mrs. Peel. Sarah's mother. Robert's brother's widow. Yes. I met her walking up the lane, but I can't think what she can have been doing here. I said: 'Robert's dead.' At least, I think I said it. I tried to say it. She didn't answer. She looked awfully queer. I wanted her to help me, you see. I would have asked anybody. I felt so awful, I felt so sick! But she wouldn't, she just went on up the lane. And I saw Jeanie—Miss Halliday, you know—looking out of the stable-loft window. And I thought: *It's no use, I must lie down.* I don't remember after that. That's all. May I go now?"

She looked piteously at Sir Henry. She was of that fair, fragile type from which tears seem to wash the last remnants of colour and vitality. She looked wretched, poor Agnes, like a doll that has been left out in the rain.

"There's only one thing," said Superintendent Finister, "that I wish we could fix, and that's the time. You say you left your room at three-fifteen?"

"Yes. Yes," said Agnes nervously.

"And went almost at once to the orchard, so that you would be at the orchard gate at three-twenty or at most three-twenty-five?"

"Well—I don't know! I didn't have a watch. I didn't look at the time. I might have been earlier." Her eyes, which had been flickering nervously about the room, shot a quick glance at the superintendent's face. "Or later," she added.

"You see, we have two independent witnesses, Miss Tamsin Wills and Sir Henry Blundell, who say they were aware of the time when they heard the shot and that it was then twenty-five minutes to four."

"That is so," agreed Sir Henry.

Agnes said tremulously:

"Yes, well—it might have been. I talked to Bates. I didn't hurry."

"Oh, it's of no great importance," Finister assured her soothingly. "But naturally we have to fix the time of the—shot, and your evidence seems to make it earlier than three thirty-five."

"No, I don't say that! I don't know! I left my bedroom at a quarter-past three, that's all I know!"

"Could you possibly cast your mind back and remember *exactly* what you did between then and coming to the orchard gate?"

"I—I suppose I can!"

Agnes paused so long that Sir Henry Blundell turned his head inquiringly from his contemplation of the last autumn leaves.

"I—I went downstairs."

"Immediately?"

"Yes. Yes, immediately. And Bates was in the hall. And he said that the Field Club had arrived. And I said: 'Where are they?' And he said: 'In the old kitchen, looking at the devil's oven.' And I said: 'We'll have tea at four; I expect that'll give them plenty of time.' And he said—oh, I expect he said 'Very good,' or something, and I—"

There was another pause.

"Well—I just looked at the flowers to see if they were fresh, and they were, and then I went out at the Tower door. I thought, shall I take a mackintosh? but it wasn't raining, so I just put on some galoshes—"

"Where were the galoshes?"

"In the lowest Tower room. It's used as a cloakroom. That's why I went that way. And I went across the lawn—not quickly, you know, quite slowly, thinking about planting some new shrubs. And—and—"

"And as you came to the orchard gate you heard a shot?"

"Yes. I should think it could easily have been three thirty-five by then, couldn't it?"

Superintendent Finister shook his head.

"No, what you've told us couldn't have taken twenty minutes. Seven at the outside, I should say. Are you quite sure, Mrs. Molyneux, you didn't do anything else? Speak to anybody else in the house, for instance?"

"Of course I'm sure!" Suddenly Agnes's pale rain- washed face flushed with uneven colour. She looked from Finister to Jeanie. Her eyes were both frightened and angry. "Why do you ask that?" she demanded shrilly.

Jeanie saw the surprise on Superintendent Finister's face give way to a grave, thoughtful look. He looked very seriously at Agnes. He only said, however, quietly: "It's important to fix the time, you see, of the shot, and I thought possibly you had had a talk with one of the staff or somebody and had forgotten it."

Agnes bent her head. Her hands were clasped tightly in her lap, her whole slight figure tense. "I see. I'm sorry. No, I don't think I did. No, I didn't, I'm sure. May I go now? I've had about as much as I can bear."

"Certainly. We're very sorry to have had to trouble you at all."

"So sorry, *so* sorry," murmured Sir Henry, turning from the window and holding out his hand. He smiled in melancholy fashion, squeezing Agnes's little fingers. Her tears brimmed over.

"Thank you, Sir Henry. No, I won't go through the hall. I can't face all those people! No, Jeanie! It's all right! I'd rather be by myself!"

She went slowly through the door to the Tower. Jeanie heard her steps dragging along the stone passage, up the wooden uncarpeted stairs, slowly, slowly, then suddenly accelerating, pattering quickly up the stairs with heels quickly clicking along the wooden passage overhead. Jeanie, listening to that sudden astonishing acceleration, saw her own surprise reflected in Superintendent Finister's look. And once again she saw his look of surprise melt into a glance thoughtful, grave, even severe.

Jeanie gave her own evidence quickly. She produced an effect, she saw, by her account of Myfanwy Peel and her antics with the revolver. Finister, Sir Henry and even the sergeant all became alert, gazing at her with a sudden bright surmise. She could not but see, herself, that around Myfanwy Peel the motive and the weapon and the opportunity all most opportunely grouped themselves. Yet she could not bring herself to believe that Myfanwy Peel was a murderess, and did her best to damp any such belief that might be taking shape in Superintendent Finister's mind. She stressed the fact that the revolver was unloaded.

"Easy enough to reload it," remarked Sir Henry.

"But of course we don't know yet," said Superintendent Finister, "that the weapon that killed Mr. Molyneux *was* a revolver. We'll know more about that after the autopsy."

Chapter Six

PRIVATE AFFAIRS

Jeanie lay awake long in her raftered bedroom at Yew Tree Cottage that night, and woke at last from an exhausted sleep to find the pale November sunlight streaming through the window opposite her bed, outlining, as a nimbus a saint, the small angular figure of old Mrs. Barchard, holding a broom as a saint his symbol.

"I knocked and knocked, Miss," said Mrs. Barchard reproachfully.

"I was asleep. What's the time?"

"Going on for ten."

"Good Heavens!"

"When I didn't get no answer to my knocking, you see, Miss, I judged it best to enter."

"And I haven't died in my sleep or anything after all," said Jeanie, and with the words came back to the dreadful realities of yesterday. Mrs. Barchard gave an embarrassed snigger and then very suddenly became grave. She had in her time swept, scrubbed and drunk tea in nearly all the houses round Handleston, a little dark woman with the sallow skin of impaired digestion and the bright prominent eyes of volubility.

"Dreadful thing happened at Cleedons, Miss," she now brought forth lugubriously.

"Yes, indeed."

"Poor Mr. Molyneux. Poor *Mrs.* Molyneux, I should say, because it's the ones that's left behind feels it most. Poor Mr. Molyneux, he's gone to his rest. But them that's left behind don't get no rest."

Jeanie took up the cup of strong tea Mrs. Barchard had placed beside her.

"Fancy, to fall out of a tree like that. I had an uncle died in a stroke. Me uncle on me mother's side, he was."

Jeanie let her run on. The village would know soon enough that Robert Molyneux had been murdered, without her information. She could not face the avid rapturous glee with which, she foresaw, Mrs. Barchard would receive enlightenment. She held her tongue, savouring on it the dark chill brew.

"To be took like that! Like being struck by lightning." A queer, half-shocked, half-amused expression came over Mrs. Barchard's thin lively face. She jabbed absently with her broom at the skirting board. "There's some people says it was a kind of lightning. They says it was old Grim."

"Who?"

"It's silly talk, really, Miss, of course. Only Mr. Molyneux he *had* planned to open old Grim's Grave to look for treasure. So they say. They say he was going to get a gentleman down from London to open it."

It was plain from the way Mrs. Barchard's voice sank that she herself was somewhat awed.

"Well, we don't know, do we, Miss? I wouldn't open old Grim's Grave, not for a million thousand pounds' worth of treasure, and plenty of people in Handleston thinks the same. Well, I mean, Miss, opening anybody's grave isn't very nice. And when it's one of these old kings, I mean to say, one doesn't know what misfortunes might happen."

"Oh, Mrs. Barchard, lots of these burial-mounds *have* been opened, you know!"

"Yes, and lots of misfortunes has happened," replied Mrs. Barchard pertinently. "Not that I believes in it meself, exactly... Still, we don't *know*, do we?"

"Yes," said Jeanie with youthful dogmatism. "I think we do know that no harm comes of knowledge. It's ignorant superstitions that do harm."

Mrs. Barchard was instantly on the defensive. Her sallow cheeks grew pink. She said in a voice that held an indignant quiver:

"It isn't only ignorant people thinks so, Miss! Mr. Fone was dead against it. He'd've done anything to stop it!"

Jeanie smiled and stretched.

"Oh, well, Mr. Fone's a poet."

"He's the best, cleverest gentleman that ever lived!" cried Mrs. Barchard vehemently. "And the kindest, too! *He* wouldn't squeeze a poor man to pay him back money he'd lent, when he'd got more than he knew what to do with! *He* wouldn't go poking his nose in a man's private affairs!"

Mrs. Barchard stopped abruptly, trembling a little.

Jeanie looked thoughtfully at the little indignant woman, remembering gossip she had heard about Hugh Barchard and his ill-starred chicken farm and ill-starred love adventure.

"Do you mean," she asked directly, "that Mr. Molyneux *did* do these things?"

The little woman was plainly disconcerted at this directness. A half-ashamed, half-sullen look came over her expressive face.

"I'm not saying so. Only, it wasn't my Hugh's fault that he couldn't make chicken-farming pay when he came back from Canada. He always paid the interest regular on what was lent him. And as for a man's private affairs, what business are they of other folk?"

It was obvious from Mrs. Barchard's unhappy rancorous tone that her son's sinful living had caused her a good deal of suffering. She had the gossip's fear of gossip.

"Was Mr. Molyneux pressing your son to repay a loan?"

Mrs. Barchard looked uneasy.

"I'm not saying so," she muttered. "I didn't say *he* did. I only said Mr. Fone didn't."

"But it *was* Mr. Molyneux who lent your son money to start his chicken-farm, wasn't it?"

"I'm not saying so."

Mrs. Barchard was evidently not saying anything at all about Robert Molyneux, now that Robert Molyneux had joined old Grim among the awful, unknown, propitiated shades.

"Still," she added resentfully, "it wasn't my Hugh's fault the bottom dropped out of chicken-farming, was it? And when everything went wrong at once like that—chickens doing no good, I mean, and that Val treating him so bad and then to be hard on the poor lad about a loan he'd never asked for—"

She glanced defensively at Jeanie, and Jeanie saw that she wanted to defend her boy against the imagined gossips who might already, with their calumnies, have assailed Jeanie's virtuous ears.

"Val?" murmured Jeanie encouragingly.

"That Valentine Frazer that treated him so bad Coming here and spending his money and making all sorts of nasty talk about the place with her silly painted face and red gloves and then to go and break his heart like that!"

"Oh dear!"

"Yes, I told him the sort she was! Often. But he wouldn't listen to me! Oh no! Red gloves, indeed!"

"Oh dear!"

"One thing I do thank Heaven for!" said Mrs. Barchard. "One thing on my knees I thank God for! He never married her."

"Oh dear."

"No. So when she went off with her painter he was well shut of her. He didn't think so, of course. Two years ago last July it was. He come to my house early in the morning, white as a sheet, poor lad. *Val's gone!* he says. *What?* I said. *Val's gone,* he said, *she's sick of me,* he said, *and she's gone up to London to be an artist's model,* he said. *An artist's model!* I said. *That's what you call it, is it? I told you what she was!* I said. *Oh, Mother, it isn't what you think!* he says, poor boy, believing the best of her even then, or pretending to. But everybody in the village knew what she was, Miss. A bad lot, that's what she was. Her and her artist! An actress she'd been and you could see it all over her!"

"An artist?"

"Yes, staying down here at the 'White Lion' he was that summer. A chap with a beard, more like a nanny-goat than a human being."

"*Not* Hubert Southey!"

"Some such name."

"Well, I'm blowed!"

Jeanie reflected how little one knew of the characters and strange private lives of those from whom one learns painting in art schools. Who would have suspected Hubert Southey, that dry and circumspect man, of an entanglement with an ex-actress in red gloves?

"Painted her picture, he did, sitting among the buttercups. And then off he goes, and off she goes. Buttercups!" said Mrs. Barchard, in a tone of extraordinary satire. "And she said her father was a clergyman."

Jeanie smiled.

"Why not? Well, I must get up, Mrs. Barchard."

Startlingly assuming a falsetto drawl as she prepared to leave the room, Mrs. Barchard remarked languidly:

"When mai fawther werz rector of Hunsley!"

Jeanie started.

"Rector of *where*?"

"Hunsley, or some such place, Miss. She was always on about it. Couldn't have gone on more about it if her father'd been a duke. Showed what a guilty conscience she'd got!"

"Not Hunsley in Yorkshire?"

"Yes, it was. On the beeyootiful moors."

"But how *extraordinary*!"

Agnes's father had been Rector of Hunsley, in Yorkshire, on the beautiful moors. Jeanie wondered if the two so very different daughters of two Hunsley rectors had ever become aware of the link between them—the only link, Jeanie imagined, from what she knew of Agnes and had heard of Miss Valentine Frazer!

It was nearly noon when she arrived at Cleedons, and Tamsin Wills met her on the stairs. Agnes, it seemed, was in her bath. She would soon be up and dressed. Meanwhile, if Jeanie cared to come to the Tower room where Miss Wills was arranging some flowers, Miss Wills would do her poor best to entertain her.

Jeanie, who found Miss Wills's ponderous pawkiness almost more embarrassing than her sulks, agreed with what, she knew, was over-effusiveness.

"Where's Sarah?"

"Reading in the school-room. Oddly enough, Sarah's lessons don't seem the most important thing in the world just at the moment!"

Jeanie tried hard not to feel abashed, and followed Sarah's governess up the newel staircase into the octagonal gun-room which, with the two rooms and the cellar below, was all that remained of the Norman tower. The high raftered ceiling, the stone walls with their gunracks and cupboards were formidable and chill. But the big sixteenth-century mullioned window which filled three sides of the octagon, and the cushioned window-seat below it, had a reassuring, kindly, civilised effect, saying that Black Ellen had been dust for centuries, and that those days were no more than a memory when men built strong towers and hid themselves therein, and that the guns in this armoury were used only for shooting coneys and wild birds. Standing by that peaceable, beautiful window, her knee on the soft cushion, Jeanie looked out. Looking down the lawn she could see, across the two low hedges, the orchard, and Molyneux's ladder still leaning against the tree. She could imagine she saw Molyneux himself lying in the grass, complaining that the broad peaceful windows lied! She turned, and met Tamsin's eyes fixed on her in a cold stare above the vases on the table.

"I've been wanting to ask you—*Don't* you think it was my duty, Miss Halliday?"

"What?"

"Why, to tell the superintendent that one can see the orchard from this window. And that I saw Mr. Fone sitting on that window-seat yesterday afternoon. Seeing that he went home so unexpectedly, I mean, and wasn't here to answer questions himself."

Miss Wills took up a chrysanthemum and slowly, as though she were cutting a living thing and rather enjoyed it, cut its stalk before sticking it in a tall vase.

"It was your duty, I suppose," said Jeanie slowly, "to tell the superintendent everything."

"Everything? Oh! I didn't know that! I'm afraid I didn't tell him quite everything."

Was this irony? Jeanie glanced at her companion, but could read nothing from the light that glittered on those large horn-rimmed lenses.

"I mean, I didn't tell the superintendent about the letter Mr. Molyneux had the day before yesterday from Mr. Fone. Perhaps I ought to have done. Do you think so, Miss Halliday?"

"No, I don't think so," replied Jeanie guardedly. "Only if he asks you. The police'll go through letters and things for themselves, won't they?"

"They won't find this one. Mr. Molyneux was so much annoyed he threw it in the fire. I wonder whether I ought to mention it. You see, I've been acting as Mr. Molyneux's secretary since Mr. Johnson went."

"Then I expect the police will ask you if you had any threatening letters."

"Well, you would call it a threatening letter—wouldn't you?—when a person says the wrath of the old gods will fall on your presumption and their heavy feet will crush your flimsy scientific superstitions. Or wouldn't you?"

"Did Mr. Fone really say that?"

"Yes, and a lot more. He's quite crazy in some ways. Especially on the subject of opening the tumulus. A more extraordinary letter I never read."

"Oh well, he's a poet, so I suppose he's allowed these peculiar feelings about tombs and things," said Jeanie placably. "I rather like him."

"There's certainly no accounting for tastes," said Miss Wills acidly, cutting viciously at a flower stalk.

"He's a clever man in his way, surely."

"Great wits to madness sure are near allied, and thin partitions do their bounds divide," said Miss Wills grimly.

"Oh well, as long as they *have* bounds, and *are* divided! Besides, Mr. Fone isn't the only person in this place with feelings about opening the tumulus. Mrs. Barchard's hair was standing on end at the idea, too."

"Oh, village people!" said Tamsin, with a disfiguring sneer.

"Anyway, I suppose the tumulus isn't likely to be opened now?"

"Not unless the Field Club find the money for it, which isn't at all likely. It was going to be an expensive business, you know. Agnes certainly won't want to spend anything on it, with death duties and everything. She doesn't care for that sort of thing, anyway."

"The opening hadn't actually been arranged, then?"

"No. The Office of Works had just given permission for it to be done."

"The Office of Works! I thought the tumulus was on Cleedons land!"

Miss Wills sneered again.

"It is, but it's scheduled as an ancient monument. In these glorious days a man can't do as he likes with his own land—did you think he could? Oh, the dear old villagers will have their way, and old Grim will sleep in peace. Perhaps it was Grim who was responsible for Mr. Molyneux's death!"

"Well, I've heard that theory uttered only this morning."

"After all, one has to dislike a man a good deal to shoot him," went on Tamsin languidly, stuffing another flower into the vase. "And as far as I know, nobody had any cause to dislike Mr. Molyneux. Except old Grim. Oh, and of course old Grim's arch-priest, Mr. Fone." "He was popular, then, was he?"

"Oh, *very*!" answered Tamsin, with an emphasis somehow more damaging than a denial. "Everybody liked him. High and low, rich and poor. *Everybody*."

Somewhat to her own consternation, Jeanie found herself responding abruptly:

"Except you."

Miss Wills seemed quite unperturbed. Her dark eyes gleamed behind gleaming spectacles. She gave a little shrug and a falsetto laugh.

"Oh well!" she said deprecatingly, and yet another mutilated chrysanthemum was crammed into a vase already overfull. "You see, I'm very fond of Agnes."

"What does that mean, exactly?" asked Jeanie somewhat distastefully. It was quite hard work being amiable to Tamsin Wills.

"Well, really, *only* that Mr. Molyneux, like most irresistible men, hadn't much resistance himself! Of course, it must be very nice to be irresistible at fifty-two, and have quite young people falling in love with one. Naturally, one would take it as a sort of joke, I dare say. But not such a joke for one's wife, after all."

"Oh surely!" uttered Jeanie, "Mr. Molyneux wasn't— didn't— he wasn't that sort of man at all!"

She flushed hotly at the unexpectedness of this attack on poor Molyneux, whom she had liked.

Lifting the jammed bunch of flowers and giving them a good shake as if they were naughty children, Miss Wills said primly:

"Oh, don't you think so? But perhaps you didn't know him so very well! *I* did. Poor Marjorie!"

"Marjorie?"

"Marjorie Dasent, you know. She'll miss her riding. I don't suppose Agnes'll keep many horses going."

"I suppose not. Miss Dasent's a great rider, isn't she?" said Jeanie, glad to turn the subject, as she thought.

"Oh, very horsy indeed! Rides to hounds, you know, and comes in all gleeful and girlish, talking at the top of her voice. Oh yes, I'm afraid our Diana of the Chase will miss the Cleedons mounts a good deal."

Tamsin buried her nose in the chrysanthemums, and glanced sideways over them at Jeanie.

"But even more she'll miss her guide, philosopher and friend! Though I believe he *was* doing his best to resign from all three posts! These police inquiries are horrible, aren't they, Miss Halliday? They make one feel so treacherous. Yet what can one do? Do you think one's justified, ever, in keeping anything back?"

Jeanie hesitated.

"I suppose not."

She was about to qualify this, but Tamsin did not give her time.

"I'm so glad! I hoped you'd say that! I had to decide very quickly, you see. Superintendent Finister was here early this morning, asking questions about—well, about Mr. Molyneux's habits and so on, and I had to decide all in a moment, and I thought, yes, it's my duty to tell everything I know. I'm so glad you think I did rightly."

Jeanie was not at all sure that she did think so. She did not like the complacent tone of Tamsin's voice. It was pretty obvious that somebody had received a nasty stab in the back and that Jeanie was being manoeuvred into condoning it.

"You mean," said Jeanie slowly, unable to endure Miss Wills's circumlocutory method of telling what was evidently going to be an unpleasing story, "that the police have been inquiring into Mr. Molyneux's friendship with Miss Dasent?"

"Isn't it horrible for poor Agnes? Only, when the superintendent asked me directly whether I'd ever seen or heard anything, well, what could I do? I felt an absolute traitor. But I'm so glad you think I did right! I don't feel quite so awful now."

"Surely you hadn't anything to tell them!"

Miss Wills turned upon Jeanie a pained, would-be ingenuous look.

"Well, I just told him what I'd heard. In the stable. Last Friday. Not quite a week ago. And it seems like a century."

"Well?" asked Jeanie abruptly, for Tamsin's circumlocutory style annoyed her.

"It was in the stable-loft, you see. I was taking milk to Sarah's kittens. It was in the evening, about five o'clock, just growing dark. I heard somebody come into the stable below. I was just going to get down the ladder when I heard Mr. Molyneux say: *Marjorie, you mustn't do this. Really, my dear, you mustn't. Can't you see how foolish it is?* He was speaking quite kindly, but strongly, you know, as if he was annoyed and didn't want to show it too much. And then I heard Miss Dasent, and she sounded very emotional, and she said: *Oh, Robert, I had to! Don't be angry with me!* And he said: *I'm not angry, but really you can't do this sort of thing. If you want to see me, you can come to the house, Marjorie.* I suppose you think that I oughtn't to have listened, Miss Halliday, but what could I do? Go down the ladder and burst in on them?"

"I suppose not."

"I'm so glad you understand! Well—and then she kind of burst out crying and became very hysterical and said she was miserable because she hadn't seen him, and what had she done to make him cross with her, and all that kind of thing, really quite incoherent! I don't remember it all. And he said she must pull herself together and not give way to silly fancies. He said: *I'm a quarter of a century older than you, my dear, and my romantic days are a long way behind me!* Which wasn't quite true, of course, because

Marjorie's thirty-three if she's a day! And then he said half-jokingly: *And anyway, I'm Agnes's property, you know, my dear.* And she burst out: *She doesn't care for you, she's heartless!* And he said quite angrily: *Please don't talk like that!* And then I heard him say more sympathetically: *You ought to go away for a holiday, Marjorie. Ask your father to let you go away on a cruise for a month or two. And when you come back we'll be better friends than ever, and laugh at all this together.* And she kind of shouted out: *Laugh! How can you be so devilish?* And then he went away, and she went on howling to herself, and I crept down the ladder without her noticing me, she was so busy soaking poor Gipsy with her tears."

There was a pause when Tamsin had brought her narrative to a close. A certain note of gloating triumph seemed to linger on the air, and Tamsin as well as Jeanie seemed to become aware of it, for hastily she added in a voice pitched so mournfully that it was almost lachrymose:

"I can't tell you, Miss Halliday, how badly I've felt about it. I'm so glad you think I did right not to try to conceal it. Though, of course, for Agnes's sake, I was terribly tempted to."

"I suppose it was right to tell the police," conceded Jeanie coldly. "But why tell me?"

Tamsin looked for a second disconcerted, but soon recovered herself and gave a somewhat artificial smile.

"I'm sorry if I've bored you, Miss Halliday."

"You haven't bored me, exactly. I'm only wondering just why you disliked poor Mr. Molyneux so much that you can get a kick out of repeating that sort of story about him."

Jeanie's voice was a little breathless. Her face was burning. The dormant hostility between the two of them awoke fully armed. They glared at one another.

"Really, Miss Halliday, I don't know why you should take that tone!"

"You're not going to tell me you didn't dislike him!"

"I certainly didn't dislike Mr. Molyneux. But as I've already explained, I'm a friend of Agnes's, and—"

"Oh, for Heaven's sake don't start all over again!"

"Very well. I'm sorry I ever mentioned the matter."

"I should think so!"

About to depart indignantly, Jeanie turned, finding a weapon to her hand:

"By the way, what *were* you doing in the lower Tower room at the time Mr. Molyneux was shot?"

Tamsin looked startled, furious and secretive all in the space of a moment.

"Looking for Sarah. I said so."

"Why?"

Miss Wills laughed somewhat harshly.

"I am her governess, you know!"

"Yes, but why the Tower?"

"It's a good look-out place!" said Tamsin defensively. Her dark, pebbly eyes snapped at Jeanie behind their horn-rimmed glasses.

"You certainly get a good view of the orchard from there," agreed Jeanie.

"What does that mean, exactly?"

Jeanie shrugged her shoulders. She remembered how Sarah had said: *Uncle Robert says I'm getting beyond her. I don't think she'll be here much longer. She adores Aunt Agnes...* Suddenly, under the cold hostile look of those dark eyes, Jeanie felt a shiver pass over her. This was not an abstract thing that they were quarrelling about. Out there in the sunny orchard under the trees, Robert Molyneux had lain dead. Perhaps out of this window, perhaps out of another, the murderer had taken aim: perhaps with one of these very lethal weapons that stood in racks and cases around the room!

Jeanie turned to go. But before she had reached the door, the other girl detained her.

"Don't go! One moment!" Tamsin cleared her throat, seemed to make a great effort to speak agreeably. "I'll be frank with you, Miss Halliday! I wasn't looking for Sarah."

"No?"

"No. I was—I was curious."

"Curious? What do you mean?"

"Miss Dasent hadn't been near Cleedons all the week-end. Mr. Molyneux went riding alone on Sunday. I knew she couldn't keep away for long. I just wondered whether *Diana* would become *Pomona* for the occasion, you know!"

"I see," said Jeanie coldly.

"I suppose you think it not very nice of me, Miss Halliday? But, after all, I *am* Agnes's friend!"

"She *is* lucky, isn't she?" commented Jeanie, and closed the door between herself and Tamsin.

Chapter Seven
UNDER SUSPICION

An hour in Agnes's company made Jeanie quite worn out. Pale and rouged, nervous as a strayed cat, she fidgeted about her bedroom, sitting down and getting up, staring in the mirror, shuddering aside from it, picking up and putting down letters of condolence, books, clothes that she seemed to be already sorting out to make room for a wardrobe of widow's black. Mentally, she seemed equally at sea, jumping from one subject to another, nervous, inattentive, strained. Only once did Jeanie really succeed in catching her friend's attention. That was when, remembering Mrs. Barchard's gossip, she was suddenly inspired to ask:

"By the way, it *was* at Hunsley, wasn't it, Agnes, that your father had his living?"

Agnes, who was standing near the fire-place at the moment, doing something to her hair, a silver mirror in her hand, became suddenly still, one hand poised at her little neck, her eyes fixed on the glass.

"Why?"

"Only by a strange coincidence, the former tenant of Yew Tree Cottage—"

Jeanie got no further, for Agnes, whose nerves were evidently very much out of order, started violently and dropped her mirror with a shattering noise on the edge of the steel fender. The glass splintered, the fire-irons fell with a clatter. Agnes, with a sharp sobbing cry, clasped her hands to her head as if driven to despair. She cried shrilly:

"There've been other rectors at Hunsley, I suppose, beside my father!"

Jeanie stared at her in amazement.

"Agnes..."

"What? *What?*"

"I didn't say—anything! I didn't finish what I was going to say! How did you know—"

Agnes lowered her clasped hands. She looked oddly frightened. She moistened her lips and uttered defiantly and yet uncertainly:

"You said that that woman's father was rector of Hunsley too!"

"I didn't! I was going to, but—"

"You did! Don't be silly, Jeanie! How should I know what you were going to say? You said it!"

"But, my dear, I didn't!"

"You did! You did!" persisted Agnes, trembling. "Oh, look at this! A broken mirror, on top of everything else! Oh Jeanie, haven't I got enough to bear without anything more? You *did* say so! You said, it's a funny thing, but the former tenant of Yew Tree Cottage said her father was Rector of Hunsley, too!"

Agnes sank down upon her knees and began, sobbing under her breath, to collect the fragments of broken glass. Jeanie stooped in silence to help her. After a moment she was surprised to hear Agnes murmur submissively:

"Perhaps you didn't, Jeanie. Perhaps you didn't say so. Only, you see, Jeanie dear, I've heard the tale so often before, from lots of people. Her father was a clergyman, it seems. He *was* Rector of Hunsley at some time or another. I just jumped to what you were going to say. You see?"

Yes, Jeanie saw. She saw the plausibility of this. What she did not see was why Agnes had been in the first place startled into dropping her mirror and asserting so frantically such an obvious untruth.

She stayed the day at Cleedons, at Agnes's request. Molyneux's lawyer had arrived, a black-robed costumier seemed mournfully to haunt the upper corridors with armfuls of black clothes, a cousin of Molyneux's had come to offer consolation and help, letters flooded the entrance hall at every post, and two policemen in plain clothes appeared and disappeared in the garden and orchard.

Agnes went early to bed, and Jeanie looked forward with relief to the prospect of her own home and hearth. She was just letting herself out of the parlour French windows on to the starlit terrace when the movement of one of the tree-like patches of darkness caught her eye, and froze her hand on the latch. It was a still, clear evening, and but for an owl calling, the country was quite silent. Though there was no moon, Jeanie could see the bare branches of trees against the sky. Standing uncertainly, half-fearful, in the doorway, she saw a man a little way down the terrace, his white face in the darkness turned towards her.

"Who's there?"

The dark figure moved, came towards her.

"I thought you were Agnes. I'm sorry if I startled you."

"No. I'm Jeanie Halliday."

"I'm Peter Johnson. I'm terribly sorry I startled you. You see, I thought you were Agnes."

Jeanie inquired with a faint smile:

"Did you want to startle Agnes, then?"

"I wanted to speak to her," said the young man inexpressively. He looked extraordinarily pale in the starlight, and lined. Jeanie would hardly have recognised the pleasant carefree youth she had met as Mr. Molyneux's secretary in the summer.

"I'm afraid you can't. She's gone to bed. But come in, won't you? We've met before, you know, in the summer."

"I remember. Before the tragic happenings of our last chapter." Peter gave a grim laugh and followed Jeanie back into the room, shutting the French windows on to the frosty terrace. He looked at the remains of the warm log fire.

"I don't know whether I ought to cross this threshold."

"You've often crossed it before."

"That was in my respectable days," said the dark young man with a sort of bitter humour. "Since the summer, I've sunk to all sorts of depths."

"I'm sorry to hear that," said Jeanie lightly, reviving the fire with the bellows.

"Yes, I've been a thief for some time," said Peter meditatively. "And now it seems I'm a murderer as well."

Jeanie dropped the bellows.

"Let me do that," said Peter, picking them up. "I'm sorry if I startled you."

"You've said that before," said Jeanie a trifle tartly. "And you know, or perhaps you don't, that there *has* been a murder here."

"Oh, I know! That's the murder I'm suspected of having done. I'm not *really* a murderer, though. Although I'm just as much a murderer as I am a thief, and everybody thinks I'm a thief."

"In fact, you're Little Misunderstood, aren't you?" said Jeanie crossly. She did not care for melodrama in real life, and Mr. Peter Johnson struck her as unnecessarily histrionic in his behaviour. He made no reply. Glancing at him as he knelt on the hearth-rug and worked the bellows, she half repented her tartness when she observed the lines in his white young face, the smudges beneath his eyes, the lips tensed so as not to tremble.

"What happened to you yesterday?" she asked more gently. He was instantly on the defensive.

"What do you mean?"

"You were here, weren't you? Sarah said you were."

"Well, I am still a member of the Handleston Field Club, you know, even though no longer a member of this household!"

Jeanie looked steadily at him. He put down the bellows and looked inimically back at her.

"What, you came all the way up from London to join the Field Club in looking at Grim's Grave and Black Ellen's Tower?"

"Well?"

"Never seen them before, had you?"

"Many times."

"So many times that halfway through the proceedings you got bored and went off to London again. You weren't here anyway when the police inquiry was going on."

Peter's face darkened.

"Thank you, I've had all the police inquiry I want at my flat in London."

"What time did you go off yesterday?"

"I left the house, madam, at about half-past three."

As soon as you'd had a good look at the medieval kitchen?"

"I didn't go near the kitchen."

"Not after coming all the way from London to see it?"

Peter Johnson put down the bellows and stood up. A bright flame rushed up around the log. Standing on the hearth-rug in his overcoat and scarf, Peter looked tall, angry, and formidable. Once again, as with Tamsin Wills, Jeanie felt a little chill of the spirit. Here the two bandied words, as if there were no realities in this peaceful, lovely place: but murder had been a reality in this peaceful, lovely place only yesterday.

Jeanie, sitting in her low chair, looked up at Peter, and suddenly thought how she scarcely knew him, how they were alone together, how somebody unknown had murdered poor Robert Molyneux. She was silent. But Peter replied after a moment:

"The fact is, as you've very perspicaciously guessed, Miss Halliday, I *didn't* come down here to see the medieval kitchen. No, I came down here to see Mrs. Molyneux." He paused. "And, having seen her, I went home."

He lit a cigarette, frowning, and offered one to Jeanie. "No, thank you. Well, it's funny, but when the police were making their inquiries yesterday, Agnes didn't say anything about seeing you."

"It isn't funny at all. It may be very tragic," said Peter, looking at her sombrely.

"Why?"

"Well, because I didn't say anything about it either to the police. When they asked me why I'd come down here yesterday I said I'd come to join the Field Club. I suppose I was a fool. I felt I'd rather leave it to Agnes to clear my character."

"Well, I'm afraid she didn't do it, Peter."

"I might have known she wouldn't," said Peter with extreme bitterness. "She let me be thought a thief. She'll let me be thought a murderer. I wonder whether she'd let me be hanged? I dare say she would, you know. Yes, I've no doubt she'd let me be hanged," said he with a sort of bitter cheerfulness that grated on Jeanie's ears.

"Aren't you talking rather nonsense?" protested Jeanie painfully, flushing, for Agnes was her friend. Peter looked at her coldly.

"Am I?"

"Well, can't you explain? Why did you come down to see Agnes?"

"Certainly I can explain," said Peter crisply, "if you've the patience to listen to me. I don't know whether you are aware of it, Miss Halliday, but you see before you a member of the criminal classes."

He paused.

"You take it very calmly, Miss Halliday. I suppose my reputation has lingered on the scene of my crime."

Jeanie said, quietly:

"I knew you'd left here, of course. I knew there'd been some trouble."

Peter threw his head back and laughed a rather forced and dreary laugh.

"Some trouble! How charmingly meiotic!"

Jeanie sat up, bristling. The melodramatic young idiot annoyed her.

"Charmingly what?"

"Meiotic. Ladylike. Euphemistic. Understated. Some trouble! Yes, there was some trouble, just a spot. I stole sixty pounds out of the wages safe, dear lady. I was a confidential secretary. I had the combination of the safe where the wages money was kept. I stole sixty pounds of it. Depravity could go no further. Didn't Agnes tell you about it?"

"No, she hasn't said anything about you."

"Surprising!" said Peter with an unpleasant sneer. He added: "And rather ungrateful, too, seeing that I stoic the money to give her. Ingratitude, your name is Agnes. However, I'm even with you now. I've divulged the secret. I will *not* be chivalrous any longer. Chivalry, Jeanie, is a mistake."

"Of course it is, if it leads you to stealing and telling lies," responded Jeanie tartly. "Do you really mean to say, Peter, you stole Mr. Molyneux's money to give to Mrs. Molyneux and then put on a tin halo and let him dismiss you for stealing? Chivalry, indeed! You must have had a fool's bringing-up!"

Peter said through stiff lips:

"Thank you, but I've been suspecting that myself for the last three weeks. You needn't labour the point."

"I'm sorry! Only, you must admit, Peter—"

"I *do* admit it. I was a fool."

"She'd got herself into difficulties over dress-bills, I suppose. Agnes is very extravagant. I dare say she used to quarrel with her husband about her bills."

"She certainly did," agreed Peter, sinking down into a chair and running his hands through his dark hair. "I ought never to have let a good job go for such a fool reason, I see that now. I ought to have told Agnes that if she didn't tell Mr. Molyneux the truth, I would. But I didn't realise at the time what it would mean. No reference. No new job. That was really why I came down yesterday. I couldn't get a job. I couldn't give Molyneux as a reference, of course, although I'd been here three years. It all seemed *too* unfair, *too* absurd! After all, to Mrs. Molyneux it was just a matter of a—a row with her husband. To me, it was my livelihood, my—my career! I thought I could persuade her to tell Mr. Molyneux that—that I wasn't quite such a hound as he thought me. She was in her room. I slipped a note under the door. After a while she came out and spoke to me in the corridor upstairs. She wouldn't listen to me. She said—I can see her expression now—she said: *But, Peter, what are you talking about?* She was wearing a sort of plum-coloured dress. She looked—like a saint. And she could do that. Pretend she didn't know what I was talking about. When—"

"Oh, Peter!" murmured Jeanie, distressed, with burning cheeks. Too clearly she could see the scene: it fitted in too well with what she had seen of the new Agnes.

"It was a bit of rotten bad luck Mr. Molyneux ever knew anything about it," said the young man gloomily. "Often he didn't go to the safe for weeks on end. And Mrs. Molyneux had some dividends coming in a few days, she said. There didn't seem much harm in borrowing the money for her. She seemed in such a state, and I couldn't help her, I hadn't a bean! I was a damned fool, I soon realised that! I used to break into a sweat whenever the old man went near the safe. I dare say he noticed, and that's what made him open it! Of course, I ought to have refused to have anything to do with the idea! Only—oh well! I don't know! She seemed so upset, and—fool!" said Peter, apostrophising himself, and became silent.

"The police know you were dismissed for theft, don't they?"

"Yes. I told them, because if I hadn't somebody else would have done."

"But they *don't* know why you came here yesterday?"

"Well, as a member of the Handleston Field Club—"

"Oh rubbish, they wouldn't take any notice of that! They probably think you came here yesterday to threaten Mr. Molyneux into giving you a character—that he refused, and you shot him in revenge. After all, a young man who'll steal sixty pounds off a trusting employer is a pretty tough guy, they probably think."

Peter winced.

"I didn't even *see* Mr. Molyneux!"

"Can you prove it? What *did* you do yesterday afternoon?"

"When I left the house after seeing Agnes it was about half-past three. I was in no hurry. I walked slowly over the common, intending to walk back to Handleston eventually and get a train. But I met a man waiting in the lane with a car, and he gave me a lift."

"Oh. Who was that?"

"A friend of Mrs. Peel's. You know, Sarah's mother. She was down here yesterday, for some reason. He was waiting for her when I came across him, and when she turned up we went off."

"How long were you talking to this man before she turned up?"

"Oh, only two or three minutes, I should think."

"And where were you when you heard the shot?"

"I didn't hear any shot."

"You didn't! But if the shot was fired at twenty-five to four, and it was about half-past three when you left the house, you must have—"

"I didn't hear a thing. I was—thinking about all sorts of things while I walked over the common. I dare say I shouldn't have heard an earthquake if there'd been one."

Peter crossed his legs and stared moodily at the toe of his shoe. He looked tired beyond measure. Jeanie said gently:

"Things'll look better in the morning. What are you going to do? You can't very well stay here, I suppose."

"I'd rather sleep in a ditch!"

"You can't do that either, it would look most suspicious."

He smiled faintly.

"Perhaps old Fone'd give me a bed for the night. He's a good sort. He wouldn't refuse sanctuary even to a—murderer. It's against his religion, or something. I'll go to Cole Harbour."

The night was crisp and frosty as they made their way down the drive to the lane that led through the farmyard and out on to the road near Cole Harbour House. They walked for some way in silence. Jeanie glanced at her companion and in the starlight as they swung along saw his face white and grim. Perhaps the cold air, chilling her skin, chilled her mind and spirit too, for of a sudden with a little thud of the heart she found herself thinking:

"Suppose this *is*, after all, Robert Molyneux's murderer?"

She found she must utter her thought. She could not let it rankle and fester in her mind.

"Peter," she said gravely, "it is true, isn't it, that you—"

She stuck. He helped her out.

"That I didn't kill Robert Molyneux? Yes, it's true. But I can't prove it, Jeanie. Perhaps the inquest'll settle it all, and I shan't have to."

"The inquest will be adjourned, I expect," said Jeanie. "I don't think they've found the weapon yet. They hadn't, this morning."

Peter Johnson gave her a sidelong look. His face looked ghostly pale in the starlight.

"I can't bear the thought of doing nothing," he muttered. "Just sticking around waiting for the police."

He broke off as the light of a car suddenly flashed in his face. It crept out of the drive of Cole Harbour House and moved off towards Handleston with gathering speed. In the back seat of the car, behind the uniformed driver, Jeanie had caught sight of the peaked cap and long saturnine face of Superintendent Finister.

## Chapter Eight
### THIN PARTITIONS

Jeanie meant to refuse William Fone's invitation to come into the house with Peter and take some refreshment, but her curiosity to see the inside of Cole Harbour House was too much for her. Mr. Fone led them slowly, jerking on his two sticks, into a long spacious room lined with books. Four tall uncurtained windows almost filled the front wall, and with their arched heads and elaborately enlaced glazing bars in the manner of the Gothic revival, gave something of the air of a chapel to the place. A great log fire burned in the wide hearth, and near it stood a wooden settle and some easy chairs.

Mr. Fone set comfortable chairs for his guests and subsided himself slowly on to the high settle seat. Seated, he was a fine, rugged-looking man whose natural background would seem to be the outdoors. He had the broad shoulders, muscular hands, finely-set head and jutting nose and chin of a strong man. But his dull skin and encircled eyes told of a life spent much indoors. He had been crippled from infancy, Jeanie had heard. Most of his forty-five years had been spent in overcoming his disabilities. He was a poet with a name in that small world in which modern poetry is read. He had written also a book on Ancient Britain which had been an unexpected success in a wider sphere, much to the amusement of Molyneux and Fone's other neighbours, who had continued to think him mildly crazy.

"Are you comfortable, Miss Halliday?" asked Fone, settling his sticks beside him. "I haven't given you the chair with the damp cushions, have I? As you can see, we've been having trouble with the roof of this room, and the rain the day before yesterday came through and soaked one of these chairs."

He pointed to a damp patch in the high ceiling above their heads.

"There is a flat leaded roof over this room, and we find it a good deal of expense and trouble."

Jeanie smiled.

"Can it be worse than stone tiles?"

"Yes, I think so, because it's not so easily repaired. However, Barchard patches it up and saves me the expense of a builder."

"May I stay the night, Mr. Fone?" asked Peter abruptly.

"Of course," replied Mr. Fone, with an equal lack of ceremony.

"Perhaps I ought to say the police suspect me of being a murderer."

"That's excellent. They suspect me too," said Fone, smiling. Meeting Jeanie's wide and inquiring eye, he went on: "The worthy superintendent from Handleston can't understand how it was that I left the party at Cleedons yesterday and went home before tea was served. I told him, I don't like tea. But tea, it seems, is a sacrament in these isles and in this age. Only one thing puzzled poor Finister more than this heathenness of mine in neglecting holy tea; and this was the problem of why I should have gone to the Tower to rest while the others were looking at the medieval kitchen. I explained that modern buildings don't interest me and also that I wanted to be alone, as I had been a good deal troubled in mind. Instantly, with the air of a man who has really thought astutely for once, he asked why I should have chosen to be solitary in the highest room in the Tower? I reminded him that when a man feels troubled, it's his instinct to climb high and look down on the world. The worthy superintendent glanced at my two sticks. I said, even a cripple is not immune from man's ancientest impulses. He looked a little ashamed, but recovered himself, for shame, you know, Miss Halliday, has no place in the soul of a superintendent of police."

Jeanie smiled acquiescently. Mr. Fone's sonorous narrative style made her feel, lying back in her luxuriously cushioned chair while he perched before her on the settle, a little like the Sultan Shahriar in thrall to the interminable stories of his crafty bride. She glanced at Peter. Peter's eyes were on Mr. Fone's face. Peter had something of the look of a frightened child trying, at the moment of danger, to read the face of the almost omnipotent grown-up. Perhaps he had never outgrown the child's early fear of the policeman. Fone, it would appear, had never felt it. He chuckled a little at Jeanie's sympathetic smile, and went on:

"He recovered himself and asked what it was that troubled me so. I replied, the proposed desecration of Grim's Grave. Finister

smiled the foolish empty smile of the man of the world, and said:
'Of course you believe in all that stuff, sir!' I replied that certainly I
believed in the sacredness of the grave. He said, still with that
vacant smile: 'I wouldn't believe it *was* a grave, just on hearsay.' I
explained that I do not hold my beliefs on hearsay. I hold them
with the marrow of my bones. When I walk upon Grim's Grave, I
do not need tradition to tell me that it is a sacred spot. The bones
buried there speak to me through the soles of my feet. He said
nothing for a while. He gave me a look as if he doubted my sanity,
which made me laugh. At this he said, like the automaton he is—I
heard the words before he uttered them—'It's no laughing matter,
sir!' 'True,' I replied. 'Robert Molyneux's death is no laughing
matter. But I wasn't laughing at Robert Molyneux's death. I didn't
laugh when I saw him fall from the tree he was mutilating, and I
don't laugh now.' Superintendent Finister quite surprised me by
the energy with which he bounded out of the chair you are now
sitting in. He cried: 'You saw him fall!' I replied that certainly I
saw him fall."

Jeanie, if she did not bound out of her comfortable chair,
certainly sat up straighter.

"Do you mean, Mr. Fone, you actually *saw*—?"

"As I sat in the Tower room," replied William Fone, "looking
out of the window, I saw Robert Molyneux mount a ladder into
one of the apple-trees; I thought of the thing he was about to do in
opening Grim's Grave, and the horror he was about to loose upon
the countryside. I tried, as you may remember doing yourself in
childhood, Miss Halliday, to influence him from afar, to will him,
as children say, to put the sacrilege out of his thoughts. I felt all
my spirit concentrate in a beam of invisible heat towards that tree,
until Molyneux turned his head as if in answer to a summons.
There was a sharp crack! and in a moment he was tumbling to the
ground. It was as if the beam of my will had caused an explosion

in that tree and sent Molyneux to his death. I descended the Tower stair and went home across the fields."

Jeanie gasped:

"But, Mr. Fone! Didn't you go to see what had happened?"

"I follow my impulses, Miss Halliday. They are a man's safest guide. As for poor Molyneux, I knew that he was dead."

"But—how?"

"A man has other vehicles of knowledge beside his faulty eyes and ears. It is the tragedy of this modern life we live that he has forgotten how to use them. I knew that Molyneux was dead as surely as I knew that my prayer was answered. *How* it happened was not for me to inquire."

Jeanie stared fascinated at this extraordinary man. He said gently:

"You think it callous of me to speak like this. But then, you think nothing of the dangers from which poor Molyneux's death has delivered us."

Jeanie glanced uneasily at Peter. As if he read her thought, Fone went on:

"I am not mad, Miss Halliday, but I fear I can't do anything to prove myself sane to you. We see with different eyes. What is life to me is the merest elaboration of cobweb work to you, and what is reality to you is a thin veil to me."

The door opened, and Hugh Barchard came in quietly, carrying a tray which he put on the table. He smiled and was about to withdraw again when Fone gestured him to a seat on the settle.

"Sit down, Hugh. We're discussing the death of Mr. Molyneux."

"There won't be much else talked about in Handleston for weeks, I expect," said Barchard, with his odd accent that was the West-country burr sharpened by long familiarity with Canadian speech.

"Tell me, Mr. Fone," said Jeanie, more at ease again, for the presence of Barchard seemed to put Fone's eccentricities into perspective as the fancies of an invalid, "tell me: did you say to Superintendent Finister all you've said to us?"

Fone smiled and poured out from the jug on the table a glass of pale golden liquid.

"You're thinking that the worthy superintendent must have thought my story very suspicious. No doubt. But it was not for me to forestall and counter suspicion, but to tell the truth. No doubt the perplexed Finister is even now at Cleedons searching all the weapons in the Tower for my finger-prints. He will not find them. I did not kill Robert Molyneux. Will you take a glass of metheglin, Miss Halliday?"

Sipping the strange, sweet drink, Jeanie had a sudden inspiration. She put the glass down.

"Mr. Fone: you say you *saw* the thing happen. You saw Mr. Molyneux fall out of the tree?"

"Yes."

"Then you can say which way he was facing when he was hit. And that means you can say what direction the shot came from. Isn't that very important?"

Fone smiled faintly.

"Superintendent Finister seemed to think so. Though, as I pointed out to him, if I committed the murder myself, as he seemed to think, my evidence on that or any other point would be unreliable, to say the least. He was rather annoyed. He seemed to think that he had carefully disguised his suspicions from me."

"What way was Mr. Molyneux facing?"

"I'll tell you what I told the superintendent. All the while I was watching Molyneux he had his back towards me. My eyes converged, as it were, on the back of his head."

Jeanie made a hasty mental sketch-map of the Cleedons orchard and its surroundings.

"He was shot in the left temple. Why then, that means the shot must have come—well, from *this* direction, as Sir Henry thought! From the south!'"

"No, for he turned his head. As I told you, he turned his head as if in answer to my silent call upon him. He turned his head so that he almost faced me. And at that moment came the crack of the shot and he fell."

"He almost faced you," repeated Jeanie, readjusting her mental picture. "In that case, it *was* from the lambing-shed direction, the north-west, that the shot came. The lambing-shed, where Sir Henry found the cigarette-end! Surely this is awfully important, Mr. Fone! Did you notice the exact time?"

Mr. Fone smiled a little at Jeanie's excitement.

"Certainly. When I got up to go home I looked at my watch. It was a minute or so after I had seen Molyneux fall, and the time was twenty-three minutes to four."

"That agrees with Tamsin Wills. She said the time was three thirty-five. Agnes seemed to suggest that it might have been earlier."

Jeanie stopped abruptly, realising that Agnes had said nothing to her or to the police about a meeting with Peter Johnson. The interview Peter had described might well account for the ten minutes' gap in Agnes's story. It was plain now why Agnes had become so shrill and angry at the end of her interview with Superintendent Finister. She had been hiding something. But, as with most cowards, it was her luck to fly from a lesser danger to a greater. For, if the police came to hear, as of course they would come to hear, of her quarrels with Robert, they might think that ten minutes' gap in her time-table hid something worse than an interview with Peter.

## Chapter Nine
## CROWNER'S QUEST

The inquest was opened the following day at two o'clock in the work-room at Cleedons, a large old barn which Robert Molyneux had converted to his uses as a carpenter's shop. The natural melancholy of the occasion was intensified by the chilled, discoloured faces of those who attended, hands nervously rubbed together and breath vaporous upon the air.

Dr. Hall, the police surgeon and amateur archaeologist, was first called. Jeanie, who had last encountered him wearing his private professional manner on the threshold of Agnes's bedroom, would hardly have recognised that mournful medico in the brisk, abrupt and cocksure little man who now cheerfully deposed to having performed an autopsy on the body of Robert Molyneux.

"—perfectly healthy, and all the organs free from disease. The left temple bone was perforated, and I found much laceration of both cerebral hemispheres. Imbedded in the right frontal lobe I found this bullet."

A small object lying on a piece of stiff paper was passed up the table towards the coroner, who, picking it up, commented curiously:

"A lead bullet, I see, somewhat flattened by the impact."

"The bullet had entered at a point on the extreme left of the frontal lobe just above the eye-socket, and travelled in a straight line through the frontal lobes, causing damage to the sphenoid bone and extensive laceration of the cerebrum. There was no scorching around the perforation."

"You were among the first to reach the body after death?"

"I believe so. I saw the body within a very short while of death."

"At what time, Dr. Hall?"

"At ten minutes to four. Sir Henry Blundell and Miss Halliday were present. The body was then lying in the orchard. It was quite warm."

"How long, in your opinion, since death had taken place?"

"Taking into consideration the damp cold earth upon which the body was lying, I should say death could not have taken place more than twenty minutes previously."

The coroner, a Mr. Perrott, a retired solicitor living in Handleston, nodded.

"That would fix the earliest possibility of death at half-past three. You heard no shot yourself, Doctor?"

"As a matter of fact, I did. I left the house about half-past three to fetch a copy of *Archaeologia* from my car, which I had left in Cole Harbour Lane near the foot-path stile. As I reached the car, I heard a shot. I did not look at my watch, but it must have been about twenty-five minutes to four."

"Did you pass the orchard gate on your way to your car?"

"No. I took the foot-path across the fields."

"Did you see anybody at all?"

"Nobody. At least"—Dr. Hall corrected himself—"that is not quite accurate. There was somebody repairing the roof of Cole Harbour House. As I crossed back over the stile I heard a hammering noise, and saw somebody on the leads. It was Mr. Barchard, I believe."

The middle-aged man who next gave evidence was unknown to Jeanie.

"You are a gunsmith, Mr. Toogood? Can you describe this bullet?"

"It's a lead bullet from a point twenty-two rim-fire cartridge. Chiefly used in miniature rifles for range practice, and also in rook-rifles for sporting purposes."

"Can they be used in any other kinds of fire-arm?"

"There are several makes of automatic pistol and similar arms on the market which use this ammunition," replied Mr. Toogood. "These arms are made for practice and target purposes, as the ammunition is much cheaper than large-calibre ammunition. They would not be likely to be bought by anyone for defence purposes.'

"Could this bullet," inquired the coroner, with a glance at Superintendent Finister, "have been fired from a service revolver?"

"No, they are all of larger calibre." Mr. Toogood hesitated, and corrected himself. "Well, there is an adaptor can be used that would make it possible to fire a bullet like this from a service revolver. They aren't exactly common."

"Now there is the point of from what distance the shot was fired."

"Well, that'd entirely depend, really, on what the weapon was. A rifle of point twenty-two calibre can be accurate up to two hundred yards or more. But in the hands of most people an automatic pistol using this ammunition would have a much shorter effective range. It can't have been fired from very close, that's the only certain thing, or the bullet would have gone clean through the head, whatever it was fired from. But it's not possible to say exactly how far. I should say that the shot must have been fired from more than twenty yards away, but I wouldn't like to be more exact than that, till I know whether it was a rifle or a pistol it was fired from."

"I see. Do you know the Tower gun-rooms, Mr. Toogood?"

"Yes, sir."

Jeanie heard Peter, who was sitting next to her, very cautiously draw in his breath. He looked flushed and strung-up.

"Are there any weapons in the Cleedons Tower gunrooms which might have fired this shot?"

A faint smile came to the gunsmith's free. "Fourteen, sir."

"Oh, indeed!"

"But not many of them could have been fired from either of the Tower rooms, if that's what you mean, sir. I mean, only the three rifles would carry the distance, and you'd need to be a pretty hot shot, even then."

"Oh," said the coroner hastily. "I was not suggesting —I did not mean necessarily *from* the Tower." He shot a glance at William Fone's impassive face, as though he already knew the nature of the evidence Fone was to give. "Still, it is in your opinion possible—I mean, it is your opinion that a rifle-shot could carry accurately the distance between either of the Tower rooms and the orchard?"

"I'm told the distance is about a hundred and fifty yards. It could be done, sir. But only by a good shot."

"Thank you, Mr. Toogood."

Mr. Toogood took his seat again in Perrott looked over the papers on the table before him.

"Now I understand that a shot was heard at Cleedons by several people on the afternoon of Mr. Molyneux's death, and I propose taking evidence on this point. Mr. Eustace Agatos."

The man who was sitting at the side of Myfanwy Peel rose and took his place at the table. He was a short, dark, sallow man, stoutly built and carefully dressed. He looked a prosperous man of business, a Londoner, self-confident, urbane, a little paunchy, a little dyspeptic, a little bald: a man of a very commonplace type, Jeanie thought, until, in a moment, she noticed his quite black, impenetrable, melancholy eyes and his immense diamond ring, and saw him thereafter as a foreigner and an oriental.

"Now, Mr. Agatos. You remember Monday afternoon, November the third?"

"The day before yesterday, yes, I remember."

"What were your movements that afternoon?"

"I was driving my car down from London. I arrived here at five minutes past three. I stopped my car in the road about a hundred yards below the entrance to Cleedons, where the little lane turns off on the opposite side of the road. I backed my car into the little lane. This was at about ten past three. I stayed there till a quarter to four. Then I drove back to London."

He spoke with composure. He seemed completely indifferent to the eager curious eyes upon him. They were strangers to him, all these country people. They were only an audience. Their thoughts meant nothing to him.

"For what purpose did you drive down here, Mr. Agatos?"

With a faint humorous pucker of his thick pale lips, Agatos replied:

"To oblige a lady. The lady who was with me, Mrs. Peel, she wished for an interview with Mr. Molyneux."

"Why did you not drive up to the house?"

"The lady who was with me did not wish to pay a formal visit. She did not wish to meet Mrs. Robert Molyneux, said Agatos simply. "She wished first to see if she might meet with Mr. Molyneux about his grounds somewhere."

"And meanwhile—while Mrs. Peel departed in search of Mr. Molyneux—you remained in your car?"

"Yes."

"Can you tell us everything that happened between ten past three and your departure for London?"

Mr. Agatos pursed his lips and looked at Mr. Perrott with a faint pucker between his dark eyebrows.

"Everything that happened?" he murmured deprecatingly. "The bluetit that sat for a moment on my windscreen? The cows that passed along the road? The dead leaf that dropped off the hedge into a puddle and got wet?"

There was laughter, instantly suppressed by a somewhat flushed and irritated coroner.

"Everything that is relevant, if you please."

"I sat in my car," said Mr. Agatos slowly. "And for a little while I read the paper. And I went on sitting in my car. And I thought: Shall I get out and go for a walk? And then I thought: No, I am too lazy. So I went on sitting in my car."

Once again there was a disposition to amusement, but it was only a titter this time, and a glance suppressed it.

"When I had been sitting there about half an hour, I heard a shot, quite close. One shot."

"You don't know exactly what time this was?"

"I did not look at my watch, no. But I would judge it to be between half-past three and twenty to four. About three minutes later a young man, Mr. Peter Johnson, came along the road and we talked for a bit."

"Do you see the young man here?"

Mr. Agatos smiled affably at Peter.

"Yes. We talked of this and that for about five minutes. Then Mrs. Peel returned and said, let us go home. And I looked at my watch as we started, and it was a quarter to four. Mr. Johnson said that he was returning to London that afternoon, so I gave him a lift."

"Thank you, Mr. Agatos. Oh, there is one thing more! Do you possess any fire-arms?"

"Somewhere I have an old service revolver. And now I suppose I shall go to prison because I have admitted this dreadful thing and I have no permit."

"Do you know where it is?"

Agatos shrugged.

"Not exactly, I am afraid. At home. In my flat, some-where. Perhaps in the tool cupboard, perhaps among my socks."

"I think that is all, thank you."

The witness made his way back to his seat next to Myfanwy. Jeanie saw him as he sat down give an affectionate touch to

Myfanwy's hand, which Myfanwy, as if in anger, instantly
withdrew. She looked sideways at the coroner, and there was fear
in her eyes. It was obvious to Jeanie that she dreaded the moment
when her name would be called. But it was not yet. The evidence
of Sir Henry Blundell was taken next. He had left the Field Club
members to go to the cloak-room on the ground floor of the
Tower. The outer passage door had been open. When he left the
cloak-room he stepped outside the passage door to examine the
ancient stone coffin that stood there and was used for growing
ferns in. While examining the coffin he heard a shot. When he
returned to the hall soon after, the clock stood at twenty to four.

Tamsin Wills followed. She had been looking out of the lower
gun-room in the Tower. She looked at her watch and saw that it
was just on twenty-five to four, and thought it was time that her
pupil tidied herself for tea. As she turned away from the window
she heard a shot. It had sounded very close, very close indeed. No,
it had not occurred to her to turn and look out of the window. Why
should it? There was nothing unusual in hearing a shot. One often
did, in the country. Yes, from the window she had seen Mr.
Molyneux standing on a ladder. His back had been towards her.

Agnes was next called. The coroner was very kind to her, spoke
gently and made his questioning as brief as possible. But even so
she shook, shed tears and made frequent use of the answer: "I
don't know."

"I don't know what the time was. I didn't look at the clock after
I left my room."

"But, Mrs. Molyneux, you went out to ask your husband to
come in—"

"Well?"

"If you wanted him to come in, didn't you know what the time
was?"

"I knew it was a quarter-past three when I left my room. And I
knew our guests had arrived."

"Did you go straight out when you left your room."

"No. I talked to some of the servants."

"Do you mind saying which of them?"

"Well—to Bates, the butler." Agnes spoke angrily. A little spot of red appeared in each wan cheek.

"Only to Bates?"

"As far as I can remember."

"Please try to remember, Mrs. Molyneux. The question of time is important."

"But I've told you I don't know what the time was when I left the house! I put on my galoshes. I didn't hurry. I went out. I walked slowly through the garden. I was thinking about planting some shrubs, and where to put them. And when I got to the orchard I saw Robert falling. And I heard a shot." Agnes's voice had sunk to a dry whisper. "I don't *know* what time it was."

Her large blue eyes looked from face to face round the table and lit on Sir Henry Blundell. She gave a little sob. Jeanie noticed the contraction of that gentleman's jaw, his almost indignant glance at the coroner, his little frown. When Mr. Perrott apologetically released Agnes from her ordeal, Sir Henry went instantly around to her and suggested that she should leave the court. Assisted by Tamsin Wills, she went.

Jeanie found her heart beating very fast when her own name was called. But, perhaps intimidated by Sir Henry, the coroner seemed, she thought, to let her off lightly. She explained how, two minutes or so after hearing the shot, she had seen Agnes in the lane talking to Myfanwy Peel, how Agnes had fainted and how Jeanie and Sarah had gone to her help and thus been brought to knowledge of Robert Molyneux's death. As she sat down, she saw Myfanwy Peel look with a slow cautious glance out of the corner of her eye at the coroner. There was terror, it seemed to Jeanie, hidden below her look. And well there might be, after her antics with that revolver! Jeanie looked forward with lively curiosity to hearing her explanation of what she was doing with the weapon.

She was, however, disappointed. Myfanwy Peel was not called on to give evidence. Neither was Peter Johnson. It seemed strange to Jeanie that these two should not be called upon to explain their somewhat unusual actions on the day of Molyneux's death, until it occurred to her that it was precisely because they were under suspicion that they were for the time being spared by the police. Against one or other of them, perhaps, the police were quietly building up a case, waiting until it was complete before the evidence of the victim, with its struggling shifts and plunging lies, should serve to bind him only tighter in the net.

It was, on the whole, a dull brief affair, the inquest, leaving, it seemed to Jeanie, more hidden than it revealed. There was but one dramatic moment, when the whole court rustled into attention and the pencils of the reporters flew joyfully over their flapping note-books. This occurred during the evidence given by William Fone. Jeanie, who guessed the nature of the evidence he was to give, hoped very much that he would see fit to suppress some of his more unorthodox reflections on the death of his friend. She rather liked the man. And by the effect on herself she reckoned the effect on this most hidebound of gatherings should the queer fellow repeat in public his opinion that Molyneux's death was for the good of the community. She stirred uneasily as the coroner addressed him. But she soon saw that she need not worry. William Fone confined himself to answering with admirable precision the coroner's questions, which seemed directed towards establishing the direction of the shot which killed Robert Molyneux.

"Then at the time the shot was fired," said Mr. Perrott, examining a large-scale plan of Cleedons which lay on the table before him, "it would seem that the deceased was facing north-east, almost towards the house."

"He was."

"Your eyesight is good, Mr. Fone?"

"Perfectly, so far as I know."

"You saw his face?"

"Distinctly. His back was at first towards me. He turned his head and the upper part of his body—"

"In which direction?"

"Towards his right. His right arm, holding the pruning-saw, swung round. I saw his face plainly. Then I heard the shot. And I saw Molyneux fall from the ladder. I sat still for a minute or two in the window-seat. Then I stood up. It was twenty-three minutes to four. I went home."

Perhaps the coroner had been coached by the police, for he did not break the ensuing startled silence by asking why Mr. Fone had not gone to his friend's assistance instead of going home. Perhaps the police, for reasons of their own, did not at this point want William Fone to be harried. All Mr. Perrott said, after a pause in which he examined his sketch-plan again, was:

"Then there seems no doubt that at the time he was shot the deceased was facing north-east. He was shot in the left temple. It seems certain, then, that the shot which killed him came from the north-west. What is this building under the north-west boundary of the orchard? Oh, I see it is marked! The lambing-shed."

It was here that the sensation occurred. A young woman in a green tweed coat stood up at the end of the table looked towards the door with a face which seemed faintly to reflect the hue of her coat, stammered loudly:

"I—I—Excuse me!" and lurching past the knees of people seated near the table with that disregard of politeness and personal dignity peculiar to those about to faint or be sick, made for the door. A police officer escorted her outside.

"Was that Marjorie Dasent?" murmured Jeanie to Peter. "Who would have thought a face as pink as hers could ever go as green?"

The inquest was finally adjourned for ten days. A flat, unsatisfying ending to a curiously and, Jeanie thought, designedly superficial inquiry. There were, however, those who had not found it dull, and to whom its adjournment seemed only to dangle the sword of Damocles over their heads.

As, in Peter Johnson's company, she emerged from the yard into the road, Jeanie saw walking ahead of her towards their waiting car Myfanwy Peel and her exotic partner. She heard Myfanwy mutter furiously:

"You *had* to say that, of course! You had to give me away!"

"Give you away!" echoed her companion in light astonished deprecation. "My dear Miffie, I only said I had a revolver. It happens to be true."

"That's all you think about! Priggish ass."

Mr. Agatos scratched his head. He did not seem much disturbed.

"No," he objected tranquilly, opening the door of their low-built shiny car. "But I know when it is no good telling lies. Also, from what I hear, it is no secret you have been going round with my revolver."

Jeanie greeted Myfanwy as she and Peter went by, but Myfanwy seemed to notice her as little as if she had been a stray sheep. She continued to objurgate Agatos.

"You're a beast! A beast!"

"We will go to Gloucester and see a nice film," said Mr. Agatos soothingly, "and then you will feel better. Only you should really say good afternoon to ladies that say good afternoon to you. Did you not know?"

"Beast! Beast!" still more furiously uttered Myfanwy. The door slammed. The car overtook Peter and Jeanie and disappeared around the bend of the road.

"Rum couple," commented Jeanie, but Peter was not at the moment interested in rum couples.

"If the police don't arrest me soon, I shall go mad."

"Oh, Peter, don't be absurd!"

"I am not absurd!" cried he angrily. Jeanie, who saw no reason why she and Peter should emulate Agatos and Myfanwy, said nothing.

## Chapter Ten
## GRIM'S GRAVE

Well, this is it," said Sarah Molyneux indifferently. She kicked the crumbling edge of a rabbit-hole, and her lack-lustre glance wandered over the bell-barrow. They were standing at the outer edge of the vallum. Grim's Grave, a tumulus of unusually regular outline, rose before them thirty feet high from the bottom of the five-foot ditch, gaining a singular impressiveness from the circle of young trees which stood upon its summit. Gaunt thistles and dry brown foxglove-stalks grew on its slopes, rabbit-holes mined the grassy surface and the scars made by old felled trees showed here and there in thicker tufts of coarser grass.

"It used to be in a coppice," said Sarah. "Uncle Robert had all the trees cut down, except the ones on top."

She spoke lackadaisically. Jeanie looked at her. It was largely for Sarah's sake that she had suggested a walk to Grim's Grave, to take the child's thoughts off the horror of her uncle's death. Poor child, she looked extraordinarily ill—haggard, if such a word could be used of so young a face. Her normal clear pallor had a pasty tinge and the shadows around her eyes were murky-coloured, as though she had not slept.

A wind blew across the country and rustled the tinder-leaved branches of the young oaks, but here in the shelter of the mound the air was still. Jeanie found suddenly that she could understand how to William Fone this was a holy place, a fearful place. What

procession had once wound its way along the track that now was a
macadam road, what gathering of priests and leaders and
common men, chanting in a strange tongue and playing queer-
shaped instruments now dimly remembered in harps and
trumpets? What fluttering of white and purple robes, what
flashing of the sun on polished metal! Almost Jeanie saw the
procession, almost she expected the child to see it too.

But turning, she saw Sarah standing limp and indifferent, her
eyes on the grass, lips sulkily parted, shoulders drooping as
though all the world's cares were on them. That long-past
procession vanished, the sound of its harps and trumpets became
only the north-west wind again playing amongst the pines.

"Sarah dear."

The little girl raised a lack-lustre eye.

"Yes?"

"You're not feeling well."

"Yes, I am, thank you."

"You don't look fit for the Girl Guide rally this afternoon."

"I'm not going."

"Oh? Isn't that rather a pity?"

"I don't belong to the Guides any more," muttered Sarah. "I've
resigned."

"What, since yesterday?" Queer child, what hyper-
sensitiveness had led her to this?

"Yes. I just wrote and said I resigned."

"But darling, you enjoyed it so!"

A slow painful colour crept up Sarah's face. Her eyelids
reddened and she frowned more fiercely than ever. She said with a
good deal of dignity, though her voice was thick:"

"One leaves off enjoying things, sometimes."

"But—"

Jeanie hesitated, uncertain whether to exhort, console or
question. She gave Sarah's hand a squeeze and dropped it.

"Well, you know best, ducky. I suppose this mound'll never be dug up now."

"I shouldn't think so." Unexpectedly Sarah added: "A good job, too! Digging things up and putting them in mouldy old museums where nobody sees them!"

"Nobody can see them if they're in the tumulus."

"And if they're in mouldy old museums nobody *wants* to see them," rejoined Sarah, unexpected young disciple of William Fone. She turned nervously at the sound of voices on the wind. When Peter Johnson and Hugh Barchard appeared upon the vallum at the opposite side of Grim's Grave, guns under their arms and a spaniel at their heels, she flinched and, suddenly turning as though she did not want to be seen, moved with deliberate unconsciousness away. Jeanie caught her hand.

"Don't you want to see Peter?"

"No!" Sarah averted her face. A sudden sob broke from her. "People shouldn't have guns. People shouldn't shoot things!" she gulped, and breaking from Jeanie's hand went off through the trees out of sight.

It was in a somewhat critical mood that Jeanie returned Barchard's "good morning" and Peter's nervous smile. To come out with guns to-day—the day after the inquest on poor Molyneux—was it not a little more insensitive than one would have expected of Peter Johnson? Her greeting to the two men was curt, and Peter looked taken aback.

"We came after rabbits, Miss Halliday," said Barchard, "but you're before us. I made a kind of promise once to Mr. Molyneux I'd shoot a rabbit here every day, and help him clear Grim's Grave of them."

Jeanie felt a sudden reaction in his favour. Life must go on as usual, after all, no matter who departed from its scene nor in what manner!

"There were lots about," said Jeanie. "But they bolted when we came on the scene. I didn't know you were a sportsman, Peter?"

The young man frowned.

"I'm not. I hate shooting at living things, as a matter of fact, only—" He glanced at Barchard as if to say that he had been prevailed upon.

"Mr. Johnson's a very fine shot," said Barchard seriously. He dangled before Jeanie's eyes a very small limp bird. "Mr. Johnson shot this snipe clean at twenty yards."

Jeanie, no sportswoman, did not find this feat impressive.

"It doesn't look very nourishing."

"I was an ass to shoot the thing," said Peter sourly. "One seems to lose one's head when one's given a gun."

Barchard smiled and shook his head.

"You're the finest shot I've ever seen, Mr. Johnson, say what you like."

"Where did you get your practice, Peter?"

"I haven't had much, except target practice. I used to practise a good deal on Mr. Molyneux's targets when I was down here," answered Peter. He spoke unwillingly, as though the subject irked him. "I've got a naturally good eye, I suppose. The snipe was a pure fluke, though."

"How's Mr. Fone?"

"Oh, he's pretty well, thank you," replied Barchard. "It's worrying for him, though, all this questioning."

"Have the police been bothering you at Cole Harbour again?"

Barchard looked across the fields through a gap in the trees towards Cleedons. He answered slowly:

"It seems there's a pistol missing from the top Tower room at Cleedons. Missing since Monday—or so the housemaid at Cleedons says."

"Monday! That's the day—"

"The day Mr. Molyneux was shot. Yes."

There was a pause. A sort of chill seemed to fall upon the three of them. Jeanie was the first to speak.

"Does the housemaid know how long it had been there?"

"Ever since she's worked at Cleedons, she says—over a year. So you can see, Miss Halliday, the police haven't done with the master yet. Seeing, you see, he was in the Tower the very time Mr. Molyneux was shot."

Jeanie uttered a little startled exclamation. Somebody else had been in the Tower at the time that Robert Molyneux was shot. Jeanie recalled the blink, the moment's hesitation with which Tamsin Wills had admitted to being in the lower Tower room "looking for Sarah." She had been first to the upper room, she had said, and found William Fone there. Had she been "looking for Sarah" then? Or for something else? A weapon? Jeanie recalled the malignant gleam with which Miss Wills had praised and vilified the dead. And she heard Sarah's reedy little voice uttering: *I don't think she's staying much longer. Uncle Robert says I'm beyond her She adores Aunt Agnes.* What if— Jeanie shivered. No, no! She must not pursue such thoughts. Tamsin Wills was, after all, a human being, not a demon.

Hugh Barchard was speaking.

"But if Finister knew Mr. Fone as I know him, he'd spare himself all this trouble. Because if Mr. Fone had shot Mr. Molyneux, he wouldn't be trying to hide it. Mr. Fone does what he thinks right and stands by what he does!"

A certain ring in the man's voice reminded Jeanie of Mrs. Barchard's vehement: *He's the cleverest best gentleman that ever lived!* The queer Fone certainly had the power, unusual in so eccentric a character, of arousing devotion!

"I'll be glad when it's over," said Hugh Barchard. "I don't like to think of the questions that'll be asked the master at the inquest

when it comes on again. He'll say a lot of things that'll sound
queer to ordinary people. He'll tell the truth, and the truth he sees
isn't the same as ordinary people's truth. Funny thing, but when I
didn't really know Mr. Fone I used to think he was crackers. Now
it seems the other people I talk to are mostly crackers, and Mr.
Fone's the only sane man among the lot of them. It's like being
with a man after being with a lot of silly sheep. He does what he
likes and he sticks by what he does."

The almost fanatical gleam in Barchard's blue eyes amused
Jeanie. How much, she wondered, of the queer Fone's character
and philosophy could this man understand? Enough, perhaps, to
give him that sense of liberation perpetually craved by all but the
dullest souls, enough to fortify him against mean gossip and the
eager criticism of the herd.

"Well," said Barchard with the sudden briskness of one who
perceives work waiting to be done, "I must be getting along. You'll
meet me in the spinney, I expect, Mr. Johnson. Come on, Rosa!"

He transferred the dangling little corpse to Peter's unwilling
hand and went off, followed by his spaniel, through the thin ring
of trees and down the slope of the meadow. Peter was left with the
snipe hanging from his fingers, a sick look upon his face which
might have made Jeanie smile had she not quickly realised it was
something more serious than this poor little bird that had brought
it there.

"What's the matter, Peter?"

"Nothing."

"But you look awfully white!"

Peter made a very obvious effort to pull himself together.

"It's only that I hate this beastly so-called sport. Shooting birds
and things makes me feel quite sick. And ashamed of myself, too,
for not having the guts to say so to people like Barchard."

"Peter, surely it's not only that wretched bird that's made you
look like this!"

"Yes, it is." His dark eyes gazed somewhat inimically into Jeanie's. His lips set sullenly. She changed the subject.

"Did you know about the pistol missing from the Tower room?"

"No," said Peter constrainedly. "I haven't seen Fone since Finister called last night. He's not up yet."

"It rather brings the thing home to Cleedons, doesn't it? I mean, if there's a pistol missing from the Tower room since Monday, it seems terribly likely that that's the pistol that was used to shoot poor Mr. Molyneux. Doesn't it?"

"I suppose so."

"But you see what that means. Mr. Molyneux must have been shot by somebody who—who was—who'd been—who might have—"

"'Had access to' is the phrase you want. The police use it a lot. Somebody who had access to Cleedons. Like me. I had access to Cleedons. In fact, I was there. Look for the motive. That's another thing the police are fond of saying. I've got a lovely motive, too, as well as access. Dismissed, dishonest secretary, not quodded, murders master. How's that? I think it would look very well on the front page of some beastly picture paper!"

His bitter voice struck harshly on Jeanie's ear. She felt sorry for him, but a little impatient, too.

"Peter," said she, "I shouldn't waste my energy feeling bitter about it, if I were you. As a sensible person you must see that you are a suspect—you can't blame Finister for suspecting you. You *have* behaved like a bit of an idiot, you know. I mean, over that money."

"I know. I was the complete chivalrous owl. You said so last night. And I quite agreed with you. Don't keep rubbing it in."

"Well, have you told Superintendent Finister about it yet, and why you came down here on Monday?"

Peter flushed and frowned.

"You haven't! Oh, Peter! Chivalry's bad enough, but pigheadedness is worse!"

"I didn't have to tell him. He asked me yesterday morning, just before the inquest, if it was so, and I—I admitted that it was. Do you think Agnes could possibly have seen the light about it?"

No, Jeanie did not think Agnes had voluntarily exonerated Peter, much though she would have liked to think so.

"I suppose the police can put two and two together," she replied. "After all, they'll have questioned everybody—gone into all sorts of things. I don't suppose it was difficult to guess the truth." She glanced up at the tall boy's brooding face. "Don't you feel a bit happier about it now? Don't you think, now that your motive for coming down here on Monday's cleared up, that Finister's relaxed his watch on you a bit?"

Peter s dark face did not clear at this suggestion. On the contrary, his unhappy frown deepened.

"I know jolly well he hasn't. I'm being sleuthed all over the place. I'm more Finister's pet suspect than ever. I—Finister thinks—they think—Oh God! I don't know what they think!"

"You do," said Jeanie, looking at him curiously. "Or you guess. What is it, Peter?"

A tide of painful red crept up the young man's face. He muttered gruffly:

"Mrs. Molyneux and I—I believe they think—"

"Oh, how absurd!" cried Jeanie, laughing. "*Agnes!* What extraordinary minds policemen do have!"

"Yes, don't they?" agreed Peter, still heavily frowning, however. "Yes, I'd laugh myself, I dare say. Only, you see, Jeanie, it happens to be partly true."

Jeanie stopped laughing very abruptly. A hot flush burnt her face. She felt an extraordinary discomfort, embarrassment and misery all in a moment for no particular reason.

"*Partly* true, I said," said Peter, eyeing her sombrely. "I felt devilish romantic about her, if you must have it, Jeanie, in a perfectly proper way. The troubadour and the Queen of Beauty touch, you know. Well, there wasn't anybody else to look at for miles around. And she *is* lovely, Agnes is. I used to gaze at her a good deal. And talk to her about my amazing exploits at school, you know, and all that sort of thing."

"Oh well, Peter!" said Jeanie, adjusting her thoughts as rapidly as possible to this little revelation. "I suppose when one comes to think of it, you wouldn't have taken the money for her, and she wouldn't have risked asking you to, unless there was some—well— some feeling in the air. I suppose—"

"What do you suppose?"

"I suppose the police *haven't* anything to go on but guesswork?"

"No. Except—"

"Oh?"

"Except I wrote a note to Mrs. Molyneux. If they've got hold of that—but she'd have destroyed it. How could they know anything about it?"

"Oh, Peter!"

"It wasn't anything much. I had to wait ages on Monday before I could see her. She was in her room, dressing. I didn't know how I could see her alone, with all the Field Club there. I pushed a note under her door. It was nothing much. It just said I couldn't believe she really meant to let me down. And that I must see her, if only for a moment. And—and didn't she realise what she'd done to me?"

"That all?"

Peter swung his snipe nervously round and round, and then, becoming aware of what he was doing, dropped it abruptly and looked down at it with a sort of horror. He cleared his throat.

"Well—yes. Except that—" His voice sank gruffly. "—that she had all my devotion, always."

Jeanie said dryly:

"Oh, had she?"

Peter gave a smile that was half-embarrassed half-grim.

"Well, I thought so on Monday."

Jeanie, looking with blank eyes at the tumulus, heard the pattering run of Agnes's feet upstairs after the interview with Superintendent Finister, the click of her heels hurrying along the corridor.

"She remembered the note and wanted to destroy it quickly. I expect she was too late. I think we can take it, Peter, that the police know all about that note of yours."

"Damn them!"

"There's only one person who need say 'damn them,' and that's the murderer. The police can't find out anything that hasn't happened, but they can, and probably will, find out everything that *has*, so for Heaven's sake, Peter, be open with them!"

"Bit late, now. They know all."

"And they've had to find most of it out for themselves without any help from you," said Jeanie reproachfully. "By the way, Peter, did you know Barchard owed money to Mr. Molyneux?"

"Yes."

"And that Mr. Molyneux was pressing him to repay it?"

"Yes. As his secretary I had to do quite a lot of the pressing myself. Not the slightest good, of course, because Barchard hasn't a bean except the salary old Fone gives him. I think it was a matter of principle with Mr. Molyneux more than anything else. You see, when Barchard came back from Canada full of some new method of poultry-keeping, Molyneux very decently lent him a couple of hundred pounds to buy some chickens with. As a matter of fact, I happen to know he regarded it at the time more or less as a gift, and never expected to get it back. Only Mr. Molyneux was pretty strait-laced about some things, you know. And when Barchard started neglecting his chickens and having a lady to live with him and spending all his money in riotous living, I think Mr. Molyneux saw no reason why he should pay for it, and small blame to him. And he'd been dunning Barchard for it ever since. Not with any hope of getting it, you know. Just a feeling that Barchard ought to be made to sit up. As a matter of fact," said Peter, "I did once suggest to Mr. Molyneux that we might as well call it a bad debt and save our notepaper and stamps, but he took me up rather sharply. He was obstinate about it. I think he'd been badly disappointed in Barchard's character, and couldn't leave off kicking himself over it, if you know what I mean."

"I suppose," said Jeanie thoughtfully, "Mr. Molyneux hadn't been specially pressing him lately? Sending solicitor's letters or threatening proceedings or anything?"

Peter smiled.

"No, he wouldn't have wasted six-and-eightpence on such a hopeless quest. I used to tip off a stiff letter to Barchard every three months or so, just to keep his memory jogged, so to speak. Oh no! Mr. Molyneux would never have gone farther. He had too much sense and too little hope of ever getting his two hundred back. And he wasn't vindictive about it, you know, only determined not to condone anything."

"I see."

"Are you thinking Barchard might be the murderer? I shouldn't think so, Jeanie. He'd know Molyneux couldn't do anything to him. I should imagine he just pitched our letters into the fire and laughed."

'Old Mrs. Barchard seems to have taken the matter a bit to heart," said Jeanie.

"I dare say. But she's a much more countrified sort of type. She'd be more frightened of the squire and the bobby than Hugh Barchard ever would. All the same," added Peter thoughtfully, "I should think Barchard almost had it in him, you know. Murder, I mean. Or anything, if it comes to that. He's a queer fellow."

"Is he, Peter? I should have thought he was an ordinary friendly sort of man."

"Oh yes, he is. But with a funny side to him, all the same. He says odd things sometimes."

Jeanie laughed a little.

"He *hears* odd things sometimes, living with Mr. Fone, I should imagine! It isn't surprising if he gets a bit touched with oddity himself! Still, I should hardly think he'd have murdered Mr. Molyneux just because he was in his debt."

Peter said slowly:

"Then you think whoever murdered the poor chap must have had a really strong motive? But when one thinks of Molyneux and the life he lived, what strong motive can anybody have had for murdering him? One would have said a more harmless man, with fewer enemies, never existed. Aren't practically all murders done for gain, or out of jealousy? Well, I was Mr. Molyneux's private secretary for three years, and I never saw a hint that anybody had it in for the poor chap on either count."

"And yet somebody who was at Cleedons on Monday *did* murder him," said Jeanie flatly. She added: "Perhaps a lunatic—"

"Like Mr. Fone?" said Peter, swinging his murdered snipe from side to side. Jeanie was embarrassed.

"No, I wasn't thinking of Mr. Fone. And of course he's not a lunatic. Only, I suppose, the queerer a person is the less you can tell what motives he might have. I was thinking of Sarah's mother, really. She seemed awfully unbalanced. And she had a revolver."

"But the murder wasn't done with a revolver," objected Peter.

"She might have had an adaptor. You see, Peter, it's been proved that Mr. Molyneux must have been killed by a shot coming from the north-west. But Cleedons and the Tower stand north-east of where Mr. Molyneux was found. That means that nobody who was in or near the house at the time can have done the murder. Tamsin Wills, for instance. It can't have been her. Nor Agnes. Nor Mr. Fone."

"But, Jeanie, though I'm very far from suspecting Mr. Fone, I must point out that we've only got Mr. Fone's word for it that Molyneux looked over his shoulder before he was shot. That theory that the shot came from the north-west depends entirely on Mr. Fone's own evidence. I don't say I don't believe him: I do. But, Jeanie, you can't really absolve a man on his own evidence!"

"No, I suppose not," agreed Jeanie. "But there was another thing. There was that cigarette-end Sir Henry found in the lambing-shed. Somebody'd been in the lambing-shed. And the lambing-shed is to the northwest of where Molyneux was found. That supports Mr. Fone's evidence, surely."

"For what it's worth, yes. But the person in the lambing-shed, whoever it was, may have gone away before Mr. Molyneux was shot and may not have been the murderer at all."

"The cigarette-end was still smouldering when Sir Henry picked it up, more than five minutes after the murder."

"Then your theory, Superintendent Halliday is that the deceased was killed by a shot fired from the north-west, probably from the lambing-shed, by a mentally unstable person with an unlikely motive?"

Jeanie laughed.

"Well, not exactly, but—"

Have you noticed how exactly *I* conform to your requirements?" asked Peter with a half-angry jocularity. "*I* was to the north-west of Mr. Molyneux at about the time he died. I was walking on the common admiring the water-fowl on Hatcher's Pond. That's what I say, but of course I might have been in the lambing-shed: who's to say I wasn't? *I* smoke gaspers, and in common with most people who have this horrid habit, I leave their ends about. *I* have two unlikely motives. One, revenge, for being fired without a reference. Two, guilty passion for employer's wife. You can choose which you like. The police incline to the latter, I believe. Finally, as you must have noticed, Miss Halliday, I am mentally unstable."

"Oh, I don't know!" said Jeanie cheerfully. "Extreme egotism may sometimes amount to mental instability, I suppose, but I don't think yours quite reaches that point."

She was irritated, and meant to show it. There was a pause. Peter kicked thoughtfully at a tussock of grass, frowning. Jeanie, a little breathless, began to repent her unkindness.

"I'm sorry," said Peter coolly at last. "But I suppose the star of the piece is liable to get a rather egotistic point of view. You notice it with leading actors."

"Oh yes, Peter," said Jeanie more conciliatingly. "But I don't see why you should think you're the star."

"Ask Superintendent Finister," said Peter. "He cast this act. Would you like this snipe, Jeanie? A small token of my esteem?"

"What should I do with it? No, thank you."

"People eat them," said Peter, holding up the pathetic little bird before her.

"I'd as soon eat a sparrow."

"I was a fool to shoot it. Do you think Grim would mind if I buried it with him?"

"Why do you shoot, if you don't want the thing when you've shot it?"

Jumping down the bank and up the side of the mound, Peter replied:

"Well, you see, I'm a good shot, Jeanie, and when one can do a thing well, one has a kind of hankering to go on doing it." He put the little corpse down an old rabbit- hole and carefully placed a sod of damp earth over the hole. "*Requiescat in pace*. Give my love to Sarah. It was sweet of her to write to me. Good-bye."

## Chapter Eleven
### IN THE STABLE

Jeanie came upon Sarah in the sloping meadow below the Cleedons garden, sitting on a sheep-trough, her chin in her hands, apparently deep in thought. At Jeanie's suggestion, she rose and went with her towards the stables. Jeanie thought that in the child's present despairing mood the silent, innocent company of horses and kittens might be more healing than that of human kind.

But when they entered the stable, with its dim light shining off time-polished silvery wood, its sweet scent of hay and pungent scent of horse-dung, they heard beside the stamping, breathing, rustling sounds of horses in a stable, a sound unmistakably human, the sound of sobbing.

Jeanie did not at first recognise who it was who stood, in a blue uniform like a policewoman's, her arm around the neck of Molyneux's bay mare, her head of shingled fair hair pressed against the great sterno-mastoid muscle, sobbing quietly and broken-heartedly to herself. Then she recognised the uniform as that of a captain of Girl Guides and the woman as Marjorie Dasent. The mare stood quietly, nuzzling as if in fellow-feeling at the hand that stroked her long nose.

Sarah stiffened and stepped back, and the sound she made aroused Miss Dasent from her sorrow. She looked up. Her long, high-cheek-boned face, with its odd faint resemblance to the creatures she so loved, was blotched, her small blue eyes drowned. She met the situation, however, with a simplicity which Jeanie could not but admire. Drying her face with a large handkerchief and coming towards them, she said in the thick voice of recent weeping:

"I—I just came over to see how poor Gipsy was, and when I saw her I—I couldn't help—well, I'm afraid I made a fool of myself."

She looked ready to make a fool of herself again. However, she blinked the new tears back and added, with a sort of shamefaced bluffness which Jeanie found touching:

"Hullo, young Sarah. What's all this about resigning? Once a Guide always a Guide, you know."

Sarah said nothing. Her arm within Jeanie's seemed positively to have shrunk to a stick, so stiff it was with some inner tension. Her lips made a thin line, she seemed scarcely to breathe. Good Heavens, thought Jeanie, glancing at her in astonishment, what's the matter now? To Miss Dasent she said gently:

"Gipsy almost seems to know what's happened."

"Almost! She does now."

Marjorie Dasent was a large-built fair young woman of about thirty, already so early putting on weight and acquiring the set, unpliable look of middle age. The only child of a local doctor, she had been born in Handleston and lived all her life here. She bade fair to live out the rest of it, when her father died, in ladylike poverty and an ever-lessening struggle against spinsterhood, loneliness and her obvious destiny, which was to join the ranks of the genteel old Handleston gossips whom now, at thirty, she was still able to deride.

"Change your mind, young Sarah, and come to the rally this afternoon. It'll do you good. We'll talk about this resignation business later."

With a grown-up wink at Jeanie, Miss Dasent stretched a large hand affectionately towards Sarah's shoulder.

Like lightning, Sarah moved away, taking her arm from Jeanie's.

"Don't! Don't!" she uttered in a cracked little voice, and turned and fled from the stable, leaving her two elders to gaze after her in dismay.

"What's the matter with the kid? What have I done?"

Jeanie sighed.

"She's taking this business badly. Better leave her alone."

"But it's good for the kid to be taken out of herself!"

"Not if she doesn't think so."

"Well, I've always thought, myself," said Miss Dasent, evidently somewhat hurt at Sarah's rejection of her well-meant caress, "that Sarah needs discipline more than most kids."

"I should leave her alone."

"Oh, I shan't interfere! I'm sorry she's having a tough time."

"We're all having a tough time," sighed Jeanie.

Marjorie swallowed and uttered huskily:

"He was—he was a good sort if ever there was one."

The words were commonplace, but there was a wild, agonised look in the poor girl's eyes, and Jeanie knew a sudden fear that Miss Dasent was about to repose in her a confidence which they would both probably afterwards regret. She took the young woman by the arm and walked her, half-unwilling, out of the dim stable into the day where the cold grey light and the chilly wind could be trusted to discourage all displays of tender emotion. Marjorie blinked and turned her tear-marred face away. Then, not without a touch of the histrionic, she squared her shoulders, sighed deeply and took a cigarette-case from her pocket.

"Gasper?"

"Thank you."

"Hope you don't mind these. I always smoke them."

"Oh, Honeybines!"

"These are just the right size, I find, if one wants a rest and smoke when one's out shooting."

Jeanie remembered how Sir Henry Blundell had picked the stub of a Honeybine cigarette up from the earthen floor of the lambing-shed in the orchard where Molyneux had met his death. A sort of tension came upon her right hand that held the little cigarette. To put it back, to put it in her pocket, to put it to her lips, to drop it: conflicting impulses held her hand poised six inches from her face. With a start as she saw the flame approaching Miss Dasent's purplish fingers, she put the Honeybine between her lips and stooped her head. Over the little flame their glances met. Jeanie's glance was guarded, but not guarded well enough, it seemed. She saw the sudden distrust spring into the blurred blue eyes so close to her own, as if her own had fired a spark there. The match dropped between them.

"I say!" said Marjorie, looking at her wrist-watch. She spoke thickly. "I shall be late! I must be off! I'm lunching early, because of this rally, you see. I'm walking back. My bike's got a puncture."

Jeanie said nothing.

Miss Dasent shot her a quick glance, distrustful, appealing, observant, all in one, and uttering again:

"I must go! Good-bye!" the turned and swung away with the long loping stride that she affected, leaving Jeanie with a scorched, unlighted cigarette between her lips.

Jennie took the cigarette from her lips and dropped it, and walked thoughtfully towards Cleedons. Her thoughts jerked disconnectedly along. Many people smoked Honeybines, after all. But not many people saw anything in this to frighten them. And Marjorie Dasent, Jeanie could swear, had been frightened just now. Many people smoke Honeybines. And one of these people had been present in the orchard at Robert Molyneux's death.

## Chapter Twelve
### TREASURE TROVE

"Can't we give you a lift?"

The offer was not very graciously made, but Jeanie, walking from the bus-stop, carrying in one hand a large bucket with a collection of ironmongery packed inside it, and in the other a shopping-basket overflowing with groceries, was not disposed to quarrel with a tone of voice. And when she found that the voice belonged to Myfanwy Peel, she was all the more ready to forgive it, for she was interested in Myfanwy Peel.

Mr. Agatos, with a smile more amiable than his companion's, got out and opened the door of the car.

"You would like to go—?"

"Oh, home, please, to Yew Tree Cottage. I've been shopping in Handleston, and these things are rather heavy."

"We have just been to Cleedons to see the little Sally, but she was not to be found."

He got into the driver's seat beside Myfanwy. Jeanie, sitting in the back, wrapped round like a queen in a fur-lined rug, surrounded, unlike a queen, with ironmongery and packets of soap and candles, murmured in some embarrassment:

"Oh, she's never where you look for her. She wanders about…"

Without turning her head Myfanwy said bitterly:

"That's their idea of looking after a child! What's that repulsive governess-creature for. I'd like to know? Education indeed! She'll be a little savage! She *is* a little savage, so far as I can see!"

Jeanie inquired:

"Did you see Agnes?"

'No, I didn't!"

Agatos shot Jeanie a deprecating, half-humorous look over his shoulder as the car slid forward. Myfanwy, evidently half regretting her own rudeness, added with an unpleasing sneer:

"Her ladyship was far too busy to see me. I saw the governess."

"Poor little Sarah's fearfully upset over her uncle's death and everything. I expect they think it better not to force lessons on her just now."

"Upset, is she?" muttered Myfanwy harshly. "Well, I know somebody else who's going to be upset quite soon."

"My dear," said Agatos pacifically, "this sounds very alarming. Let us hope we are not going to be upset in this very wet road."

"Oh, don't be an ass."

"I cannot help it. God made me an ass for His purposes."

"You can help continually talking rot!" said Myfanwy. Jeanie saw her profile turned for an instant towards her companion, and it looked both haggard and furious. Jeanie hoped that Agatos would abstain from further persiflage, for she was convinced that it would take very little to make his virago strike him. But in the next moment these apprehensions of a road accident fled away as a new thought struck Jeanie into a kind of dismay. What of the child Sarah's future? Must she return to the care of this neurotic woman? Jeanie wondered whether Robert Molyneux had made any provision for his niece. She was soon enlightened.

"Of course, I'm nobody! A child's mother is nobody when there's anybody else that wants her! But when she's not wanted any longer, then it's, 'Oh, you're her mother, aren't you? You take her back, you ought to be pleased to have her!' Well, if Saint Agnes thinks I'm going to be made a convenience of in that way, she's mistaken. And you can tell her so, Miss Halliday! You're a friend of hers, aren't you?"

"My dear, Miss Halliday will not know what you are talking about," murmured Eustace Agatos, crawling at a snail's pace through a herd of milch cows. He added gravely: "Miffie is cross, you see, because the governess has told her that in the poor uncle's will there is no fortune left to the little Sally."

"Not a penny!" exclaimed Mrs. Peel. "Not a farthing! Not that *I* care for money! But what gets my goat is that *that's* the man who pretended to think that the child's mother wasn't responsible enough to look after her! That's what he calls responsible!"

"Is there no provision made for Sarah at all?" inquired Jeanie in a casual voice that did not altogether match her feelings.

"*Agnes* is left her guardian. Agnes! And not a penny, not a penny to the child, after all his cant about responsibility!"

Jeanie's heart sank. Robert had had more confidence in his wife than Jeanie had, that was evident.

"You are a strange woman, Miffie," Agatos remarked sadly. "Only a very clever man, like me, would understand you. A week ago you wanted nothing but your child. You could not have her, and you were not pleased. Now, you can very likely have your child, and still you are not pleased. Not exactly pleased, it seems to me."

As he spoke, they drew up before Yew Tree Cottage.

"That's a nice little place," said Mr. Agatos. Standing back from the road behind a long and rather neglected garden, with the old tree from which it took its name humped darkly behind the stone roof, Yew Tree Cottage certainly presented an inviting picture. Agatos evidently had an eye for an old cottage, for he added: "There are plenty of pretty little places round this part of the country, but this is the prettiest yet I've seen."

"Oh, then, won't you—?"

Jeanie was about to invite them in when, to her surprise, Myfanwy Peel forestalled her. Myfanwy was still flushed with temper, but she spoke in those peculiar, insincere and honeyed tones which an ill-tempered person adopts when he feels that he has, for once, perhaps gone too far and wishes to make amends. She smiled in a stiff grimacing fashion, showing her teeth. She held the door open and one slender leg stretched to the footboard.

"It's the sweetest little place, Miss Halliday! Could we, I wonder? Just for a moment? Wouldn't you just adore to see the inside, Eustace?"

Agatos, looking speculatively at Mrs. Peel as if he wondered what she were after now, agreed that he would, indeed, adore to.

"Eustace is quite nuts on old houses," prattled Myfanwy, as the three of them walked up the path between the wintry shrubs and the roses where one or two hips and even a wind-pinched leaf and flower or two still hung. "He's always buying them and selling them again. Oh, did you ever see such a sweet little porch!"

Her eyes travelled restlessly over the front of the cottage she was pretending to admire, but it did not need great acumen to see that her thoughts were otherwise. Jeanie awaited developments with mild curiosity.

She did not have to wait long. After many perfunctory glances and loud but hollow exclamations of rapture over the front door and hall, after expressing an ardent desire to see the rest of the dear little place, Myfanwy sank on to the settee in the little parlour and held her hands to the blaze and refused to be dislodged.

Agatos protested:

"My dear Miffie, you have not seen half this nice place!"

He was hovering in the parlour doorway, looking into the hall. His pale fleshy face with its dark sleepy eyes had quite a pleased, lively look.

"Do you like it?" asked Jeanie eagerly. She loved Yew Tree Cottage so much herself that to hear its praises was sweet to her.

"Indeed I do! It has the makings of a very, very nice little place. One could put a gallery round the hall—a kind of minstrels' gallery, and move the back hall-door. Yes, the back hall-door should not be there."

"It always has been there!" said Jeanie, a trifle indignantly.

"Ah yes, very likely! The people who built these places did not mind draughts. May I go and look at the kitchen while Miffie warms her bones and tells you the story of her life? I think she wants to tell you the story of her life. She has been silently willing me to go away for a long time now."

"Really, Eustace, you fool, what do you mean?"

"Oh yes! I am very psychic. Then I will go and look at the kitchen—may I, Miss Halliday, all by myself?"

Jeanie wondered, as he went off, what Mrs. Barchard would make of him.

"Eustace is crazy about old cottages," murmured Myfanwy as Jeanie looked in the wall-cupboard for some refreshment for her guests. "It's a hobby of his to buy up the most awful little hopeless hovels and do them up and sell them again to quite civilised people—for weekends, you know. And although it's just a hobby, you know, he doesn't do badly for himself out of it." Jeanie could well believe it. Mr. Agatos did not strike her as a man who would in any circumstances do badly for himself.

"Will you try some of Mrs. Barchard's special sloe-gin? I'm sorry I haven't anything else to offer you," said Jeanie as her guest seemed to hesitate.

"Well, just a very, very little. I don't really take stimulants at all," explained Myfanwy in an odd, mincing tone. "But as it's home-made..."

She sipped the beautiful plum-coloured liquid.

"I do certainly feel worn out, Miss Halliday. Perhaps it'll do me good. I don't know how I lived through that awful inquest. And then to have it adjourned, all to go through again! If they wanted me to give evidence, why didn't they take my evidence yesterday and let me go? Keeping one hanging about like this!" She dropped a spot of gin on her dress and swore irritably. "I'm not really at all well, and the doctor says I ought to go away for a thorough change. I ought to be in Bournemouth at this moment—I'd booked the rooms and everything. Only I wanted just to come up and see Sally before I went, and look what I landed myself into!"

Her voice had risen now to a high complaining note like a sulky child's. She looked at Jeanie with what was intended to be a rueful smile, but there was fear between her eyes. This was what she had come for, then, for reassurance, for counsel, to talk over the horror she had involved herself in, to remove, if possible, a bad impression and to hear somebody else beside her Eustace say that she had nothing to fear from the police. I wonder! thought Jeanie. A neurotic woman like this is utterly incalculable, one can't tell what she might do!

"After all, Mrs. Peel, you had a revolver with you. And those letters you wrote to Mr. Molyneux. You can't expect—well, can you? to get off without any inquiry."

"Oh, that revolver!" Myfanwy gave a little tinkle of meretricious laughter which might have done well enough on the stage. "That museum piece! I could hardly lift it! As for firing it— well, my dear, have you ever tried to aim straight with a gun you can hardly lift?"

Jeanie said quietly:

"But, Mrs. Peel, a service revolver's a dangerous weapon. It isn't a joke. It's no use trying to pretend it's in the same class with a pea-shooter!"

"It wasn't loaded! You saw that for yourself!"

Jeanie did not reply to this childish protest.

"And anyway," pursued Myfanwy Peel, "the bullet was a point twenty-two. They said so. That queer man at the inquest said so. You can't use a point twenty-two cartridge in a service revolver. Except with an adaptor, or some such thing that I never even heard of or knew existed till the day before yesterday!"

She broke off and looked at Jeanie defiantly with great tears in her eyes.

"I don't think you've got anything to fear," Jeanie soothed her.

"Then *why* have I got to attend next Friday? *Why* do they keep me hanging about here? I shall go raving mad before then! That business about Sally was enough to drive anyone mad! And now this beastly inquest! Could I have another weeny glass of your delicious sloe-gin? And do tell your Mrs. Barchard from me that it's absolutely delicious."

Refilling the little glass, Jeanie murmured:

"The whole thing's horrible, of course."

"Cheerio," murmured Myfanwy drearily. She sipped. "Miss Halliday, may I talk to you frankly? I feel you'll understand. I *never* meant to use that revolver. Of *course* I never did!" She put her glass down. Two tears slid over on to her cheeks, and with a forefinger wrapped in a handkerchief she quickly removed them before they could damage the elaborate arrangement of red, orange and blue on her cheeks and eyelids.

"You don't know—nobody knows what I suffer with my nerves! How wretched I feel sometimes! Almost as if I could kill myself! I was looking in Eustace's chest-of-drawers for a jumper of his I wanted to borrow to drive down in, and I saw that damned revolver! I wish to God now I'd never seen the thing! And I just snatched it up and took it with me. I thought, when I saw Robert I'd bring it out and make him think I meant to kill myself with it. I thought that might startle him out of his damned freezing politeness!" She made a strange sound, half sob, half laugh. "But of course I never really meant—I made jolly sure there were no cartridges in it, can tell you! Then when you saw me in the yard, I was looking for Robert. Like a fool, I was rehearsing what I'd say to him. How I'd take the revolver out and show it him and see him drop his pukka sahib tone for once! It wasn't loaded, though. Of course not! And I never even saw Robert! You spoilt that!" She gave another dreary half-laugh strangled into a sob. "You and that little bitch Sally! I'm damned if I'll have her thrown back on my hands at Agnes's convenience! When I'm so beastly ill!"

Myfanwy put her glass down on the table, crossed her slender legs and looked at Jeanie with hard defiance. The next instant she was shaking with sobs.

"Oh, why do I behave like this? I feel so rotten! You don't know what it is, Miss Halliday; nobody does who hasn't felt it! Oh, it is dreadful of me to come into your house and behave like this! But, oh God! I feel so rotten, I feel so tired!"

Jeanie's attempt at consolation was interrupted by the return of Mr. Agatos from his tour of the kitchen quarters. Myfanwy controlled herself at once, sprang up and went to the window, where she opened a handbag that resembled a small suitcase and started to re-make her complexion in a businesslike and accomplished fashion strangely at variance with her former misery. Jeanie turned to her other guest.

"And what would you like to do with the kitchen?"

Agatos smiled and replied promptly:

"Put the kitchen range out in the scullery and turn the kitchen into a dining-room. Enlarge the window, move the staircase..."

Jeanie laughed.

"And then what would be left of Yew Tree Cottage?"

"A very nice, saleable little place," said Agatos seriously. "Oh, *Miffie*! You have been drinking gin!"

Mrs. Peel, now fully repainted in the gayest colours, turned insouciantly from the window.

"*Sloe*-gin, darling. It's practically a temperance drink."

"You promised the doctor and you promised *me* that you would not touch such stuff!"

"Really, Eustace, what will Miss Halliday think of me if you talk like that?"

"You are very bad, Myfanwy. You have no self-control. You will soon be crying all over me, if you drink gin. Ah, I see you have already been crying all over poor Miss Halliday. Yes, thank you, I will try a little. It does not make *me* cry."

"Ass," said Myfanwy indifferently. She looked ill-tempered enough, but she seemed determined not to disturb with frowns and tears the beauty of her new complexion. "I love your fire, Miss Halliday. Adorable little grate. So cosy."

"It's new. I only lit a fire here for the first time yesterday. There used to be an open hearth here, and it smoked and smoked."

"Ah, that's where the fine andirons under the stairs come from! It seemed a pity to me they were put away," said Mr. Agatos regretfully. "An open hearth is very nice, you know. People who buy week-end cottages like open hearths."

"I dare say. But nobody likes smoke. Something had to be done about it. And raising the grate seemed the best way to do it. The draught wasn't strong enough, you see."

Running his hand under the mantel, Mr. Agatos inquired:

"Do you think it quite safe to have a big coal fire raised up so high in a fire-place that was made to have wood-fires on the hearth? Feel the chimney-beam. It is quite hot. I think your builder has taken a great risk. You do not want your pretty house burnt down."

"That's what Hugh Barchard said. The beam's going to be cased in asbestos. Then it'll be all right, won't it?"

"Yes, but I should not let your builder dilly-dally over it. That beam is very, very hot. This old wood, it is like iron in some ways, but it will not stand constant heat. It dries and dries, and one day it starts to smoulder and to smoke. And then a little wind comes and there is another old house burnt down. And Miss Halliday in her bed with the stairs all burnt away, perhaps, what does she do?"

"Gets out of the window, I suppose."

"Ah, talking of stairs!" Agatos put his hand in his pocket. "I have found a great treasure in the cupboard under the stairs."

"What on earth were you doing there, Eustace?" drawled Myfanwy.

"Just looking at the stairs and wondering why they are as they are and whether they would not be better if they were different," replied he. "You are very negligent with your jewellery, Miss Halliday. See what I have for you!"

With some ceremony he laid a broken string of pearls on Jeanie's knee.

"Genuine Woolworth's?" murmured Jeanie, picking it up. There was only a length of about five inches, with a small brilliant clasp.

Agatos shrugged his shoulders.

"Perhaps—who knows? Even Ciro! I am not an expert in pearls."

"Pretty anyway. But not mine. They must be Valentine's."

"Valentine's?"

"A former tenant."

"I think anyway you can justly keep them, if you wish. Do you know," went on Agatos dreamily, "I often think, when I am having alterations done to one of these old cottages that are a hobby of mine—suppose there is treasure hidden under the floor or up the chimney? There never is. But there might be, you know. Why not?"

"Why not?"

"Once I did find a penny of the reign of William the Fourth. It was very exciting. And once I found a halfpenny of King George the Fifth that had been in a bonfire, and that was very exciting, I can tell you, until I had cleaned it. And now I have found a pearl necklace, but I think it is not very ancient and I fear it is not pearl. Never mind. One day I will find a golden torque and a fibula and a great jar full of golden coins of King Cunobelinus."

He rose as he spoke. Myfanwy had been on her feet some time and obviously anxious to be gone now that she could no longer have Jeanie to herself. Watching them into their car, Jeanie thought them a queer couple.

Recalling Agatos's warning, Jeanie damped her parlour fire down with the contents of the sink-strainer before she went out, later that afternoon, to see Agnes. As she did so, she felt for herself the hidden beam behind the mantel. It was certainly hot. She determined to write a curt note to her builder this evening, reminding him that he had not finished his job, for her builder, in the fickle way of builders, had temporarily deserted Yew Tree Cottage for some other more alluring case of dilapidation.

As she walked along the road her thoughts shifted uneasily to her little friend Sarah, about, it seemed, to be used as a missile in the warfare between her mother and her aunt. It had been foolish of Robert Molyneux to leave the child dependent on her aunt's goodwill. But wiser men than he, Jeanie supposed, had had illusions about their wives!

The sun was setting as Jeanie walked towards the west, and a cold wind blew fitfully down the road, as though it did but wait for darkness to become a gale. Cole Harbour stood silhouetted black against the wanly luminous sky. The sun, going down behind heavy clouds, pointed a last finger of light towards the clump of conifers on Grim's Grave, plucking forth tones of red from the black boles and muted tones of green from the black needles. Loitering along the road, watching the slow withdrawing of the sun's finger and the fading of red and green out of the black trees, Jeanie saw a human being come with a queer furtiveness along the vallum look round and begin to walk up the tumulus. Jeanie's heart gave a little throb of alarm, as though her own thoughts might have brought a dead man forth from Grim's Grave. But no, this was a child, it was—surely! Sarah. Jeanie could see her now walking awkwardly up the slope, holding one arm very stiffly at her side, as though she had something concealed beneath her coat. Jeanie was about to shout to her, but something in that furtive awkwardness prevented her. She lingered in the road, unwilling to go on, yet loth to interfere. What could a child, and a nervous child too, be doing at this hour alone among the conifers on Grim's Grave?

Jeanie hesitated and then, opening the gate into Cole Harbour meadow, made briskly for the tumulus. She was a little breathless when, having rasped her legs on a bramble, stumbled in a rabbit-hole concealed in a tussock of coarse grass, and clambered up the irregular, coney-mined side of the mound, she found herself inside the ring of pines. On the summit there within the circle of trees, Sarah Molyneux was kneeling, digging with furious energy in a rabbit-hole. Her face was red with her efforts, but her lips were a thin set line, her eyes fixed. Her mackintosh lay in a heap on the grass beside her. Jeanie heard her utter suddenly in a cracked voice:

"Oh hide it for ever, Grim! Don't let anybody ever find it! Oh, Grim—"

She caught sight of Jeanie and with a little shaken cry jumped to her feet, putting out her hands as if to fend Jeanie off.

"It's only me, Sarah, it's only me!" said Jeanie, stepping out from the shadow of the pines on to the summit of the tumulus. Sarah's face had gone quite white, the sweat of her exertions stood on her forehead like sickly pearls.

Jeanie spoke as matter-of-factly as possible:

"What are you doing, ducky, in this queer place?"

"Go away, go away! Can't I be left alone? *Do* go away, Jeanie!" cried the child in a cracked hysterical voice. She took up the earthy trowel she had instinctively tried to hide at Jeanie's approach. "I— I'm just playing a game. By myself. I don't want people. I'm all right. I—"

She glanced with an obvious agony of anxiety towards her mackintosh lying there on the ground. But it was too late. Jeanie had approached close enough to see that something long and straight lay hidden beneath that mackintosh.

"Oh Sarah, something's worrying you!"

"It isn't! *Do go away*, Jeanie!"

"How can I, and leave you like this? It's nearly dark! What *are* you up to? What've you got under your mack?"

Instantly Sarah flew to stand guard over her mackintosh.

"Nothing!"

"Oh, Sarah, surely you can trust me!" uttered Jeanie. "I'll help you, whatever it is!" she rashly added, and saw Sarah waver.

But there was a third upon the scene. As if one of the trees had taken on human life, Superintendent Finister moved quietly forward from among them. Turning, Jeanie saw him standing there, tall, narrow and saturnine in his blue cloth which in this last lingering of daylight had an intense deep quality of colour. Poor Sarah, to her the appearance of the tall policeman upon the scene was, it seemed, like the signing of a death-warrant She swallowed once, stood up straight, letting her trowel drop, and stood very still.

"Rabbiting, Miss Molyneux? Or what?"

Superintendent Finister looked pointedly at Sarah's mackintosh.

"Rabbits have been a perfect plague here this year," he went on. "The country's stiff with them. If you've been for a walk round Cleedons, Miss Halliday, I expect you saw our men?"

"Your men?" echoed Jeanie blankly, but Sarah, she noticed, flinched.

"Our men dragging the pond on the common."

With the fear of new horrors as yet unknown to her, Jeanie stammered:

"No. What for?"

"For the weapon, you know. It must be somewhere."

"Oh, the weapon! Of course!"

Sarah was as still as a stick. Her stillness was more noticeable than movement. Jeanie, putting an arm around her shoulders, felt her whole body stiff as wood.

"We think now the murderer probably hid it immediately after the murder. And of course the pond's the obvious place. Too obvious. Still, a criminal in a panic doesn't always avoid the obvious so well as he'd like to. But they haven't found anything yet."

The superintendent spoke with a kind of dreamy detachment.

"What do you expect to find?"

"Well, there's this pistol missing from the gun-room at Cleedons, and nobody seems to know anything about it. There on the morning of the murder, so the housemaid says. Not there since. Somebody must know something about that. A Colt automatic target-pistol. That's what's missing from the gun-room, and that's what we should expect to find. But I keep an open mind. It wouldn't surprise me to find a miniature rifle. Not so easily hidden as an automatic, you know. More likely to be thrown away on the spur of the moment. This Colt automatic that's missing from the gun-room is only ten and a half inches long. It would go in a coat-pocket. But a miniature rifle's a thing you can't hide so easily. You might easily get in a real fright and throw it in a pond or push it down a drain."

He spoke gently, sadly, and his eyes never left that mackintosh of Sarah's.

"Or a rabbit-hole," he added softly.

He looked thoughtfully at Sarah, who was staring straight in front of her. The trees that ringed the three of them round were quite dark now. This is the hour, thought Jeanie, for witchcraft and the visiting of tombs. She glanced at Sarah, and saw her lips silently move, and wondered whether she were appealing once again desperately to the spirits of the tumulus to help her. She shivered.

"It's cold."

"Yes, and will be dark soon," agreed Superintendent Finister. He looked paternally at Sarah. "I shouldn't do any more digging now. Let old Grim sleep in peace for to-night."

He spoke kindly, and picking Sarah's mackintosh up from the ground held it out for her to put on. She made one jerk to prevent him, then gave it up and stood quite still.

"Hullo!" said Superintendent Finister without great surprise, looking at the small rifle which lay exposed upon the grass.

Sarah said nothing for a moment. She shoved her arms down the sleeves of the coat that Finister still held out for her, and wrapped it round herself and remarked in a high, unnatural voice:

"I suppose we might as well go home, Jeanie. It's too dark to do any shooting now."

With exaggerated nonchalance she stooped to pick the weapon up from the ground, but Finister was before her.

"Shooting!" echoed he with a faint smile, looking at the label on the stock. "You're a bit young for handling fire-arms, aren't you, missie?"

"Perhaps," conceded Sarah. With dignity she added: "Could I have my rifle, please?" Her voice trembled.

"This isn't your rifle, my dear."

"It is."

Sarah held out her hand and looked Finister straight in the eyes. Her own eyes looked small and very dark. His were thoughtful, not unkindly. Jeanie murmured:

"Oh, Sarah dear!"

"It is," repeated Sarah brazenly. "So give it me, please. I suppose a person can shoot rabbits on their own uncle's farm—" her voice faltered—"without being a criminal?"

"I suppose so too, my dear, but you haven't been shooting rabbits, and this isn't your rifle."

"It is."

"Come," said Finister kindly. "Miss Molyneux, this is no use. I shall find out soon enough, you know, whom this rifle belongs to."

"My uncle. It's not *exactly* mine, but—"

"Missie, we know all the guns your uncle had at Cleedons, and only one of them's missing, a target-pistol."

"This is a new one. He bought it a day or two before he—before he—"

Finister shook his head.

"Is this any use, ducky?" asked Jeanie. She was startled at the look the child threw her.

"You said you'd help me!"

"But, Sarah!"

Feeling a traitor, Jeanie looked helplessly at Finister.

"Come," said he briskly. "Why do you suppose I followed you up here, my dear?"

"Don't call me your dear!"

Taken a trifle aback, Finister laughed shortly.

"Well! Why do you suppose I followed you up here? I was watching my men at work on the pond on the common. I saw you come out through the gap in the hedge of the Cleedons orchard. You looked around. I shouldn't have noticed you particularly, perhaps, only you looked around you as if you didn't want to be seen. You couldn't see me, I was among the trees at the edge of the pond. I saw you stoop down and disappear. You crawled under the culvert, didn't you, that crosses the ditch there? When you came out, you had something in your hand—a rifle, I thought. You put it under your coat very quickly and sauntered off. I followed you. I followed you through the orchard and the barnyard and across the road. So you see, my d— Miss Molyneux, it would really be better to tell me all about it."

There was a pause. Two little spots of red burnt in the child's pale cheeks. She did not look at Finister nor at Jeanie, but at the tree-tops as if she envied the birds. She said brokenly:

"I shan't tell you a damned thing."

"Well, miss, you know we can easily find out."

"Find out and be damned. Can I have my rifle?"

"No. I'm keeping that."

"Keep it then, and go to hell with it."

"Oh Sarah!" murmured Jeanie, as they made their way down the side of the tumulus and up the bank among the tearing brambles and spiky sapling-stumps almost invisible in the dusk. "What's the trouble? Hadn't you better tell me?"

"So that you can go straight and tell Finister, I suppose," said Sarah coldly. She stumbled over a rabbit-hole and recovered herself, with dignity.

Jeanie sighed. Confederacy between the adult and the child had its difficulties.

"I might want to," she admitted. "But I could promise not to, if you liked."

"To the death?"

"Well—it would depend whose death," said Jeanie, feebly joking.

They passed out of the gate of the Cole Harbour meadow on to the chilly, wind-whistling road. Sarah paused, carefully replacing the chain.

"No, Jeanie, I can't," she muttered at last. "It isn't only me, you see. There's another person."

Jeanie stopped and looked at her young friend's face, pearly white in the dusk with huge dark eyes that evaded her glance.

"Have you promised that other person not to tell?"

"No, but—"

"Then change your mind and tell me!"

Something in Sarah's nervous contraction when Jeanie laid a gentle hand upon her shoulder, something in the sudden focusing of her cold, fearful glance, her movement like a startled animal's woke an echo in Jeanie's mind. She remembered how she had seen Sarah shrink and run from another person's well-meant caress. Her hand on Sarah's stiff shoulder became very still. They looked at one another. A sick depression came upon Jeanie, a premonition of horror. All very well to offer so genially to disperse poor little Sarah's worry! What if it should prove undispersable, a horror capable of enveloping Jeanie and Cleedons and all Handleston in its foul mist?

"Oh Sarah," uttered Jeanie. "Was that rifle Marjorie Dasent's?"

It did not need Sarah's too quick, too violent denial, the terrified contraction of her pupils, to tell Jeanie that indeed it was. They stood in silence, looking at one another. Jeanie recalled Marjorie's collapse at the inquest, the obvious fear that had looked out of her eyes at Jeanie over the lighting of a cigarette, Tamsin's story of her scene with Molyneux. Oh, the thing was horrible, and going to be worse! In the midst of her horror Jeanie noted it as an odd thing that she felt no particular moral revulsion from Marjorie Dasent now that she saw her as a murderess. She thought of her with the mixture of pity, aversion and embarrassment with which a healthy person may contemplate one hideously ill.

"She'll be hanged!"

It was Sarah who spoke, suddenly abandoning pretence in a dry whisper soft as the beating of a moth's wing.

"How did you know?"

"I saw her, Jeanie," said the child in a hoarse whisper.

"You can't have done, dear! You were with me in the hay-loft!"

"It was afterwards," uttered Sarah, still in that ghostly whisper. "When you were with Aunt Agnes in the lane. I went to fetch some water, and I couldn't find a bucket. You remember. I went behind the barn into the orchard to fetch the chicken's basin. And I saw Marjorie crossing the orchard. She had a gun. She came from where the lambing-shed is. She looked awful. I saw her look at where Uncle Robert was. She just looked at him. She looked awful. And then she went out quickly through the gap. She didn't see me. She seemed to look round, and then I saw her stoop down. And when she stood up, she had no gun. She'd buried it under the culvert. She looked so *awful*, Jeanie! But she'd just done a murder, so of course—and she went away. Oh Jeanie, Jeanie! She'll be hanged, if they find out, won't she?"

The two walked slowly on.

"Do you think the police will know it's Marjorie's?" asked Sarah fearfully.

"I'm afraid they'll easily find out. What made you interfere, my dear?"

"I couldn't just let them find it! And they were dragging the pond. They were looking everywhere; I knew they'd find it soon! I thought I'd hide it in a better place. Grim's Grave. I thought it might be safe there. If I prayed to Grim—"

"My dear kiddie!"

"Well!"

"Oh well, it's natural, I suppose! I wonder," speculated Jeanie, "how many things are buried there on top of Grim? If it occurred to you so easily, you won't have been the first to think of it in all these centuries!"

## Chapter Fourteen
## BIRD-BOLTS

Agnes was in the little panelled parlour, and alone, for once, when Jeanie arrived at Cleedons. A glittering tea-equipage fit for a reception stood on the low table beside her, with enough untouched bread and butter, cakes and little sandwiches to feed a party. The crimson curtains were drawn to shut out the dusk.

"Alone for once, Agnes?" asked Jeanie a little timidly, not quite certain of her welcome, for she had come uninvited.

A rueful expression came over Agnes's face.

"You may well say 'for once'!" she murmured. "What with policemen and relations and the doctor, I get no peace. Dr. Hall's so determined that I ought to be ill that he calls every day—to make me so, I suppose. And as for Tamsin Wills! Really, Jeanie, I don't know what to do about that girl! She fusses over me and follows me about till I'm nearly crazy. What have I done to arouse all this horrible devotion? Really, it's like being a schoolmistress again."

Jeanie winced, for there had been a time when Agnes had roused her devotion, and she had not thought, then, that Agnes found it horrible.

"We had a fearful row here about ten minutes ago. Tamsin flung off out of the house. Really, Jeanie, I don't know what's the matter with her! She'll have to go. She's been getting more and more peculiar ever since she made that dead set at Mr. Fone, and he had to show her so plainly he didn't like her."

"Mr. Fone! I wouldn't have thought Tamsin was exactly in love with Mr. Fone!" said Jeanie, a trifle uncomfortably, for there had been real malice in Agnes's tone.

"Of course not, now! She hates him, no doubt. Because he didn't agree with her about their being soulmates. I believe he said they were on quite different spirals or something."

Jeanie laughed.

"*I* believe you're just making that up!"

Agnes smiled, taking the accusation as a tribute to her powers of entertainment.

"She'll have to go. I've had enough of it," said she, stretching a little in her low chair and yawning delicately, like a lazy cat. "We had that awful Peel woman here this afternoon. Tamsin saw her. That's really what started the row. Naturally, Tamsin's very anxious that Sarah shan't go back to her mother and leave Tamsin out of a job. But after all, as I told her, a mother has the first claim on her own child."

"Oh, surely," said Jeanie uneasily, "if you're Sarah's guardian, Agnes, you wouldn't—"

A fretful look came at once, at this hint of criticism, to Agnes's face.

"Of course I wouldn't, but I wanted to annoy Tamsin, because I'm sick of her bullying and fussing, and I won't have her dictating to me. Of course, if I'm Sarah's guardian I'll carry out Robert's wishes. I don't like children, and Sarah doesn't like me, but of course I do as Robert wanted. But it's no pleasure to me to have Sarah here; it's a duty, and I wish somebody could convince Mrs. Peel of it. I shall keep the child simply, simply because Robert wished it!" said Agnes, searching around among her cushions for a handkerchief.

"I'm sorry, Agnes," said Jeanie penitently.

"Oh, it's not you, Jeanie. It's Tamsin. She's really quite intolerable!"

"Why not send her away?"

"I'd like to, only well, what could I do with Sarah? All the bother of finding another tutor or deciding on a school. I really feel I haven't the strength to make any changes just yet."

Agnes blew her nose and, standing up, poked a log down in the fire with the toe of her shoe. She looked very frail standing there in the firelight in her long black gown, and Jeanie looked at her with a half-unwilling admiration. A beautiful dress: and why should not a dress of mourning be beautiful? Must death be surrounded everywhere with ugliness? Thin lips, drooping at present, beautifully touched with artificial colour: and why not? Thin, fine-cut eyelids, with nature's somewhat earthy shadows beautifully transformed with mascara to a frail violet: and again, why not? Well, it was only four days since poor Mr. Molyneux's death: how could so newly-widowed a wife as Agnes find heart for that elaborate study of her own appearance?

"Tamsin didn't like Robert," said Agnes suddenly. "And of course he couldn't endure her, really. She wasn't his sort of girl. And lately he'd begun to think she wasn't up to her job. I think he was wrong there. Tamsin's very well qualified, and not at all a bad teacher. Only of course Sarah's never liked her, and that weighed a lot with Robert. He was thinking of getting rid of her, I know. And she knew it, of course. Anyhow, she didn't like him. She was jealous of him, too—you know, Jeanie, what extraordinary notions these repressed kind of girls like Tamsin can get in their heads! Only I didn't realise till lately how abnormal she was. She's getting worse, I suppose. Really, I don't think she's quite sane!"

Agnes's voice went on in a low peevish tone, with little fretful sighs. Evidently, Tamsin had behaved very badly that afternoon.

"Oh Agnes, why not tell her to go, if it worries you so?"

Agnes's eyes turned, wide and dark, upon Jeanie's face. She said with a little sob:

"I used not to mind her disliking Robert. But now— it seems too horrible! Too horrible, that she shouldn't like him, and he's dead! Oh Jeanie!"

She half-turned, and let her face sink for a second upon Jeanie's shoulder.

"When we had that row this afternoon—when she was so unbearable—I felt quite *ashamed* of the suspicions that came into my head. But I can't get rid of them! I keep thinking, *Tamsin* was in the Tower room. *Tamsin* could have—oh no! No!"

"But Agnes, it wasn't from the Tower that the shot came. It was from the other side of the orchard."

"Who says so? That lunatic William Fone! Who would take any notice of him?" asked Agnes scornfully.

"But there's no reason why he shouldn't be speaking the truth, Agnes, even if he is a lunatic! Unless of course he shot Mr. Molyneux himself."

Agnes raised wide, frightened eyes from Jeanie's shoulder. She looked paper-pale and fragile in the firelight.

"Tamsin tried to make us think he did," she uttered slowly. "Don't you remember? Right at the beginning, Tamsin tried to make us suspect Mr. Fone? Oh Jeanie! Was it because she had done it herself? Did she know how easily it could be done from one of the windows in the Tower?"

They looked at one another. Jeanie felt quite a little chill of horror. What more likely than that crime should flower in the soil of malice? And had not Jeanie herself thought Tamsin Wills a very spring of malice? Then her common sense reasserted itself.

"I don't think you need torture yourself with that suspicion, Agnes. The truth's bad enough. The police have found a rifle that was hidden in the orchard-ditch."

"Do you mean, they know who did it?"

"No, they don't *know*, but—"

But Agnes, when Jeanie mentioned Marjorie Dasent's name, looked first a little contemptuous, then amused, and then, drying her eyes, laughed the whole idea to scorn.

"Marjorie! Oh no! She hasn't enough imagination even to *think* of—oh no! It's absurd! I don't care how many rifles of hers they've found! Somebody else must have been using it!"

"But Sarah said—"

"Sarah! Now, *she's* got too much imagination. She probably made up the whole thing. She's a little romancer, that child, Jeanie!"

"I dare say. But there's a difference between romancing and—"

"No, there isn't. Look at that mother of hers! Hardly knows what she's saying half the time!"

"Yes, but—"

"Oh, no, Jeanie! Marjorie Dasent! It's ridiculous! She simply hasn't got it in her! But Tamsin—"

Agnes shuddered.

"Oh, I suppose I'm an imaginative fool myself! Sarah and I are a pair, aren't we?"

She sank into her low chair again, and leaning her elbows on her knees looked, as if for comfort, into the roaring fire. She loved heat, and shut windows and drawn curtains, and scented rooms, and cushions. She was like a sleek, thin cat in her tastes and her delicate ways. Jeanie, who was not, was beginning to feel oppressed in this hot-house atmosphere. She unbuttoned her knitted jacket.

"My dear, don't keep Tamsin here! Tell her to find another job!"

"She'll have to stay till after the inquest, anyway. I can't suddenly turn her out of the house!"

"Shall I come and stay here?" suggested Jeanie, with a good deal of self-sacrifice, for she did not relish the idea of being a buffer between Agnes and Tamsin. The days were past when making herself a slave to Agnes's imperious whims would have been happiness to her. "I could keep Tamsin away from you. And take the housekeeping off your hands."

Agnes replied wearily:

"Oh, Tamsin does that. She's marvellous at any sort of organising. You wouldn't think it, but she is. It's sweet of you to suggest it, Jeanie, when I know how you'd hate it. But it's all right, thank you. I mustn't encourage myself in these stupid fancies. Besides, darling, Tamsin hates you, and I don't think you like her much. You'd probably quarrel."

Jeanie flushed.

"I think you consider her too much. If you feel about her as you say you do, you ought to get rid of her!"

"There! See how nicely you'd get on with her!" murmured Agnes with a faint sparkle of mockery. "No, Jeanie, to be fair to her, she's marvellous in lots of ways. She saves me no end of bother. And I suppose there's always something one has to put up with. But it's sweet of you to suggest coming here, Jeanie. You are kind."

It was odd how her caressing voice suddenly broke off sharp on a kind of gasp. Jeanie, who was standing up divesting herself of her jacket and laying it over a chair-back, looked at her friend in surprise to see what had startled her.

Agnes was still sitting with her elbows on her knees, but all the relaxation of her pose was gone. Her arms were rigid, her hands contracted, her chin lifted from them and averted, as she stared with eyes that looked suddenly dark and large at something on the floor. Her lips were parted. She looked quite foolish—stupefied or half-witted. She looked as though she had suddenly seen an adder on the floor by her feet, head raised to strike.

All Jeanie could see was the contents of her jacket-pocket which, as she hung it over her chair-arm, had emptied itself upon the floor. There was a shilling, a pencil, a lipstick and the broken string of pearls which Eustace Agatos had found under the stairs at Yew Tree Cottage. Jeanie stooped to pick them up. But Agnes was quicker.

"Pearls, Jeanie?" she asked, in a strange, uncertain voice.

"Don't I wish they were! I'd sell them to pay some of the builder's bills!"

"But—are they yours?"

Jeanie laughed, though she was a little surprised, too.

"Do you suspect me of burglary?"

"No, but—"

"They're treasure trove. They were in the cupboard under the stairs at Yew Tree Cottage."

Still holding the pearls in her hand, gazing as if hypnotised at the little brilliant clasp, Agnes repeated, still in that slow, uncertain way:

"At Yew Tree Cottage?"

She raised her eyes a moment from the pearls and looked in front of her, frowning slightly. Her lips formed the word:

"But—"

"They're only Woolworth's!"

"Are they?"

"Surely they're not real?" asked Jeanie. "You know more about pearls than I do."

"Oh—no," said Agnes uncertainly. "No, of course not. I shouldn't think so. How could they be? Is this all there were? I don't know anything about pearls. No, of course they couldn't be real. Only this clasp looks rather good. I'll tell you what, Jeanie. The man in town that set my opals knows quite a lot about pearls. Next time I go up I'll take them to him. He wouldn't charge anything for valuing them. If you leave them with me, I'll see to it."

"I shouldn't have thought it was worth the bother," said Jeanie, somewhat puzzled. "Anyway, I think I'll have them back now." She held out her hand. "They're just what I want for a still-life I'm painting," she said mendaciously. She was determined, she knew not quite why, not to leave the pearls with Agnes. Agnes obviously wanted them and would not say why. Very well, Jeanie would keep them until she had found out why Agnes wanted them. To this queer distrust, their one-time friendship had descended.

Very unwillingly, it seemed to Jeanie, Agnes surrendered them.

"You can have them when I've done my painting. I'll make you a handsome present of them, Agnes!" Jeanie dropped them back into her pocket. She stayed at Cleedons another half-hour or so, chatting to Agnes, and often during their talk she found Agnes's eyes fixed speculatively and, she thought, even greedily, upon that pocket.

"Well, don't lose your valuable pearls," was Agnes's remark as she rose to go and put her jacket on; but Jeanie felt that the half-joking tone in which it was uttered covered a real concern. Indeed, Jeanie had the odd persuasion that it was the pearls, rather than herself, that Agnes was seeing off when she rose and went with the departing Jeanie into the hall.

"Oh, Jeanie, it's dark and windy! Poor you, going out into it!"

"I've got my torch."

"Here's a letter—from Tamsin!"

"Tamsin?" Jeanie, doing up the collar of her mackintosh, had an instant premonition of trouble. Agnes's little face was quite white under its dark, startled frown. She gasped:

"Oh no! This is too much! She's mad! Oh Jeanie, I really can't stand any more! Oh, the silly fool! Of course, she doesn't mean it, but—oh Jeanie! I simply can't cope with any more of this sort of thing."

"Well, let me look."

Violently, as if she repudiated every connection with it, Agnes thrust the letter into her hands.

"*You will not see me again. When you read this, I shall have done what you told me to do*. Oh, Agnes! What did you tell her to do?"

Agnes, leaning against the table, looked hunted, miserable and furious all at once.

"I can't re—"

"Oh my dear, of course you can!"

"Well, I suppose she means—I told her to go and drown herself in Hatcher's Pond! Oh Jeanie, but I won't be held responsible for what that idiot of a hysterical girl does in one of her fits of mania!"

Jeanie felt a little sick. How like Agnes, that her first thought should be to disclaim responsibility!

"I'll go and see if I can find her. I've got my torch. The police were dragging Hatcher's Pond. Perhaps they'll have seen her."

"Oh, surely you wouldn't tell them!" exclaimed Agnes, taking fright.

"Not yet. I suppose we ought to give her a chance to come quietly home by herself. But if she's really drowned herself, we'll have to tell them."

"Oh Jeanie, haven't I enough to bear without this?"

"Well, I'm sorry, but I can't help it," replied Jeanie, with less than her usual gentleness. "I should go to bed if I were you. I'll be back as soon as possible, whether I find her or not."

Outside the sky seemed full of noise and the tossing boughs of trees. The wind had risen and backed to the north and snow was surely in the offing. It was not, in Jeanie's opinion, at all a night for drowning oneself.

## Chapter Fifteen
### CANNON-BULLETS

Nor was it a night in which to indulge in emotional conversations out of doors. For this, and not a plunge in the uninviting waters of Hatcher's Pond, was Jeanie's fate. She found Tamsin, sooner than she had expected, leaning against one of the trees near the pond's edge. At the flashing of Jeanie's torch she turned as if to hide, to run. She looked white in the torchlight, strained and blind and wildly dishevelled, as though she had let the wind and brambles have their way with her.

"Tamsin!" cried Jeanie, and at her voice the girl checked her impulse of flight, stood in miserable uncertainty trying to pin up one of the loose coils of her hair.

"I thought—you were a policeman."

"What are you doing?"

"Just—thinking."

In Jeanie's torchlight the boles of the little group of silver birches in which they stood gleamed like ghosts, but everything else was dark, except Tamsin's white face and the moon, very high up and small and continually obscured by quickly-moving clouds.

"You come home and think there," said Jeanie, rather feebly jocose.

"Home? Cleedons, do you mean?" responded Tamsin with a haughtiness that Jeanie might have found funny had she been less perturbed. "Cleedons isn't my home."

"Where is your home, then?"

"In Westmorland."

"Don't be silly!"

Tamsin muttered furiously:

"Please leave me alone!"

Controlling herself, Jeanie said:

"You want a hot bath and a good night's sleep."

"Not under *that* roof!" muttered Tamsin dramatically. Jeanie had turned her torch off, for she doubted the battery, and they spoke to one another in the blackness, seeing one another's outlines in the dim moonlight and the dimmer reflections off the iron-grey water. As if to match their voices to their outlines, they muttered.

"Oh nonsense. Because you and Agnes quarrelled, do you mean? Surely you can forget that! After all, there's some excuse for Agnes! Her husband's only been dead four days, remember!"

"I don't forget it. It's she who's more likely to forget it."

"Whom do you mean?"

"She married him for his money, and she'll marry her next husband for his title."

Jeanie gasped.

"*What?*"

"Sir Henry Blundell's a widower, isn't he? And *so* sympathetic," muttered Tamsin tensely, with a vibrating sneer in her voice.

"Oh, how horrible! And how ridiculous, Tamsin."

"Well! When Agnes becomes Lady Blundell, remember I was the first to tell you of it," said Tamsin. She made a hoarse sound, half-dreary laugh, half-Sob. "Oh, *I* saw them, after the inquest, talking in the panelled parlour! What's going to happen was as plain as the nose on your face! Some women can't live without a man hanging round them!"

Jeanie might have retorted that Agnes had lived thirty-eight years without any such encumbrance. But Agnes had altered, whispered a little voice in her brain. Yes, Agnes had altered in all sorts of ways. Robert Molyneux's widow was a very different woman from Miss Agnes Drake.

A startled moor-hen rustled the rushes and whirred away across the pond, reminding Jeanie that the place and the time were no more suitable for contemplation of Agnes's character than for scandal about her doings.

"Come along back! You'll be having pneumonia and catching your death."

"I shouldn't care!"

"I should."

"You! I don't see why *you* should care," uttered the girl. Her voice was scoffing, yet wistful too, as if she longed to take Jeanie's response at its face value. Jeanie, who had intended only to remind Tamsin that her death would be a great nuisance to all concerned, felt quite ashamed. One assumed too readily that the Tamsin Willses of this world were immune from the human longing for affection and approval. Too readily one gave aversion for malice and dislike in exchange for mistrust. Tamsin said very low:

"I meant to die to-night, but I couldn't. I couldn't. I was a coward! I made a mess of it, as I make a mess of everything. The water looked so awful. I thought of how one would struggle. I couldn't."

"I don't think you really meant to die, just over a quarrel with Agnes!"

Tamsin's arm stiffened.

"A quarrel! You don't know what she said!"

"Yes, I do." As she spoke, Jeanie realised that, had it not been for the events of the afternoon, she might herself have half believed Agnes's words. She might now have been afraid to walk with Tamsin Wills over the dark and gusty common.

You do? Oh, how can she? How can she? Without anything to go on!"

"Well, Tamsin, how could you say the same thing about Mr. Fone, without anything to go on?"

Jeanie was startled by the effect of her words. Tamsin stopped dead and dragged her arm from Jeanie's. She swallowed once or twice before she was able to speak. In the darkness, with her hair blown into wild disorder and her white face, she looked like a maenad. She seemed stiff with anger.

"I know Agnes tells everybody I'm in love with Mr. Fone!" she said at length in the rapid, shaken low tone of extreme emotion. "All because I once asked him to lend me some books! All because I was interested in his ideas! I never liked him in the way Agnes pretends! I didn't! The man's a lunatic, anyway! I've never even pretended to like him! I—"

Jeanie, astounded at the passion with which the girl was speaking, a passion blown on the gusty wind which made her words now loud and full, now weak and blown away, as it whipped her black hair across her face and then caused it to stream out into the night, tried to throw cold water on these green fires.

"I don't see that it would matter if you did like him. It's not a crime, to like people. Nor even to love them. Is it?"

"How do I know she doesn't even—say it to him?"

"Who? Mr. Fone? It wouldn't matter if she did."

"It would!"

"Nonsense, it wouldn't. People are always saying all kinds of things," replied Jeanie soothingly, if vaguely. "One does oneself. No sensible person thinks a thing about the things people go round saying."

"If I thought Agnes had said—that, to Mr. Fone, I should die!" was shaken tensely from between Tamsin's cold lips.

"Then you *do* love him?"

"No! No! No!"

"Well, I don't see why you should mind him thinking you love him, if you don't. Nor if you do either, so—"

"I dislike him extremely," said Tamsin with a quite extraordinary cold venom. There was a pause. White and stubborn, Tamsin stared into the darkness. Jeanie touched her arm and found it stiff and hard as iron, all the muscles contracted. She felt as if she had been sent out into the night to tame a savage, and did not know in what language to make the appeal. She tried again.

"I don't think Mr. Fone ever thinks about anything but his Ancient British tracks and his pagan gods. And I don't think poor old Agnes means half she says, she's so shaken up. Why worry your head about what either of them says or thinks? You've got more sense than either of them, or you would have if you didn't let yourself be so sensitive!"

Tamsin relaxed a little, but she said nothing.

"I'm sure," continued Jeanie, "Agnes is very sorry for everything she said. And I'm sure you ought to be, if you said to her anything like what you said to me! So why not come home and apologise to each other and sleep on it? After all, Tamsin, poor Agnes *has* had a dreadful time! And you're supposed to be looking after her!"

This more skilful appeal made its mark. Tamsin consented to fall into step beside Jeanie and walk on towards the road.

"But it's horrible," she muttered, "the way people talk as if every unmarried woman thought of nothing but *luring* some man into marrying her!"

The notion of Tamsin luring anybody struck Jeanie as comic. She replied gravely, however:

"What's horrible about it? Sometimes it's true, because in lots of ways married women have a much better time of it than single ones."

Tamsin in the darkness made an extraordinary scoffing sound interrupted by a shiver.

"*Do* they indeed! Well, it depends what you call a good time! They're dependent for their happiness on the behaviour of some man who may be a perfect brute, instead of being dependent on themselves!"

"Even spinsters aren't that. We're all dependent for our happiness on other people."

"Not in the same way. A friendship isn't supposed to be— exclusive. A marriage is."

At the peculiar tone in Miss Wills's voice, Jeanie stopped on the gravel under the tossed and noisy elm-trees.

"Oh Tamsin! You've just been complaining yourself about people's unkind tongues! Don't for Heaven's sake start talking to me again about poor Mr. Molyneux and Marjorie Dasent!"

Even to utter Marjorie's name made her coldly unhappy, as though the hideous future were all written for the wretched girl, and only Jeanie knew it.

"I wasn't thinking of Marjorie. I don't really think Agnes minded that much, she knew how silly Marjorie was. It was that woman at Yew Tree Cottage."

"The woman at Yew Tree Cottage?"

"Yes. The woman who lived with that man Barchard. Before your time, Miss Halliday. Perhaps you didn't know Yew Tree Cottage had a rather unsavoury reputation before you came to live in it!"

"Oh yes, I knew! You mean Valentine Frazer."

"That was her ridiculous name. Or so she said. I expect it was a stage name, really."

"What about her?"

"Only that she made Agnes very unhappy."

"Valentine Frazer made Agnes unhappy?" asked Jeanie incredulously.

"Yes."

"But how?"

"In the way married women can easily be made unhappy," replied the virtuous spinster Tamsin with some complacency.

"I didn't know Agnes even knew her! How do you know she made Agnes unhappy?"

"She came up here one afternoon, I don't know what about, of course, and Agnes saw her in the garden. And I saw Agnes crying afterwards."

"And you think it had something to do with Mr. Molyneux?"

"Well, what else could it have been?" said Tamsin. "Considering what the woman was!" she added with a vindictiveness marred by a sudden shiver.

Jeanie was silent as they walked up the windy drive. It seemed strange that Agnes had never mentioned Valentine Frazer to her.

But there were probably a great many things Agnes had not mentioned to her erstwhile protégée and friend. And why should she have mentioned her acquaintance with Valentine Frazer? She would not have been proud of it!

"What was she like, this Valentine Frazer?"

"Like? Oh, like you'd expect. A vulgar, noisy kind or creature. The sort of person you can see and hear from miles away. If she were shopping in the village everyone knew it. Used to go and drink port in the saloon bar at the 'White Lion.' That's how she met her painter, I suppose."

"Was she good-looking?"

Tamsin turned a chill shiver into an ostentatious shudder of aversion.

"If you like chemical golden hair and lots of pink paint!"

"But she was young?"

"Oh no, nearly forty, I should think. She was good- looking, I suppose," admitted Tamsin grudgingly. "Or what most people would call good-looking, when she took the trouble. She was supposed to have been some low-class kind of actress and she just looked it and behaved like it. A chorus-girl, as people used to say, only it sounds rather old-fashioned now."

"She was popular, was she, in the village?"

Tamsin laughed ill-naturedly.

"You can't live in sin, and be popular, in a village," said she. "But she had lots of money, Heaven knows how she got it, and spent it at the village shops and was friendly to everyone in a noisy kind of way, so she was quite decently treated. To her face."

"I see. Good Heavens! I wonder what Harmless Hubert's done with her!"

"Harmless Hubert?"

"Hubert Southey. I know him a bit. He taught at the Art School I went to."

"Oh, the painter she went off with! Probably murdered her by now, I should think. But he was very much smitten at the time."

"Smitten! How marvellous, and how very, very odd, to think of Harmless Hubert being smitten!"

"He painted her sitting in a field, with half the village kids looking on," said Tamsin. "You can imagine the chatter! I don't think Agnes need have made herself unhappy. Obviously it wasn't Mr. Molyneux, it was this painter Southey, who was the favoured one. But being a married woman, you see, and dependent, she did make herself unhappy."

"I don't think you can say that. I don't see that there's any reason to suppose that there was anything at all between Mr. Molyneux and this woman, and I do think, Tamsin, you ought not to suggest such a thing without more to go on," said Jeanie uneasily. Tamsin stiffened again, and spoke coldly.

"There was an awful quarrel between Mr. Molyneux and Hugh Barchard, anyway. I do know that."

"But that was about the money Mr. Molyneux lent Barchard! Peter Johnson told me."

Tamsin shrugged her shoulders.

"I'm afraid I'm not so pure-minded as you are."

"I'm afraid you're not."

They walked on in silence, but Tamsin could not long restrain herself from self-justification.

"All I know is, Agnes used often to go down to Yew Tree Cottage, although officially, of course, she didn't even know the woman. And she was always nervous and wretched when she came back. In fact, she seemed nervous and wretched most of the time the Frazer woman was here. She's been a different person since. It just shows you—"

"It shows me, anyway," said Jeanie, smiling, trying to make amends, "that the former tenant of my cottage must have been a formidable woman."

"Formidable! Oh no! Just handsome in a *very* vulgar kind of way, and loud and noisy, and immoral and impertinent!"

"I should think the average English matron *would* find that a bit formidable," said Jeanie. "And she wore red gloves, didn't she? Because Mrs. Barchard said so. And a pearl necklace from Woolworth's."

They were upon the door-step of Cleedons and Tamsin had her hand outstretched towards the bell when, perceiving what Jeanie had in her hand, she paused with an exclamation:

"Those! Let me look!"

"Why, have you seen them before?"

In the light over the door Tamsin peered at the broken string of beads, held them up and examined carefully the brilliant clasp.

"Of course! Where did you find them? Have you shown them to Agnes? They're hers."

"Whose?"

"Agnes's."

Oh no, because—"

"Oh yes! I couldn't mistake them. The clasp was specially designed for her. And I remember the way the safety catch had got bent. Where on earth did you find them?"

Jeanie looked incredulously at Tamsin.

"But I showed them to Agnes, and she didn't say they were hers! Surely she wasn't shy of saying to me that she wore artificial pearls!"

"Artificial pearls!" echoed Tamsin. "They're not artificial! That string cost fourteen hundred pounds!"

"What!"

"It did. Mr. Molyneux bought it cheap, through a friend, too. Agnes lost it, about three years ago, and there was a fearful to-do. Is that all you found?"

"But Tamsin! I tell you Agnes saw them, and she didn't say they were hers!"

"I can't help that. They are."

"But how extraordinary! I'll ask her! I can't possibly keep them if they're as valuable as that, even for a day or two!"

"Oh no!" cried Tamsin. "Don't tell her I said they were hers! Perhaps I oughtn't to have said anything! She'll be furious with me! And everything seems to be going wrong between me and Agnes! Give me a chance to make it up with her!"

The girl's distress was so genuine, her nerves so obviously unstrung, the happenings of this queer evening so conducive to folly, that Jeanie agreed. After all, if Agnes had denied knowledge of the pearls before, she would do so again. What could have been her motive?

## Chapter Sixteen
### THE PORTRAIT OF A LADY IN RED GLOVES

"Do you know a good jeweller in Gloucester, Mr. Fone? I want some pearls valued."

"I should imagine a pawnbroker's would be a suitable place. We must look out for the sign of the three golden balls. The human love of adornment," continued Mr. Fone thoughtfully, "has led to many curious proceedings, but to none more curious than the wearing around the female neck of strings of morbid growths from the bodies of oysters."

Jeanie laughed, but Mr. Fone seemed perfectly serious.

"I am told that the inducing of morbid growths in unfortunate oysters is quite a profitable industry among the Japanese. In my view it is not an occupation worthy of man."

They were sitting in state under a fur rug in the back of Mr. Fone's old touring car. A landscape of Jeanie's had been accepted for an exhibition in the Guildhall of paintings by Gloucestershire artists, and Jeanie had gladly accepted Mr. Fone's offer to drive her in to the private view. He had some business in Gloucester, he said, and would drop her and Peter at the Guildhall.

Peter was at the wheel. He was gayer than Jeanie had known him since before Molyneux's death. He looked serene and happy, like a seaman in his boat or a painter before his canvas.

"I too, by the way, have some shopping to do in Gloucester," said Mr. Fone. "I want to buy a pair of sighting staves, such as Boy Scouts carry about with them. Or, if these aren't procurable, broom-handles would do, I dare say."

"Staves?" echoed Jeanie, with vague thoughts of cowled pilgrims or of medieval gentlemen smiting one another over the head in single combat.

"Yes. Such as surveyors use, and such as were used by the early inhabitants of these islands to make those straight roads afterwards metalled by the Roman invaders. I have been trying to get the local antiquarians interested in the subject of early British trackways. But there is nothing more stubborn than an antiquarian asked to reconsider his notions. Sir Henry Blundell, especially, appears to suffer from a kind of Romanophilia that amounts to a mania. He appears to think that these islands hardly existed before the Romans set their heavy feet on them. No argument, however strong, would ever convince Sir Henry that the Romans were a poor, unimaginative, material-minded, slavish race of men, inferior in both physique and spirit to the people they conquered, superior in only two things—mechanical skill and the discipline of the trained slave. I am hoping to give a demonstration of the theory of the old straight track one day soon to some of the Field Club members. If you are interested in the subject, I hope you will join us. I don't expect to convert Sir Henry Blundell from his worship of Roman militarism, but if I induce a few of our members to prefer the culture of our own early ancestors to that of our dull-souled invaders, I shall have done something."

It depressed Jeanie, but after what Tamsin had said it did not surprise her, to hear that her half-string of pearls was worth between four and five hundred pounds. The man behind the counter showed a certain curiosity as to the whereabouts of the other half.

"For, of course," said he, "the whole string, if well matched, would be worth much more than twice that."

"I see. I'm afraid I haven't got the other half."

A pity, remarked the jeweller, in a voice interrogative with curiosity. Jeanie did not attempt to satisfy it. Her own mind seemed starred all over with interrogation-marks, so starred that she could not think clearly enough to answer anybody else's questions.

"What's the matter?" asked Peter, looking at her quite anxiously as she reached the street where he was waiting for her. "You look all kind of dazed, Jeanie. Pearls only Woolworth's, after all?"

Jeanie shook her head.

"No, they're worth five hundred pounds."

"Five hundred pounds! Then why the tragedy effect, Jeanie? Did you hope they'd be worth more?"

"No, I hoped they wouldn't be worth anything. They're not mine. They're some that were found in my cottage. Tamsin says they belong to Agnes. Agnes doesn't say they belong to her. I don't know how they got in my cottage. It's all very complicated."

"Agnes did lose a string of pearls about three years ago," said Peter. "I remember. Mr. Molyneux was rather annoyed about it, because he hadn't bought them long, and the insurance people were rather sticky about paying up."

"But Agnes doesn't say they're hers. Tamsin says they're hers."

Peter looked in a somewhat puzzled manner at Jeanie's grave face, and laughed.

"You'd better come and have some lunch with me somewhere and we'll try to solve the problem, Jeanie. It sounds like the beginning of a brain-twister out of the Week-End Agony Book."

They rejected several tea-shops of varying allure, and settled themselves in the sombre dining-room of an old-fashioned hotel, where the service was slow and the food conscientiously boiled, but where they were at least free from hustle, noise and the close propinquity of other lunchers. Over a plate of brown and glutinous soup, Jeanie told Peter about Agatos's finding of the broken string of pearls, about Agnes's surprise and hesitation when she had seen them, and Tamsin's positiveness as to their ownership.

"It doesn't sound much like Agnes to repudiate a five-hundred-pound string of pearls," commented Peter a little grimly, when she had finished.

"No, I know. And yet, Peter, I believe they *are* hers, or she knew something about them, anyway. She behaved so oddly."

"And Tamsin says, does she, that Agnes was acquainted with the lady who used to live at your cottage? I didn't know that, but she may have been."

"Tamsin says Agnes went to see her several times."

"Then she must have left her pearls there. Or had them stolen there. Or given them away to Barchard's lady."

"Not very likely, is it?"

"Or perhaps," said Peter thoughtfully, crumbling bread into his soup in a vulgar manner, "it was some nefarious scheme for collecting the insurance money. Agnes lent the pearls to this Miss Frazer, and—"

"Oh, surely Agnes wouldn't do that," murmured Jeanie, pained.

Peter was expressively silent.

"Besides," said Jeanie, "one'd have to know a person awfully well before one would take her as a partner in a—a swindle, wouldn't one? No that's impossible, Peter. But I should like to know Agnes's pearls got to Yew Tree Cottage."

"Better find Miss Valentine Frazer and ask her."

"I wonder where she is. I wonder if one could track her down. I wonder whether one could ask Hubert Southey if he knows her whereabouts."

"Why not?"

"I don't know," said Jeanie, smiling slightly. "Hubert Southey is such a *very* proper little man. Oh, Peter!"

"What is it?" he asked anxiously. "This fish?"

"No, no, that's all right. It's only—oh, I wish, I *wish* I knew who killed Mr. Molyneux."

Peter said:

"*I* didn't, Jeanie. And I believe even the idiot police are beginning to realise that. I don't think I'm their pet suspect any more. Young Sarah told me about—"

"Oh dear, I'd managed to forget Marjorie Dasent for a whole hour."

"I'm sorry."

"Not your fault. I started this conversation. Only—
it *is* horrible, isn't it, to think of evidence like that against a girl one knows?"

"Very. But, candidly, it's not half so horrible as evidence like that against oneself," replied Peter grimly. "Probably she didn't do it any more than I did. But it'll give old Finister something to think about for a day or two. Did you notice how I passed that bobby in the street just now, Jeanie? Almost without quivering. You don't know what it means, to be able to pass a bobby without a quiver."

"Do you really think Marjorie didn't do it, Peter?"

Peter put a lot of salt thoughtfully on his well-boiled fish.

"I shouldn't have thought she had it in her. But one never knows."

"*I* think she must have done. She had a rifle, she was in the orchard. Sarah saw her, you know. And she had a motive, of a kind."

"Yes. All that's against her. Anything in her favour?"

Jeanie thought.

"Only that Agnes, who knows her fairly well, I suppose, says she can't have done it, she hasn't got it in her, and nothing will induce Agnes to believe she did it. Agnes seemed to think—"

Peter looked up sharply.

"Yes?"

"Well—that Tamsin—but of course it's absurd!"

"Why? Tamsin's a very erratic type of young woman, if you ask me. And Mr. Molyneux didn't like her at all and intended to sack her, and she knew it. And being Sarah's governess is a good well-paid job, and Tamsin isn't exactly the sort of girl who falls easily into good jobs. And she's devoted to Agnes and would hate to leave her. And she was stupidly jealous of Molyneux; anybody could see that. And she was in the Tower room overlooking the orchard when Robert Molyneux was shot."

"Yes," agreed Jeanie. "All that's against her. But Mr. Molyneux can't have been killed by a shot from the lower Tower window, and that's in her favour."

"Who says so? Only Fone! Nobody else professes to know which way Mr. Molyneux was facing when he died. Nobody else saw him die. Perhaps Mr. Fone's mistaken."

"Or perhaps," said Jeanie, with a certain malice, for Peter had an admiration for Mr. Fone, and she hoped to make him rise, "Mr. Fone shot Mr. Molyneux himself. Why not?" she went on quickly, as Peter frowned and made a little movement of protest. "Mr. Fone was in the Tower room overlooking the orchard when Mr. Molyneux was shot. Mr. Fone had written a letter to Mr. Molyneux which Tamsin described as threatening— oh, not threatening him with death, more a sort of gipsy's curse affair, as far as I could gather. Mr. Fone was determined the tumulus shouldn't be opened if he could help it, and really seems to have believed hell would be let loose if it were! Also, by his own account he behaved very oddly in going straight home after he saw poor Mr. Molyneux die, without doing anything to help him. Well? All that's against him. What's in his favour?"

Peter smiled, helping himself to a drowned potato.

"Merely that one can't imagine him telling a lie about such an exploit. If he'd been mad enough to think that the end of saving the tumulus justified the means of killing Robert Molyneux, he'd have said so. He's not like ordinary men. Barchard's right there."

"Ah! Barchard! No, no potatoes, thank you. What about Barchard? He had a motive. He owed Mr. Molyneux two hundred pounds."

"And where was *he* at the crucial moment?

Jeanie's face fell.

"No good. He was mending leads on the roof at Cole Harbour. He couldn't even have seen Robert Molyneux from there, all the farm buildings are between Cole Harbour and the Cleedons orchard. Besides it's the wrong side. Mr. Molyneux was shot from the northwest and Cole Harbour's more or less south-east."

"But that's only according to Fone!" Peter reminded her.

"I know, but unless we're to believe Mr. Fone did the murder himself, surely we must accept his word," said Jeanie a little warmly.

"No, he may have been mistaken."

"I don't see how. He says Mr. Molyneux looked round towards Cleedons just before he was shot. He says he saw his face. You can't be mistaken about a thing like that."

"Perhaps not," said Peter in a rather unconvinced tone. "Are you sure Barchard was on the Cole Harbour roof?"

"Yes. Dr. Hall saw him when he went to fetch
his *Archaeologia*."

"Well, now, what about Dr. Hall?"

Jeanie laughed.

"Well, of course Mr. Molyneux didn't like doctors, did he? But
no, Peter. I think we can leave Dr. Hall out of it. No motive."

"Any other member of the Field Club behave in a suspicious
manner?"

"Not as far as I know."

Jeanie remembered Tamsin's innuendoes about Sir Henry
Blundell, but firmly suppressed them. They were too absurd!

There were already quite a lot of people wandering pensively
around the sky-lit gallery when they entered. These wore, for the
most part, the peculiarly subdued, pale and dejected look of
people at picture-shows, who move as if the top-light intimidates
them, as well it may. The pictures were ordinary, and Jeanie could
sympathise with Peter's remark when they had been half round
the gallery.

"Oh, Jeanie, how I do long for a few triangles!"

"Triangles, Peter?"

"Eyes, you know, and triangles, and flashes of lightning, and
cubes, things that make you think. I like art to be serious, Jeanie."

Jeanie smiled.

"Poor Peter, you won't find any abstractions here!"

"No. Nature-lovers to a man, I see," replied Peter sadly as they
moved on. "Hullo!"

He paused, with a look of amused attention, before a painting
which was certainly very far from the severe abstractions he had
been humorously extolling. It was a portrait, one of those skilfully
arranged and careful paintings which induce a slight spiritual
nausea in others beside ardent modernists. Jeanie glanced at the

catalogue. For Hubert Southey, this was quite a daring portrait. The setting was at least unusual. But how he had subdued the brassy glitter of buttercups in a field, the deep blue of summer shadows on grass, to the polite tints of his own studio-bred and timid mind! Poor old Southey, thought Jeanie, with the friendly scorn of the pupil for the teacher.

"Lady in Red Gloves. It's awfully daring, as a matter of fact, for poor old Harmless Hubert. That little bit of red, you know. I expect he felt awfully dashing putting that together."

"But, Jeanie, don't you realise? It's the Handleston Helen!"

Jeanie started, and looked at the picture with a livelier interest.

"Of course! Mrs. Barchard told me he painted her picture sitting among the buttercups! She's attractive, isn't she?"

"Yes. Lots of glamour."

"Is she a little like somebody I know?"

"Yes," said Peter at once. "She's a little—a *very* little—like you."

"Like *me*? Oh no, Peter!"

Jeanie flushed and stared at the portrait, half flattered, for it was of a pretty woman, half irritated, as one is at the thought that one may not, after all, seem quite unique to one's friends.

"Oh yes, Jeanie! Not really like, just a chance resemblance, but her face is the same shape as yours, and her eyebrows are a little bit the same."

He spoke seriously, as though he had made a study of Jeanie's eyebrows, and she blushed still deeper.

"*I* think she's a little, weeny bit like—Agnes."

"Agnes!"

Yes, it was a remote likeness to Agnes Molyneux that Jeanie had seen in the portrait. There was a distinct look of Agnes about the straight delicate nose, the cleft narrow chin.

"I don't see the slightest resemblance," said Peter.

"Well, it's not a very good portrait, anyway," said Jeanie. "But the buttercups are awfully like buttercups, and the gloves are awfully like gloves, and the brooch is—good Heavens! It's awfully like a brooch I bought once!"

Jeanie leant forward to have a closer look. Hubert Southey, though a landscape painter by profession, was by nature, his critics often to his disgust remarked, a painter of still-life. His buttercups might be dulled, his sunlight dimmed, and the faces of his sitters stiff with fatigue and strain; but his jewels were jewels that their makers would recognise with pleasure, his gloves were calculated to rouse the enthusiasm of a leather-worker, his hats were models from which milliners might copy and never be in doubt over the choice of straw. He could, in his way, paint.

And he had painted at Valentine Frazer's white neck a large star-shaped brooch of zircons.

Six years before, when Jeanie had first heard that her beloved Miss Drake was to be married, she had much exercised her youthful mind over the subject of what to give as a wedding present. The school was of course making a presentation, but Jeanie longed to give some personal thing by which Miss Drake could always remember her. And at the Caledonian Market one day in the holidays she had seen just the thing—a star-shaped zircon brooch in a setting of Indian silver of distinctive and charming design. Jeanie had bought it, spending a great deal more than a schoolgirl could properly afford. And Agnes had said that she adored it and could never have a brooch she would like better.

And now that very brooch of glittering zircons was painted at the neck of the Handleston Helen, as Peter had called her. There was a little stone missing from one of the rays, as Jeanie well remembered. Jeanie stared and stared at that painted brooch. The provoking, naughty, if somewhat fixed smile above the brooch drew her glance upwards, the painted eyes twinkled into hers.

"Ah, how do you do, Miss Halliday. I hope that look of dismay doesn't mean you don't like my picture?"

Jeanie turned with a little start.

"How are you, Mr. Southey? No, I'm admiring your picture, and so is my friend, Mr. Johnson. He knows the model."

As she spoke, Jeanie suddenly became acutely aware of the local gossip, and a stupid feeling of embarrassment came over her. She began to utter quickly platitudes about the exhibition. She saw a faint surprise at her manner reflected behind Hubert Southey's spectacles, and after a few reciprocal compliments upon Jeanie's work he returned to the subject of his own.

"Yes, rather a new departure for me," he uttered complacently. "I enjoyed doing it, too. One gets sick of studio portraits, don't you know. One wants the sunlight."

*Yes, one does*, silently commented Jeanie's professional mind, looking at those buttercups, *and one doesn't get it*. Her unprofessional mind noted Hubert Southey's extraordinary unconcern. Anybody might think from his carefree manner that the man was a regular Don Juan!

"That was a wonderful sitter, too," went on Hubert Southey, stroking the back of his head. "She had a great capacity for sitting still without losing sparkle, don't you know."

He spoke as if regretfully.

"I should have liked," added he, "don't you know, to have kidnapped her!" He gave a little laugh at his own daring. His mild eyes behind their horn-rimmed spectacles shone with a boyish and innocent mirth. "Yes, don't you know, I should have liked to have packed her up among my gear and taken her back to Chelsea!"

"Oh yes?" uttered Jeanie faintly, summoning a responsive smile. Yes, certainly she must revise her careless estimate of Hubert Southey's character. Why, the old villain seemed positively to be enjoying his own disingenuousness!

"Only," said the villain, putting the crowning touch to his mendacities, his neat pointed beard fairly twitching with naughty merriment, "what would Dora have said? Eh? What would Dora have said, don't you know?"

With this piece of daring, he took his leave and went off to greet another of his many friends, leaving Jeanie and Peter gazing after him.

"Dora?" echoed Peter interrogatively.

"Miss Southey."

"A cool hand, isn't he, Jeanie? Don't you know?"

Jeanie smiled, though she felt troubled, too, not liking the slight earthquake feeling of insecurity which accompanies the readjustment of one's ideas about a respected teacher.

"Yes, indeed he is."

"Well, I suppose Handleston gossip doesn't reach as far as Chelsea. He probably doesn't realise what a Byronic reputation he's got in these parts."

Chapter Seventeen
MADAM, WILL YOU WALK?

When Jeanie, about to close her garden gate behind her and go for a lonely walk in Cole Harbour woods, saw a blue-clad stiff figure approaching up the road, she nearly dashed the gate to and ran back up the path to hide. It was Marjorie Dasent, and Jeanie did not want to see her. She did not know how she should greet her. She could not speak to her naturally, knowing what she knew.

But it was too late to retreat. Marjorie hailed her from fifty yards away, and she had to wait at the gate until the other girl came up, her hands thrust into the pockets of her mannish navy jacket, her black felt hat well crammed down on her head. Marjorie looked much as usual. Her rather self-consciously long masculine stride was the same as ever. Her complexion had its usual somewhat wind-nipped, ruddy look. Her greeting to Jeanie was as self-confident, as loud and hearty, as though in some other avatar she had walked the quarter-deck.

"Good afternoon! Heel, Caesar!" cried Miss Dasent sternly, somewhat to Jeanie's surprise. The words, however, were addressed to no illustrious shade, but to a barrel-shaped old black spaniel who had been doing his best to keep up with his owner's stride and now came sniffing and wagging hopefully towards Jeanie as though he thought she might set a kinder pace.

"You walking my way, Miss Halliday? Lovely day for a walk, isn't it? Aren't dogs a nuisance?"

"I've always thought so," replied Jeanie with sincerity.

Marjorie smiled, for in her innocence she thought Jeanie was indulging in facetiousness. Mechanically returning the smile, Jeanie thought: Is this the girl I'm suspecting of murder? Is this the girl whose rifle was found hidden under a culvert? The girl who saw Robert Molyneux die and said nothing about it? It seemed impossible to believe such things of this innocent, middle-aged child, with her wind-nipped, high-bridged nose, mild diffident blue eyes and circumscribed set of ideas! Perhaps a shadow fell upon Jeanie's face and Marjorie saw it, for her smile faded. She said uncertainly:

"I really don't know what I'd do without Caesar. It's rather lonely for me now that Father's getting so old. Caesar's practically my only companion. You'd probably think me quite demented if you heard me talking to Caesar sometimes."

A little irritated by this dog-talk, Jeanie agreed.

"I expect I should." She eyed the shuffling spaniel without enthusiasm as he sniffed at a rabbit-hole and decided that it was too much trouble to do more than sniff. "He must be a perfect store-house of interesting information. Do tell me what you talk to him about."

Marjorie looked at Jeanie dubiously. Her good-humoured blue
eyes seemed of a sudden cautious and grey. She said with doubtful
jocosity:

"Oh, all the secrets of my life, you know!"

"Such as?"

"Well!" Miss Dasent laughed uneasily, stealing a hurt,
frightened look at her unresponsive companion, who was
swinging along at her side at a pace that almost outmatched her
own. "All sorts of things! I don't know!"

Jeanie contemplated the obese and unhappy creature
labouring along in front of them. She was irritated and
embarrassed. She did not want Marjorie Dasent's company. She
wanted to be alone. She hated walking along with a person at
whose eyes she dared not look for fear of the distrust and horror
that might be read in her own. Her resentment made her take the
cold plunge that the turn of the conversation suggested.

"Did you tell him about the rifle you hid under the culvert the
day poor Molyneux was murdered?"

There was a silence. Still Marjorie swung along and still Jeanie
swung along beside her, and still the spaniel sniffed desirously at
the road and dragged himself past delights in the pursuit of duty.
They walked thus in silence for a moment. Then Marjorie said
with a great gulp, slowing down:

"Superintendent Finister knows about that!" A little muscle
worked in her cheek. "He knows I didn't do it, though! He doesn't
suspect me! He'd have arrested me if he did!"

"Not necessarily," said Jeanie brutally, also slowing down. "He
might be keeping you in cold storage."

Caesar, released from duty, found a horse-dropping and
occupied himself voluptuously with it. A car passed and the two
ladies moved towards a field-gate and stood on the grass verge
and faced one another. Marjorie was flushed, hostile, hot-eyed,
Jeanie pale, cold and distrustful.

"Why do you speak to me like this, Miss Halliday?" asked Marjorie with a sort of trembling resentment.

"I don't know why I'm speaking to you at all," said Jeanie gloomily. "It can't do any good. That *was* your cigarette-end that was found in the lambing-shed wasn't it?"

"Yes. Oh, I was a fool. I know I was a fool!" said Miss Dasent brokenly. "But, Miss Halliday! You can't—you *can't* think that I— that *I*—"

"Why on earth not? I do think it!"

"But I—but I was *pals* with Robert Molyneux!" protested Marjorie with a trembling chin. "How can you? Oh, I know I was a fool and hid my rifle! I lost my head, I saw he was dead, I was terrified!"

Her large hand positively dragged at Jeanie's arm in her attempt to carry conviction, to make Jeanie turn and look at her.

"Miss Halliday! You can't—nobody could think *I* wished Robert any harm! We were the best, the best of pals!"

She wept.

"Why didn't you come forward at the inquest?"

"How could I? I'd been a fool and hidden my rifle. I thought I'd go back one night and fetch it, and nobody would ever know I was in the orchard that day. Only, whenever I went to fetch it, there seemed to be policemen about. Or people I was afraid were policemen. I was afraid to get it in case I was seen! Oh, I've been through Hell!"

"What made you hide it in the first place? Wasn't it a frightfully stupid thing to do?"

"Yes!" whispered Marjorie, wiping her eyes on a large handkerchief. "But I was so frightened. Nobody knew I was there. In the lambing-shed. And with a rifle. *He* didn't know. Nobody knew. How could I have proved that—that I only wanted to look at him? Just to look at him and to say good-bye in my own mind to—

oh, to some silly thoughts I'd had! How could I have proved it? How could I have explained even? Without making things seem horrible that weren't horrible at all? I was watching Mr. Molyneux pruning his trees. I was saying good-bye to a lot of nonsense in my heart, and resolving to be sensible. And suddenly I saw him falling out of the tree, and I realised that there'd been a shot. I—it seemed ages, years before I could move. I felt as if I'd imagined the whole thing. As if it couldn't really have happened and if I shut my eyes and looked again there'd be still on his ladder. At last I went as near him as I dared. I saw the bullet-hole in his temple. I knew that he was dead. I was terrified! I couldn't wait and be found there! I couldn't take my rifle with me, I was frightened—oh, of everything!"

"Sarah saw you hide it."

"Sarah? Oh, poor kid," stammered Marjorie. She wept a little, leaning on the field-gate, and then polished her eyes and face thoroughly on her gentlemanly white handkerchief.

"I'm sorry to make such a fool of myself. Come here, Caesar! Bad, dirty dog!"

Caesar, disconcerted perhaps by his owner's gruff broken tone, paused for several last sniffs before lumbering up, and received a half-hearted welt over the back which made him wag his tail even more amiably than before.

"What are they going to do?" asked Marjorie. "I go on and pretend everything's all right and nothing's going to happen. Only, how do I know whether Superintendent Finister believed me yesterday when I explained? I had to tell him things I could hardly bear even to think of! And even then, how do I know he believed me?"

A sudden horrible thought seemed to strike her.

"How do I know *you* believe me? Perhaps you don't!"

She waited for a protest, but Jeanie did not make it.

"Perhaps nobody would believe me! After all I was there, in the lambing-shed, secretly, and with a rifle. And I'd been very unhappy. And that awful man Fone said at the inquest that Robert was facing towards Cleedons when he was shot. Making the coroner say the shot must have come from the direction of the lambing-shed! Who'd believe me after that?"

"Why? Didn't it?"

"Didn't what?" asked Marjorie, blowing her nose. "Didn't the shot come from the lambing-shed direction, then? Was Mr. Molyneux facing towards the house when he was shot, or was he not?"

"I don't know," stammered Marjorie. "I couldn't see him, then. The boughs of the tree were between him and me. And I heard the shot without noticing—you know how one does when it's quite an ordinary noise that one's accustomed to. I was so surprised at seeing him fall I didn't realise for a moment that there'd been a shot, my first thought was he'd been taken ill. I suppose if that man Fone says he was facing the house when the shot came, he *was* facing the house. Only, that means the shot must have come from quite near me, and I should have thought I would have heard it instantly. I should have thought it would have quite startled me."

"Didn't it?"

"No. I—I'm telling you, I hardly noticed it until afterwards."

"I heard it plainly enough in the stable.

"The worst part of all this for me," cried Marjorie suddenly, "the horrible part, is, that I'm thinking all the time of myself and what may happen! Whether the police will find the murderer in time to save me from being arrested! I think so much about it that I haven't time to be properly sorry about poor Robert. It's horrible! And by the time all this is over and settled, I shall have got used to him not being there, and perhaps I shan't be able to be properly sorry!"

"Being sorry doesn't do anybody any good. I shouldn't worry about that," said Jeanie, and turned off at the gate into Cole Harbour woods. And as she walked up the foot-path she wondered whether Marjorie Dasent had it in her to be "properly sorry" for Robert Molyneux's death. She had her pal Robert for ever enshrined now in her probably somewhat embellished memories. Perhaps that was where she wanted him. Perhaps, in fact, in spite of her very natural denials, that was where she had put him...

Chapter Eighteen
A DISTURBING VISITOR

Jeanie had her walk in the woods and returned to make herself an omelette for lunch and a cup of tea. She was just pouring the water on to the tea when a loud sudden knock on the door caused a spurt of water to jerk from the spout of the kettle. Conscious that her face was flushed by the fire and her hair untidy, she was not in the mood for visitors, but putting down the kettle and tucking in a stray lock of hair, she went to the door.

Superintendent Finister stood on the door-step, watching a robin hop from clod to clod of the turned earth. Jeanie felt an odd little twinge of nervousness at the sight of him. Her feelings towards the police had undergone a change since her meeting with Finister and Sarah on Grim's Grave. She knew vicariously now a little of the fear of the law-breaker. It was a queer sensation, to feel afraid of a policeman!

"'Morning, Miss Halliday." The ghost of a smile, perhaps at Jeanie's unwelcoming and distrustful look, was permitted to lighten for a moment the perennial melancholy of the Superintendent's face. "I hope I'm not disturbing you, but as I was coming this way I thought perhaps I might have a word with you."

"Of course, Superintendent," replied Jeanie, with an alacrity she was for from feeling, and led the way to the parlour. Hostile she might be, but she was curious too, or she felt positively disappointed when Finister, refusing a chair, said:

"I just wanted to inquire how little Miss Molyneux is? I've not seen her since the other night and I'm afraid I gave her rather a shock then."

"Oh, I think she's all right, thank you."

Jeanie looked warily at Finister. Sarah's health, she perceived, was not really the man's preoccupation. Why come to Jeanie to inquire about Sarah's health?

"You won't—I do hope you'll see your way to leave Sarah out of your inquiries!" she said anxiously. "Children oughtn't to be mixed up in this kind of thing!"

"Nobody," responded Finister with sad reasonableness, "ought to be mixed up in this kind of thing. This kind of thing oughtn't to happen. We all know that. As for that rifle, we needn't trouble little Miss Molyneux about that. It belongs to Miss Dasent."

He looked quickly at Jeanie as he spoke, and she saw how acute and observant his long face could suddenly appear. The impersonal ruthlessness of the law was suddenly brought home to her. She felt almost as if she herself were guilty.

"I know. Sarah saw her hide it under a culvert." Finister nodded.

"Extraordinary thing to do," he commented. He corrected himself thoughtfully after a moment. "*Not* extraordinary. Idiotic."

There was a silence, while he appeared mournfully to contemplate the ordinariness of idiocy.

"I interviewed Miss Dasent yesterday afternoon," he went on. "But I don't propose to go any farther at present. Her explanation seemed quite satisfactory."

"Oh, good!"

A wave of relief broke over Jeanie, then subsided again as she met Finister's direct, watchful glance. She hesitated. Finister had not yet come to the purpose of his visit, then.

"Why do you tell me this, Superintendent Finister?"

He replied with calm evasiveness:

"I thought you would be interested to know. Of course Miss Dasent's behaviour was very suspicious. Very foolish. But there really isn't enough evidence to arrest her on. Or rather, there's evidence which seems to point in quite another direction. And we policemen can't afford to make mistakes, you know."

"Another direction?" stammered Jeanie. His dark, direct glance actually made her feel as though it might be in her direction that this evidence pointed. She flushed and was furious with herself for doing so.

"Well, there is the question of the Colt automatic target-pistol, you know, Miss Halliday."

"Oh yes?"

"It's been missing, you know, since the day of the murder, from the Tower room. And no one has come forward to explain its disappearance."

Jeanie felt inclined, as Finister paused, to cry: *Well, I didn't take it! Why come to me?*

But it was her turn to maintain silence when the superintendent asked suddenly:

"You've known Mrs. Molyneux a long while, haven't you?"

Jeanie stared at him in surprise.

"Mrs. Molyneux?" she echoed at last. "Yes. Ten years or so. Why"

Finister nodded indifferently.

"Mrs. Molyneux is a very attractive lady."

Jeanie hardly knew whether to laugh or be indignant at this unexpected remark. Finister went on:

"Do you know if Mrs. Molyneux's friendship with Mr. Johnson is of long standing? Did they know one another before her marriage to Mr. Molyneux?"

Now Jeanie saw where Finister's questions were tending. He was still, was he, obsessed with the notion of Peter's guilt! She felt herself flush hotly. She felt extraordinarily and very suddenly angry with this lanky saturnine know-all.

"Not as far as I know."

"Mr. Johnson had been secretary to Mr. Molyneux for three years. They had been on friendly terms, anyway, for that length of time?"

"Very likely," replied Jeanie with extreme hostility. "But if, when you say 'friendly terms,' you mean a love affair, why not say so? And let me say that if you do think that, you're quite mistaken!"

Even as she spoke, Jeanie saw her own folly. She foresaw, before he uttered it, Finister's bland question: "But, Miss Halliday, why do you suppose I should think such a thing?"

Jeanie stammered defiantly:

"The way you spoke just now! It was obvious!"

"Because I said that Mrs. Molyneux was an attractive lady?" uttered Finister in mild but, Jeanie was sure, assumed astonishment. "It was obvious to you that by that I meant that she and Mr. Johnson were lovers? Surely, Miss Halliday, if that was the sequence of your thoughts, it can only have been because such a suspicion was already in your mind?"

Jeanie realised that she had fallen instantly, obligingly, headlong into a trap. She detested, she loathed the tall and mild-eyed Finister. His feet polluted her carpet. His breath poisoned her domestic air. With a rising pulse and temper, she scarcely cared how she floundered farther into the trap he had set for her.

"Well, of course it was in my mind! Mr. Johnson told me himself about the questions you'd been asking him!"

Finister murmured blandly:

"Oh, but we didn't ask any questions about the state of Mr. Johnson's affections, I assure you!"

"Perhaps not," cried Jeanie angrily. "But no doubt it was obvious what you were driving at!"

"Obvious?" echoed Finister gently. "Mr. Johnson found it obvious, did he, that we suspected him of a liaison with his employer's wife? That is interesting."

Jeanie, bursting with fury, with difficulty held her tongue. She had said, she perceived, too much.

"It may interest you to know that we have a note written by Mr. Johnson to Mrs. Molyneux which is in somewhat remarkable terms, considering their respective positions. One of my men found the letter crumpled up on top of some rose-leaves in a bowl on a table in the upstairs gallery, soon after the murder was committed."

"I know. It didn't mean anything."

"'You have all my devotion, always,'" quoted Finister reflectively.

"Why not? A romantic devotion."

'Plenty of crimes have been committed under the influence of a romantic devotion."

Jeanie sat down. She felt suddenly limp and depressed. The man had made up his mind, it was obvious, that Peter Johnson was Molyneux's murderer, and Jeanie's championship was doing only harm. Let her say no more. What did it matter in the long run? There could be no real evidence brought against an innocent man. Let Finister run his silly obstinate head against the brick wall of Peter's innocence if he chose!

Finister walked to the window and stood for a moment, hands clasped behind him, gazing out into the quiet garden.

"You know," he said at last gently, "or rather, you probably don't know, that yesterday my men fished up the Colt automatic from the bottom of Hatcher's Pond?"

Jeanie said:

"Oh?"

She found herself shaking a little all over.

"Yes."

A silence fell.

"Well," said Jeanie at last, for obviously somebody must say something: the silence was becoming unbearable. "Well, it was clever of you to know it was there."

"It was simple. If people want to lose things they always throw them in water if they can. And Hatcher's Pond is the only water near Cleedons. And when Mr. Johnson first approached Mr. Agatos on the day of the murder, he came from the direction of Hatcher's Pond."

"That doesn't sound very incriminating," said Jeanie, trying to speak lightly.

"Not in itself, perhaps, no," replied Superintendent Finister politely. He added: "The pistol is one which Mr. Johnson was in the habit of using for target practice. Didn't he tell you?"

"Why should he?"

"No reason, of course. I just thought he might. I'm told he's a brilliant shot."

"I know." In spite of herself, Jeanie's voice sounded defensive and unhappy.

"Well," said the superintendent, giving Jeanie a melancholy valedictory smile, "I'm glad little Miss Sarah wasn't too scared the other night. Thank you, Miss Halliday. I can see myself out."

Jeanie pulled herself together and accompanied her detestable visitor to the door.

"I'm afraid I've disturbed you," said he apologetically.

Jeanie felt sure that he was as well aware as herself of the double meaning of the words.

He had, in fact, so much disturbed her that she found herself when he had gone unable to settle down again to her lunch. She had a dry taste in her mouth and an uneasy feeling in her heart. She made herself some tea, and stood at the window looking dismally out at the half-dug garden and sipping an infusion that tasted like sawdust.

"But damn it, Peter!" she cried angrily to the indifferent garden. "You said you'd told me everything!"

A robin perching on her spade cocked his head at her movement and flew off. Jeanie put down her cup, put on her coat and went out. She had had enough of innuendoes and suspicions and suppressions of the truth. She would ask Peter, who was supposed to be a friend of hers, a plain question about that pistol. And she would ask Agnes, also supposed to be a friend of hers, a plain question about that zircon brooch. It would be something to do, anyway, Jeanie told herself miserably, tramping along the damp road towards Cole Harbour. She could not go on placidly eating her lunch and digging her garden and waiting to hear from Mrs. Barchard or some other gossip that Peter was arrested. She thought of Peter, gay, casual and talkative, as he had been in Gloucester. She did not know whether she felt more frightened, angry, or sad. Her heart ached extraordinarily.

Hugh Barchard, in his character of houseman, opened the door.

"Is Mr. Johnson in?"

"He'll be back soon, I expect, Miss Halliday, if you care to wait. Mr. Fone's at home. He's on the library roof."

"The roof? Why?"

"There's going to be a meeting of the Field Club gentlemen there next Wednesday, and Mr. Fone's going to try and convert them to this old straight track theory he's taken up. You can see over the country in most directions from the library roof. Perhaps you'd like to go up there yourself, Miss Halliday? It's quite safe behind the balustrade. The roof's quite flat."

"No, Mr. Fone's invited me for Wednesday, and I think I'd better not anticipate the meeting. I'll wait till Mr. Johnson comes back."

But perhaps Peter Johnson would not be coming back, except to collect whatever few things a man under arrest is allowed to take with him to the police station. Jeanie had little doubt, after her interview with the superintendent, that Peter's arrest was impending. The only thing that puzzled her was why Finister should have allowed her to know of it. Perhaps, after all, the police were not quite sure of their man, and Finister hoped to get from Jeanie some further incriminating evidence. If so, she flattered herself he had not got it!

Barchard showed her into the little white panelled parlour where an ordnance survey map lay open on the table with a ruler and pencil beside it.

"I'm just working out some leys for Mr. Fone," explained Barchard, indicating a network of pencil lines drawn across the map. "Mr. Johnson's been helping me."

He put a chintz-covered chair for Jeanie by the fire and was about to depart when it suddenly occurred to Jeanie that if she wanted to spend an embarrassing afternoon asking plain questions of people who did not want to answer them, here she had a victim ready to her hand. She flushed, plucked up her courage and called him back. He turned and awaited her pleasure, friendly, incurious, at ease.

"I expect Mr. Fone told you," said Jeanie, in an unexpectedly loud voice which she instantly toned down. "We went to a picture show in Gloucester. I had a picture hung there."

"I congratulate you, Miss."

Leaning against the table, his pose was easy, but his blue eyes set in their nets of crow's-feet were watchful. No doubt he wondered what on earth Jeanie was leading up to, blushing like an idiot and shouting at him like a sergeant-major! Oh dear, thought Jeanie, I shouldn't make at all a good detective! I don't how to handle people.

"So had—so had Mr. Southey a picture there. Hubert Southey."

Jeanie turned upon Hugh Barchard an eye which, she hoped, was not too fixed and stern. His watchful look relaxed, and he smiled faintly as if he guessed at her embarrassment and its reason.

"Yes, I know the chap you mean. He used to stay down here in the summer."

"Yes. Well, this picture he's exhibiting in Gloucester is a portrait."

"Of Valentine?" asked Barchard simply. "I know the one, I expect. With her sitting in a field, wearing red gloves. It was a very good likeness."

He spoke calmly, gently, as of someone dead. And after all, as Jeanie reminded herself, the trouble had occurred two years ago: there was no need for her to feel this excessive embarrassment.

"Hubert Southey was there," added Jeanie. Barchard showed no emotion.

"Was Valentine there?"

"No."

"I'd like to see her again."

More freely now that the ice was broken, Jeanie stammered:

"In this picture, she's wearing a zircon brooch."

"Zircon?"

"Cingalese diamonds. A star-shaped brooch, quite large."

"Oh yes, I remember it. Her diamond brooch."

For the first time a sort of emotion showed itself in Barchard's bearing. The brooch perhaps recalled some words, some scene he had forgotten. His voice went oddly gruff. He cleared his throat and as if to cover his emotion took a ruler from the table and played with it, bending it backwards and forwards.

"Well—diamonds! It isn't real diamonds, you know."

"Not?"

"Zircons like those, small ones, have hardly any value."

"Val always spoke as if it was very valuable. She used to say they were real diamonds." He looked at Jeanie thoughtfully. "How do you know about that brooch, Miss Halliday, if it isn't a rude question?"

"I'm afraid it's I who am going to ask rude questions!" replied Jeanie, and they both smiled. "Well, you see, Mr. Barchard, I recognised the brooch. I bought it."

"You *bought* it, Miss?"

"Yes. A long time ago. Six years! And I couldn't be mistaken. It's too well painted for that. And so I wondered—I thought perhaps you might know how Miss Frazer came by it, and wouldn't mind telling me," faltered Jeanie, for now that she had come to the point the question seemed a rather impertinent one. The brooch had long ago passed out of her legal possession! She felt a little qualm when Barchard, frowning a little and bending the ruler like a bow in his strong fingers, said slowly:

"I don't quite understand, Miss Halliday. Did you lose the brooch, then?"

"No, I gave it away. I bought it to give away."

"Oh?"

Rapidly thinking things over, Jeanie saw no reason why she should not reply to Barchard's unasked question. She owed candour, if she expected it.

"To Mrs. Molyneux."

This, it seemed, did startle him. The ruler dropped with a little clatter on the polished boards. He looked blankly at Jeanie.

"Mrs. Molyneux?" he repeated.

"Yes."

"Mrs. Molyneux? But what had Val to do with Mrs. Molyneux? As for that brooch—"

He paused so long that Jeanie prompted him.

"Well?"

"I thought the painter fellow gave it her. In fact she told me he did. As a sort of payment for sitting to him. We quarrelled a bit about it, because I thought it was too valuable, thinking it was real diamonds, you see."

"I gave twenty-five shillings for that brooch in Islington cattle-market."

"Well, I don't know anything about diamonds and their value, and neither did Val, evidently. She certainly thought it was valuable, because we had a bit of a row about it. The painter chap had given her a pearl necklet already. Not real ones, you know, but still I didn't like her taking jewellery from the chap. Not that I minded her sitting to him. Only I didn't like her being paid for it. Well, it's ancient history, now. This chap Southey flattered Val, and told her she was a marvel to paint. And she got the idea that all the big artists in London would come falling over themselves to paint her. And so off she went. Poor Val! I bet she didn't find being a model all she thought it'd be."

At a loss, Jeanie stared at Barchard. Lolling against the table, fiddling with his ruler, he wore a thoughtful, regretful look, as though his mind were occupied with pleasant memories.

"But—"

He looked up mildly.

"Yes?"

"Well, for one thing, the pearl necklace. That *was* real. It was quite valuable."

Barchard frowned, and after a pause asked slowly:

"But, Miss Halliday, how do you know?"

"That's the extraordinary thing. I found a piece of it, about half the string, in the cupboard under the stairs at Yew Tree Cottage."

"At Yew Tree!" echoed Barchard. He stared in the fire as though he might find the answer to this puzzle there, and found it not, and with a shrug appeared to give it up. "Well, I certainly understood from Valentine they were a cheap cultured string. And you say they were valuable?"

"Quite valuable. Worth about fifteen hundred pounds."

"Good Lord! Miss Halliday, there must be some mistake. Val can't have thought they were valuable, or why should she have left them behind? Perhaps they're not the same string!"

"Is it very impertinent of me to ask if you know who Valentine Frazer was? I mean, where she'd lived and what she'd done, and so on?"

Barchard looked thoughtful, and taking his pipe from the table began to fill it.

"I'm afraid I don't know much about her. It's queer how well you can know a person and still not know much about them. I met her in London. She'd been on the stage. She'd been abroad, dancing in shows at cabarets, though she hadn't done anything in that line for years. I never asked her what her life had been, and she never asked me." He smiled faintly. "When two people who've knocked about the world a bit and aren't so very young any longer—Val was thirty-three when I first met her—take a fancy to one another, it's generally better for both of them not to be too inquisitive. Or so we thought."

"I see."

"Poor Val, I hope she's happy. I'd like to see her again. I wonder if Mr. Southey would know her address."

"But—"

Barchard looked at Jeanie and smiled a little ruefully.

"I suppose folks have been telling you she went off to live with Southey?"

"Well, as a matter of fact, your mother—"

"Mother's never set foot farther than Gloucester in her life," said Barchard tolerantly. "And she just loves gossip like all the rest of them. After all, it makes life interesting for people that haven't had many interesting things in their own lives. But Val never felt like that about that little painter chap! Not she! No, she got tired of me and the quiet life down here, and she got it into her head to make a fortune as an artist's model and have her portrait in the Royal Academy every year, and off she went. If you listen much to Mother, you'll hear all sorts of interesting things," said Barchard, smiling. "But I'd advise you not to believe too many of them, Miss."

He puffed at his pipe and smiled at Jeanie, as one citizen of the great world to another.

"Had you any reason except Mother's gossip to think that?"

"No. I hadn't, really. In fact, on Saturday Mr. Southey spoke as though he hadn't seen Miss Frazer since he painted that portrait."

"Oh? That's funny! He was going to introduce her to other artists, she said. Surely she went to see him when she left here!"

"Didn't she write to you at all after she left?"

"No. I didn't want her to go, you see. We argued and quarrelled about it for weeks. And then suddenly, without telling me she was going, she went. If she had to go, I was glad it was that way. And I didn't want letters from her. I hate sentiment and letter-writing and all that stuff. I like to go straight on from one thing to another. Like Mr. Fone's straight tracks that don't curve nor go back themselves. And she was the same. Still, I'd like to see her again, now I've got over her leaving me like that. There's Mr. Johnson just come in at the gate."

## Chapter Nineteen
### I'LL TELL YOU EVERYTHING!

When she saw Peter's radiant face Jeanie was tempted to put Finister's warning and all thoughts of Molyneux's death out of her mind, and throw herself with Peter into the game of old-straight-track hunting.

"Jeanie, there's a ford at Whitley. And if you stand at the ford and look at the clump on Lady Hill, you look right over Whitley Church. Isn't that thrilling, eh?"

"Is it, Peter?"

"Scientifically thrilling, Jeanie. It's an old straight track. The Neolithic people used to walk along it."

"What, over Whitley Church?"

Peter looked a little pained.

"Jeanie, Jeanie, think again. The church may be an ancient specimen of masonry, but it's not Neolithic. They didn't walk over it, because it wasn't there."

"Then how do you know where they walked?"

"All Christian churches," said Peter, with the sweeping dogmatism of one who has just adopted a new theory, "are built on the sites of pagan churches, and all pagan churches were built on the sites of Neolithic temples."

"Ah!"

"Yes. Ah!"

"And the Neolithic people always took their Sunday walks past the temple, naturally. I get you, Peter. But then, why on a hot Sunday afternoon, did they struggle up to the clump on Lady Hill?"

"To get to Droitwich."

"Droitwich?"

"Salt, you know. It's probably a salt-track."

"A salt-track?"

"The track which brought the salt to this part of the country from Droitwich. Salt's very important to primitive people. Look at India," said Peter, who had obviously accepted Mr. Fone's theory in no carping spirit.

Jeanie would much rather look at India, and at Mr. Fone's collection of ordnance survey maps, and at Peter's carefree face, than at the picture she had set herself to look at. The mere sight of Peter had lifted her load of care. It was foolish, but she could not help it. She longed to forget Superintendent Finister's visit to Yew Tree Cottage. But she could not.

"Peter."

"Yes, madam? What can I do for you?"

"Oh Peter, there's something I came to say to you. I must say it. I wish I needn't."

The radiance departed from Peter's face. He looked at Jeanie with apprehension, though he spoke playfully.

"What is it, Jeanie? You sound rather portentous."

He laughed a little nervously.

"You haven't got anything horrible up your sleeve, have you, Jeanie?"

"I'm afraid I have, Peter."

Peter looked at her with a frown, his hands in his pockets, his shoulders defensively hunched, his foot beating nervously on the oak floor.

"Can't you keep it there, Jeanie dear?"

"I'd rather not."

"All right. What is it, Jeanie?"

Now that she had come to her plain question, Jeanie felt strangely unwilling to ask it. She felt afraid of the answer. Her pulse had actually quickened. She could feel its beat all over her.

"Won't you sit down, Peter?"

"No thanks, I'd rather stand up to be shot at."

As he spoke the words he crimsoned. It was not, perhaps, in the circumstances, a very fortunate figure of speech. He made a little nervous grimace and went over to the window and leant against the sill.

"Well, Peter," said Jeanie, and her embarrassment made her voice more incisive than she intended. "You remember that day last week we met on Grim's Grave?"

"Yes, of course."

"We talked a bit, and you told me what you'd done on the day poor Molyneux was killed?"

"Yes."

"You didn't have to tell me. But you did tell me. We were friends. And you swore you'd told me *everything*."

"Well, come, now, Jeanie! *Everything* is a tall order!"

"Everything that had to do with Molyneux's murder and your movements that day. Don't quibble."

"I'm sorry," said he coldly.

They might have been friends that day on Grim's Grave. They were enemies now.

"I wish you wouldn't stand with your back to the light, I can't see you at all!" cried Jeanie suddenly, with more exasperation in her voice than she intended.

"I'm sorry," said Peter woodenly and made a pretence of moving to one side.

"Well, Peter, it's just this. You said that day you'd told me everything. And you told me, among other things, that there was a pistol missing from the Tower room at Cleedons. You didn't tell me—"

Jeanie had meant to say: *You didn't tell me that it was the one you used for target practice!* She found herself saying instead:

"You didn't tell me it was you who had taken it! You didn't tell me you threw it in Hatcher's Pond. You didn't tell me anything about that pistol!"

Her face was burning. What had made her speak like this? Had she been asked five minutes ago she would have said that she did not believe any of these charges against Peter. Yet she had herself uttered them, ruining—if Peter were, as she believed—surely she believed!— innocent—their friendship for ever.

But Peter seemed in no hurry to repudiate her words, and her friendship and her. He did not, in fact, move nor speak at all. Jeanie saw, though, how his hands slowly grew tense and gripped the sill at each side of him.

"Oh," he said at last. He spoke in a queer thick cautious voice. "How do you know the pistol is in Hatcher's Pond?"

"It isn't, any more."

"What?"

"Peter, do you mean that it *was* you who threw that pistol in the pond?"

"What do you mean, it isn't there?"

"The police have got it up. Of course. You must know they've been dragging the pond. What did you expect?"

"I thought they'd finished dragging and hadn't found it," said Peter thickly. "I've bathed in Hatcher's Pond. I know what that mud is. I thought it had stuck there. I thought when they found that rifle they'd stop bothering their damned heads about my pistol."

"Oh, Peter, *your* pistol?"

"Well, the one I used to practise with."

"You said you'd told me everything and you were keeping all this back?"

"What would have been the good of telling you? What would you have thought? What do you think now? Look at you! You think I'm a murderer! Don't you? And the police think I'm a murderer!"

He turned, and Jeanie saw his face white and distorted in the cold November afternoon.

"Oh God!" he cried. "I wish I *had* murdered Molyneux! Then I'd just let them take me and hang me and have done with it!"

"Peter! Oh Peter! What were you doing with that pistol?"

"I suppose I might as well tell somebody before I'm arrested. Perhaps you'll even believe me—who knows?"

"Only tell me everything, this time. Unless—"

"Unless I really murdered Molyneux, you mean?" finished Peter for her with a very bitter-sounding laugh. "Don't worry, Jeanie. I *might* have murdered Molyneux, and the police think I *did* murder Molyneux, and I shall no doubt be *hanged* for murdering Molyneux. But, as it happens, I *didn't* murder him. I'll tell you everything, Jeanie."

"For the third time!"

"Yes, only it really will be everything this time. You don't mind if I make it short as possible, do you?"

He came forward and sat down on a foot-stool in front of the fire, and held his hands to the flames.

"I like fires. I might as well make the most of this one. I suppose they have radiators in prison."

"Peter please!"

"Why the hurry? Old Finister's not on the door-step, is he? Or is he? Are you an agent of the police, Jeanie? Oddly enough, I rather like Superintendent Finister. It'd give me great pleasure to hear at this moment that he had fallen dead. But I like him. In happier times we should be brothers."

"Peter!"

"All right. I'm coming to it. Well, Jeanie." His voice trembled, and he fished in his coat-pocket for cigarettes and matches. "When I'd seen Agnes and she said she didn't know what I was talking about, and she'd told me to go back to London and not make a fool of myself, and I had made a fool of myself without impressing her in the least—well, then Agnes went downstairs. And I was left in the corridor upstairs. Have you ever thought about suicide, Jeanie? I don't mean academically, but as something that might happen to you?"

"Never."

"Well, then, you're not a good person to tell this to. I don't suppose it's any good trying to explain suicidal feelings to a person who's never had them. Even a person who *has* had them can hardly believe in them, when he recovers. The despair, the awful empty tediousness in front of one—"

Peter broke off, for his voice was trembling.

"Anyway, when Agnes went downstairs, I just stood there, listening to her footsteps going away. I thought about suicide. It wasn't only that I was out of a job and in disgrace, and with a pretty poor outlook in front of me. It was that awful emptiness and tediousness. I went and got the pistol out of the Tower room and put it in my pocket and went down the Tower stairs and out. Mr. Fone was just coming into the house as I went out. I meant to shoot myself. Only I couldn't decide where to do it. And there was no hurry. I had the pistol ready, and I went over the common. I was kind of waiting for inspiration, really. I knew inspiration would come. And then I'd finish everything. I went and looked at the pond, and thought what a mug's game drowning was compared with shooting—how one would struggle, I mean, and the mud and the foul taste of the water. And suddenly I was inspired. Only instead of shooting myself I found myself chucking my pistol right out into the middle of the pond. And I knew, in an odd kind of flash, as if I could read the future, that I should never be a suicide. And it's funny, Jeanie, but even now I don't feel in the least inclined that way. When I'd chucked the pistol in the pond I stood around for a little, kind of wondering what on earth had made me do it. I don't remember hearing any shot all this time, but I was in the state when one doesn't hear things. And I felt sort of calm, as if things were all fixed up for me somewhere, and all I had to do was just to wait. And I went off, meaning to walk to Handleston and get a train back to London. And I found Agatos in his car. That's all. Do you believe me?"

"Yes of course."

"I don't know why you should. After all, Jeanie, I could easily have murdered Mr. Molyneux. And if I had murdered him, this tale I've just told you is just the sort of tale I should make up. That's how Finister'll argue. Isn't it?"

"I shouldn't be surprised," replied Jeanie, trying to speak lightly. "Unless—won't they be able to tell that the pistol hasn't been fired lately?"

Peter shrugged.

"I shouldn't think so. It's been in the pond a week. It'll be all chugged up with mud. It only had one cartridge in it, anyway. I thought that would be enough to kill myself with. It seemed more final and fatal, somehow, to take only one." Peter gave a somewhat hollow laugh. He rose to his feet and as his face drew out of the circle of firelight into the cold light of the window his glance seemed to rest nowhere, but flickered round the room as if he thought an enemy might be hidden behind some piece of furniture. "Let's go and find Fone, shall we, Jeanie, and help him scan the horizon for tracks?"

"I don't think I will, Peter. I've been invited for Wednesday, and I think I'd better wait for then."

"Wait for then!" echoed Peter. "I don't like that word wait! I've got to wait now, I suppose, Jeanie. I've got to wait to find old Finister standing at my shoulder uttering the well-known words, 'Anything you say will be used in evidence against you.' Do you think it would be any good my running away?"

"Oh Peter, no!"

Peter, prowling restlessly about the room, stopped and looked down at her. His face was pale, his dark eyes contracted.

"I can't—just wait."

"Oh please do, Peter! Running away wouldn't be the slightest use!"

"Perhaps not. But it'd be something to do."

"It would be my fault. What should I do when I heard you'd been—arrested?"

Peter's frown relaxed as he met her protesting, tearful eyes.

"Come with me, Jeanie! I've often thought it'd be fun to flee from justice, but justice has never given me the chance before."

He smiled, but there was still a wild, tense look about him. Jeanie knew that at a word's encouragement he would be off on a mad, useless flight which could only make his arrest more certain. Was it for this that Finister had been so confiding to her about the pistol? She was Finister's ferret, was she? He put her down the rabbit-hole, in the hope that the scared bunny would bolt into the line of fire. Then, when the wretched Peter was well on his way to London or Timbuctoo, the saturnine officer would step in and calmly take his man, his criminal fleeing from justice! Jeanie sat up with sudden energy.

"No, Peter, no! You mustn't! Promise me!"

Peter's smile faded. He looked at Jeanie as though her vehemence surprised him.

"Mustn't I? Must I wait for old Finister to jump out on me? All right, Jeanie, if that's what you want me to do."

"Oh, Peter," cried Jeanie, the tears spilling over her lids, "it isn't what I *want*, it's what's the safest thing for you!"

"Don't worry, Jeanie," said Peter gently, clasping one of her hands in both his for a moment. "What is there to worry about? After all, aren't we both forgetting. I *didn't* murder Molyneux."

## Chapter Twenty
## MADAM, WILL YOU TALK?

"What, Peter? Oh no, Jeanie! You must have misunderstood Superintendent Finister! How could he suspect Peter, of all people? What on earth sense could there be in such an idea?"

Agnes had gone very pale at Jeanie's news, and although she had quickly recovered her poise, little drops of sweat actually stood now on her fine-skinned, finely-wrinkled forehead. She cared so much, then, for Peter's safety? It was not like Agnes to care so much about another person's safety! Was it possible that the detestable Finister's loathsome fancies might have after all some foundation in fact?

Jeanie was once again with Agnes in the little parlour at Cleedons in which Agnes spent most of her time. The room, as usual, was over-heated, over-cushioned, over-scented, stifling after the cool airs and fresh clean scents of Cole Harbour House.

"But Agnes, Superintendent Finister as good as told me himself that Peter was their man! I know they'll arrest him! He doesn't deny that it was his pistol that was dragged up out of the pond! He doesn't deny that he threw it there just about the time Mr. Molyneux was killed! He doesn't deny that only one cartridge was in it!"

"Does he deny anything?" asked Agnes, speaking in a cold sarcastic tone that brought back to Jeanie memories of Agnes the schoolmistress, much admired of the few, much hated of the many. "Does he deny, for instance, that he shot Robert?"

"Yes. He says he took the pistol out intending to commit suicide."

"What a pity he didn't carry out his intention!"

"Agnes!"

Agnes had spoken with a sudden vehemence, a cold anger, which startled Jeanie. They looked at one another. Agnes's blue eyes were dark and cold. Her broad low forehead on which the thick greyish-blonde hair was parted and waved back had usually a suggestion about it of Greek art, a Clytie or a Sybil. But now as she stooped her tense head and looked angrily up at Jeanie under her brows, that low wide forehead gave her the look of a snake.

"I mean it. What a pity he *didn't* commit suicide, and save himself the trouble of being hanged, if he had to play the fool at all! What's going to happen now? It'll be pleasant for me, won't it, the trial?"

"For you?" stammered Jeanie, aghast as much at the vindictive expression upon her friend's face as at the cold egotism of her words. Evidently, Jeanie could put Finister's suspicion of illicit love quite out of her mind. This was not love. It was the meanest sort of fear.

"Yes, for me!" cried Agnes shrilly. "So nice having one's dirty linen washed in public, isn't it? Has it escaped your memory that Peter was my husband's private secretary? And that he was dismissed for taking money out of the safe? All that'll be gone into publicly, I suppose! I shall have to give evidence at the trial. That'll be delightful for me, won't it? Probably my photograph will be in the picture papers!"

"Oh, Agnes!" said Jeanie. She felt a little sick. Did no feeling for Peter touch Agnes's heart at all? Was there never room at all in that queer, acute but blinkered mind for any generous thought, for any interest that was not of self? She pulled herself together and spoke firmly.

"Oh, that. I know all about why he took the money, Agnes. And so do the police, of course."

"And so will all England, soon! That'll be charming for me, won't it?"

Agnes's little face was quite distorted with fear and fury. The fine lines which were as a rule almost invisible on her delicate, well-cared-for skin all had grown dark as if a malicious pencil had been at work about her face. She looked lined as a little monkey, venomous as a little snake. All kinds of abuse seemed to hover about her lips, but suddenly she paused. She put her hands over her eyes. There was a silence. In the silence Jeanie heard footsteps on the gravel terrace. Somebody passed the window. Jeanie recognised the loping stride of Sir Henry Blundell.

Slowly sighing, Agnes withdrew her hands from her eyes, cupped them around her chin. She seemed to have wiped away in that gesture most of the lines upon her face and all the snake-like anger of her look. Exhausted, pale, tragic, fragile as a late autumn flower, she gazed at Jeanie.

"I'm sorry, Jeanie. I hardly know what I'm saying. That was Sir Henry, wasn't it? He said he was calling here at half-past three."

Evidently Jeanie was expected to take her leave. So strong was the force of suggestion that seemed to emanate from Agnes's sudden silence and quiescence, that she almost did so. But she remembered her errand here, and suddenly determined that she would not be driven away until she had fulfilled it.

"I want to ask you something first, Agnes."

Agnes frowned.

"Some other time."

"No. Now."

If you'd only let me know you were coming! I haven't time now!"

I want to ask you a question and it won't take long," said Jeanie, breathless with nervousness, for never in her life had she defied Agnes before, and the submissive habit of years is not easily broken. "Sir Henry can wait."

"He can't! There's the bell! I shall ask Bates to show him straight in here!"

"Then I shall ask my question in front of him, and you won't like it. You'd better do as I want, Agnes."

"Jeanie! Do you know what you're talking about?"

"Perfectly well. I'm not a schoolgirl now, Agnes, and you're not a school-mistress, and it's not the slightest use putting on that tone!"

"I think you're mad, Jeanie."

"Listen, Agnes. I gave you a zircon brooch once; do you remember?"

"Really, Jeanie, is this the moment for your reminiscences?"

"Agnes, the question I want to ask you is about Valentine Frazer."

There was a pause, as Bates entered the room. At last Agnes said:

"Show Sir Henry into the hall and tell him that I shall only be a moment."

"Very good, madam."

The door closed. On the instant the calm employer's mask fell from Agnes's face. She turned furiously upon Jeanie, then checked as if she found something formidable in Jeanie's look. Her limp:

"I don't know what you're talking about, Jeanie!" fell unconvincingly from her lips.

"Why didn't you tell me that pearl necklace was yours?"

"Mine? What pearl necklace?"

"The one I showed you the day before yesterday. The one I found at Yew Tree Cottage."

"Really, Jeanie, haven't I got enough to think about without—"

"If Sir Henry has to wait hours in the hall it won't be my fault. Don't waste time, Agnes. You gave your pearl necklace to Valentine Frazer, and I want to know why."

There was a pause. Agnes took a cigarette from a box on the mantelpiece and searched nervously around for something to light it with.

"Really, I think you're demented, Jeanie," she said. "Valentine Frazer. That's the woman who lived with Hugh Barchard at Yew

Tree Cottage. What conceivable reason could I have had for giving her a pearl necklace?"

"That's what I want to know."

"I lost my necklace, it's true. Possibly she found it."

When you saw it the other night you pretended not to recognise it."

"I didn't recognise it. One pearl necklace is very like another, if one isn't an expert. Oh damn. Must these damned housemaids leave empty match-boxes all over the place?"

She flung a brocaded match-box into the fire.

You gave Valentine Frazer your pearl necklace, and you gave her your zircon brooch."

"What in Heaven's name are you talking about?" cried Agnes angrily.

"I've seen a portrait of the woman wearing your brooch. How did she get it if you didn't give it to her?"

"Don't be a fool! As if there can't be two zircon brooches in the world! They're the commonest kind of rubbish travellers in Ceylon bring back with them!"

Absurd Jeanie! This description of the lovely brooch she had given Agnes cut her to the quick!

"You didn't think it was rubbish eight years ago!" she cried.

"It was sweet of you to give it me. I still wear it sometimes."

"Show it me, and I'll believe you!"

"Really, Jeanie, you said just now you weren't a schoolgirl!"

"You gave that brooch to Valentine Frazer!"

"I did not." Again Agnes put her cigarette between her lips and looked about her for a match.

"Here's a match, if you want one!"

"What on earth should I be giving things to that woman for? I didn't even know her! I never met her! How should I? What had we in common, I should like to know? Perhaps you can tell me that, as you seem to know everything! Would I be likely to meet a woman like that?"

Agnes held out her hand, but Jeanie struck a match. Frowning, Agnes stooped to the flame.

"Why not? She was a tenant of your cottage, wasn't she? And I think you had a good deal in common! You'd both been professional women—you a school-mistress and she an actress! You were both daughters of clergymen who'd held the same living!" said Jeanie, remembering Mrs. Barchard's gossip. "You—"

She broke off sharply, gazing at Agnes's face, her straight, delicate nose, her thin pink-stained lips pursed lightly around the already pink-stained cigarette. A puff of smoke came sharply into her face.

"Sorry," said Agnes, as if she had not done it on purpose. But Jeanie scarcely noticed it.

"What the devil is the matter with you, Jeanie? You look semi-idiotic with your mouth open like that!"

There was a mirror over the mantelpiece, and Jeanie found herself looking at her own face in it, thinking of the painted smiling face of the lady in red gloves.

"*Is* she like me? I don't think so, but Peter saw it. So I suppose she must be. And I thought she was like *you*. Agnes, she's your sister, isn't she? Your sister, that was supposed to be dead!"

Agnes stood very still. Her protest when it came sounded oddly half-hearted.

"What are you talking about?"

Her cigarette dropped on the fur rug. It was an appreciable moment before she picked it up. She seemed suddenly all at sea, ill-co-ordinated, lost. She was wondering wildly, Jeanie knew, whether to confess or deny. Jeanie decided to save her the trouble.

"I know she is, by the way you're behaving! I hadn't even thought of it a moment ago, but now I know! Your sister, Agnes!

The sister who died young, soon after she'd started her stage career! The sister you sacrificed so much to! The sister I reminded you of. Only it seems she didn't die! You were quite broken by her death, you said. Nine years younger than you, almost more like a daughter than a sister—"

"Jeanie, don't."

To Jeanie's astonishment, Agnes spoke quietly. She had dropped her cigarette into the fire. She had turned and laid her arm upon the mantelpiece, her head upon her arm. One appealing hand stretched out behind her as if she actually expected Jeanie to take it. Disconcerted, ashamed of what seemed of a sudden cruel jeering, Jeanie became silent.

"You know as well as I do, Jeanie, that a schoolmistress can't afford to have disreputable sisters. Vera—Valentine, she called herself, it was her stage name—*had* to be dead. I paid for her to go to Canada. I hoped she'd stop there, never be able to raise the passage home. But she got home somehow. You see, Jeanie, she knew what a handicap she could be to me. She only had to appear, and—"

"What would it have mattered?" asked Jeanie, feeling clumsy, awkward and at sea in the face of Agnes's mournful quietude. Agnes raised her muffled head to answer with spirit:

"You didn't know Vera! She was impossible! She was everything you can think of that's impossible! We never liked one another. Well, was it likely? She had a kink. She used to behave outrageously from her childhood. And she hated me, she was always ready to do some malicious thing to annoy me. I'd have left her alone. But she wouldn't leave me alone. And I knew it. And she knew that I knew it. And when she took up with this man Barchard, and then came to live here on purpose to annoy me and frighten me, although she promised me when I married Robert that as long as I gave her a hundred a year she'd never so much as write to me—! Of course she knew she could break her promises as she pleased. She knew I couldn't do anything! I believe she only ever got hold of Barchard because she found out he was a tenant of ours!"

"But what were you afraid of, Agnes? She couldn't hurt you!"

Agnes raised her head and turned. She looked outraged and indignant.

"She could tell everyone she was my sister! And I shouldn't have been able to deny it! She could prove it! She could make life here impossible for me, that's all! If you call that nothing! My sister, a common woman, who lived with a working man without being married to him! My sister, turned out of the village inn for using bad language! Delightful it would have been for me, wouldn't it?"

"She couldn't *hurt* you."

"Don't be silly, Jeanie! She could have ruined me socially, made Cleedons impossible for me, spoilt my marriage—"

"Hadn't you told your husband about her, then?"

"No. I—I didn't want Robert to be worried."

"I see."

"It's all very well for you, Jeanie! You didn't know Vera!"

"What did you expect to happen in the end?"

"I thought if I could keep her quiet for a bit, she'd get tired of annoying me and go off, as she'd done before. And as she did, this time, in the end. I gave her things. Money, when I could manage it. And bits of jewellery—in the end, even my pearls. I had to pretend they were lost, because Robert missed them, and we got insurance for them."

"So your sister had to pretend the pearls were a cheap artificial string, and lie low about them. I see. And the zircon brooch?"

"If Vera was fool enough to think they were real diamonds, I couldn't help that! It kept her quiet for a whole month, anyhow!

And I kept on hoping that she'd get tired and go! It wasn't to her advantage, after all, to quarrel with me! Kill the goose that laid the golden eggs! Only I had to be very careful not to snub her or irritate her too much, for fear she got into a temper and forgot where her advantage lay! Oh, Jeanie! It was too awful the time she was here! She'd do all kinds of tricks! Waylay Robert at the gate and let me see her talking to him! Write to Robert, and I'd see the envelope and—and then it'd be just a tenant's letter to say the tap wanted a new washer or something. When she went, it was too heavenly, too good to be true! I couldn't believe for weeks that she wasn't coming back. But she was always like that. When I married Robert I hadn't heard of her for three years. I was really beginning to hope she was dead. Only she saw a notice in the paper, and turned up at my flat two days before the wedding, wanting to be introduced to Robert! You can imagine what I felt! Oh, my whole life's been spoilt by that horrible girl!"

Jeanie would have liked to tell Agnes that it was not her sister, but her own cowardice, that had spoilt her whole life and would probably spoil the rest of it.

"I see," she said. "Well, thank you for telling me, Agnes. I *was* puzzled about those pearls. I'll bring them back to you."

"For Heaven's sake bury them! Or bring them to me, and I'll do it! Jeanie, you won't—"

Agnes lifted a face flushed by the heat of the fire and her own emotion.

"You won't, Jeanie, tell anyone?"

"But surely it's awfully silly to try to keep it a secret, Agnes! It's turning your life into a misery for no reason at all!"

A flash of irritation and fear came over Agnes's face, but she controlled herself and said softly:

"Vera drinks too much and leads a stupid life. She'll probably die quite suddenly one of these days. And then I shan't have to worry about her any more. You won't, will you, Jeanie, breathe a word?"

"No, then."

"I know I can trust you," said Agnes, with a melancholy sweet smile. With just that smile she greeted Sir Henry Blundell when he entered.

"You two have met before, haven't you?"

"Of course." Sir Henry shot at Jeanie that keen, direct, somewhat alarming glance which was, Jeanie suspected, a mere mannerism, meaning nothing, not even observation.

"We shall meet again on Wednesday at Cole Harbour, shan't we, Sir Henry? Mr. Fone's invited me."

At the name Cole Harbour, a slight contemptuousness spoiled Sir Henry's friendly look.

"Indeed! Then your presence will be the one cheerful feature of a tiresome afternoon, I'm afraid. I'd almost made up my mind not to go. But I suppose, as one of the committee, it's my duty."

"You don't agree with Mr. Fone's theory of the old British trackways, then?"

"I do not," replied Sir Henry incisively. "Fone's enthusiasms are apt to be fantastic as well as tiresome, and in this case he really surpasses himself."

"Well," said Jeanie crisply, "*I'm* looking forward to a very interesting afternoon."

She spoke in defence of her friend Fone and his enthusiasms. She had no head for archaeology. She did not really think Wednesday afternoon would be very interesting. No premonition as she spoke the word "interesting" came to warn her of its inadequacy.

A smaller party than Jeanie had expected was gathered at Cole Harbour. Perhaps the cold north wind had kept many of the Field Club members at home. Beside Mr. Fone, Barchard and Peter, Mr. Harrison was there, and Sir Henry Blundell, little Dr. Hall, young Denham the journalist and two or three others whom Jeanie did not know. Tamsin Wills, Sarah and Jeanie herself were the ladies of the party. Tamsin wore a rather self-conscious air and avoided Jeanie's eye: perhaps the daylight memory of that night on the common embarrassed her.

On the leads of the library roof, the air had that peculiar harsh nip in it which tells of coming snow. Barchard helped the ladies climb from the ladder over the stone balustrade on to the flat leads of the roof. A kitchen table stood incongruously in the middle of the roof, and upon it several ordnance survey sheets were spread and drawing-pinned down. A chair stood beside the table, and pencils and rulers lay ready.

There was a polite altercation on the ground between William Fone and Sir Henry Blundell, the former insisting that he, being slow and awkward, should climb up last, the latter conceiving it his duty to steady the ladder on the ground for his crippled host. Jeanie, watching over the balustrade, felt irritated with Sir Henry. Could not the fool of a conventional polite man see that poor Fone would prefer to make the awkward accent in private and keep such physical dignity as a cripple could?

Eventually, with the smothered ill grace of a man accustomed to his own way, Sir Henry had to give in. He came lightly up, swung his long body over on to the roof and began at once to adjust a pair of field-glasses. Fone, when at last he appeared, protested half humorously at those glasses.

"Megalithic man used his own eyes, Sir Henry!"

Sir Henry laughed.

"I am glad that I have *one* advantage, then, over megalithic man! What a wonderful view to the south! I didn't realise how steeply the land slopes away from here! What tower is that I see on the sky-line?"

"That's the castle ruin on King's tump. And I am glad you have drawn our attention to it. For the most important of the megalithic trackways which I am hoping to point out to you this afternoon runs in that direction In that direction lie the Wiltshire downs. And a straight line drawn from Grim's Grave through the castle ruin, which, though itself a medieval structure, no doubt stands upon a prehistoric earthwork, through Whitley Church, Stonebarrow, Brendon Camp and many other significant places, reaches, eventually, Avebury."

Jeanie, with most of the others, gathered at the balustrade and looked southwards over the wintry fields. They were glad of the excuse to turn their backs on the drear north.

"Avebury!" echoed Sir Henry. "You're not going to persuade me that megalithic man could see Avebury from here without field-glasses?"

"No," said Fone with restraint. "And nor can modern man see it with them. But he can find his way to Avebury without map or guide if he makes his way by his own eyesight from one to another of the ancient landmarks I have mentioned. And I have no doubt that in megalithic times a road ran straight from one to another of them."

In Cole Harbour Wood, which lay beyond Grim's Grave, and hid her own Yew Tree Cottage from Jeanie's view, somebody was once again felling trees. How long ago, how very long ago it seemed since Jeanie, walking peacefully along the road to Cleedons, had heard that sound! The only care in her mind then had been for her smoking parlour fire. She saw two or three felled trees now lying on the cleared ground, the piled-up frith waiting for the fire. Larches, they were, she could see now. She saw a man wielding an axe. She liked the intent, bent look of him, the rhythmical swing, the hard loud sound of impact. Lift, swing— thud! Lift, swing— thud! Queer, how the ear expected the thud before it came! One saw the axe-head sink into the wood, on an under-cutting stroke one actually saw the white chip fly out, before one heard the thud that sent it flying.

Jeanie found Peter Johnson standing near the balustrade beside her. He looked pale and stern, and seemed to have aged in the last two days.

"I hope they're not going to cut down all those trees, Peter."

"I don't suppose so, Jeanie. Just getting a few larch poles for fencing, I expect."

"Listen!"

"To what?"

"The axe. It's funny how you don't hear the thud till after the axe has hit the tree."

"Not really. Light travels faster than sound, and the wood's some distance away. I haven't seen anything of Finister, Jeanie. Have you?"

He spoke jauntily, but when Jeanie looked up at him, she saw that his eyes were haggard. Her heart contracted.

"No, Peter."

"I wonder what he's playing at. I wonder all the time. I'm only just managing to hang on here, Jeanie. Sometimes I feel I *must* run off somewhere—anywhere, and hide. You don't know what it's like!"

"Oh!" murmured Jeanie, for he was raising his voice and the strong wind was blowing his words across the roof, and she saw Tamsin Wills look curiously across at them. "I do, Peter. Try to take it easy."

"But my dear sir," they heard Sir Henry utter in tones of bland surprise. "Are we to understand, then, that in your view the Watling Streets were not made by the Romans?"

"Re-made, yes. Not laid down. The tracks were already here, and had been in use for centuries."

Sir Henry shrugged his shoulders very slightly.

"I wish I understood," murmured Jeanie to Peter, "what Mr. Fone is talking about. Who were the megalithic people?"

"Why, the men who put up the megaliths, Miss Halliday," replied Hugh Barchard, who was standing near and who, perhaps because he had heard it all before, was not attending very closely to Mr. Fone's lecture.

"The megaliths?"

"The stone circles. And the barrows. Grim's Grave."

William Fone was defying the wind and facing northwards now, while he was pointing out to a somewhat sceptical audience a sighting notch on distant Herry Hill, just visible over the rising land.

"Apart from Herry Hill, there is not much of interest to be seen in that direction," said Mr. Fone, "although a great many interesting landmarks exist. The rise of the land blocks our view of the interesting circle of barrows on Treinton…"

Once again Jeanie lost the thread of her host's lecture. Not much of interest to be seen, he said. There was a good deal of interest to be seen. There was a heron flying over Cleedons with its peculiar slow flight. Cows were coming with the slow indifferent motion of their kind down the lane to the milking-shed. A boy in a faded crimson shirt was watching them in. The dairyman in his white coat crossed the chilly stone yard. Across the paddock a cart was rumbling slowly, piled high with bracken, which now looked purplish and cold in tone, lacking the sun's rays. Was it only nine days since Jeanie had with such pleasure watched this very scene, admired the warm brown of the bracken, the green of the orchard grass, the soft autumnal glow upon the scene? Where now in this chill wind was that soft autumnal glow? Where kindly Robert Molyneux, the owner of that wagon, the master of these men?

She watched the bracken-wagon drawn up inside the barn. She noted how the dried light-coloured mud upon the wheels made a harmony in cool tones with the light corduroy trousers of the wagoner, the grey of the stone buildings, the chill blue of the sky. She watched the bracken unloaded into the barn, watched the wagon rumble off again behind the tall open barn-doors, watched a white hen scratch and peck about in the orchard grass for seeds or insects which might have fallen over the wagon-side. Jeanie was idly glad the hen was white. It gave just the needed point to the picture in cold tones she was painting for herself.

It gave just the right note to the picture in cold tones she was painting for herself. And the tones of the picture were very cold. Unnaturally cold. Fearfully cold. They seemed to grow colder and colder every second. Or was it Jeanie herself who grew colder and colder every second? The axe in Cole Harbour Wood thudded through the background of her thought. She stared across the road.

"What's worrying you, Miss Halliday? You look as if you'd seen a ghost," murmured Hugh Barchard jocosely.

"I have," replied Jeanie. Her voice sounded strange in her own ears. "I've seen a white hen."

She heard her voice as if it were someone else's. Had she spoken rather loudly? She became aware of eyes looking at her—surprised, curious, observant. Even Mr. Fone had paused in his discourse and was looking at her. Had she said something odd?

She had said something rash. She must be careful what she said. She had better say nothing at all. She had a feeling that she was surrounded by enemies. She looked for Peter, and found him

looking at her with a concerned expression. What was the matter
with them all? What was the matter with her looks? She saw Dr.
Hall looking at her concernedly. She tried to smile at him. She
thought she succeeded, but Dr. Hall evidently thought not.

"You're not well, Miss Halliday!"

"Yes, I am, thank you."

Did she say that, or only mean to say it? Dr. Hall did not seem
to hear her.

"The wind's too cold for you. You'd better sit down a moment.
Here—this stool."

Obediently, Jeanie sat.

"I'm perfectly all right. I wish you'd all go on with your
meeting. Please, Mr. Fone. Please do. I shall be quite all right in
half a jiffy."

She had to submit to Dr. Hall's adept grab at her wrist. She
remembered how Agnes had said that before she fainted in the
lane she had felt that she must lie down. Jeanie knew now how she
felt. For two pins she would have laid her sick, heavy head against
the cushioned waistcoat that appeared on a level with her
dimming eyes. Had Dr. Hall not been inside the waistcoat, in fact,
she would have done so. Everything went black.

But not for long, because when she opened her eyes Peter was
still kneeling beside her and holding her hand, and Dr. Hall was
still leaning solicitously over her. She saw them all standing
round, and felt both ashamed of herself and oddly frightened. She
longed for warmth, a soft chair to lie in, and solitude.

"I'm all right now. Quite, quite all right. I think I'll go home."

She refused with vigour Sir Henry Blundell's offer to drive her
home to Yew Tree Cottage.

"No, really, thank you very much. I can walk. It'll do me good."

"Certainly I'll drive you, Miss Halliday," protested Sir Henry
with the crisp determination that characterised him. But Jeanie

was equally determined that he should not, and for the second time that afternoon Sir Henry was forced to yield. It was Peter who helped her down the ladder and walked along the road with her towards the sanctuary of Yew Tree Cottage, leaving the rest of the Field Club to stamp their cold feet, wipe the moisture from their noses, listen to Mr. Fone and long for the moment of descent.

Peter slipped his hand through Jeanie's arm.

What's the matter, Jean? Nothing serious, I hope?" His dark eyes were kind and anxious. Jeanie looked at him gravely. She still felt a little queer, and a heavy headache had settled over her eyes.

"Well, it is rather, Peter. I think I know who murdered Molyneux."

She felt his hand tighten over her wrist.

"What?"

"I think I know who—"

"Jeanie! But—"

"I think I'll go home and sleep on it, Peter. I feel in too much of a muddle to talk about it now. It's rather sudden, you see. I'll tell you about it in the morning."

"But Jeanie, can't you just—"

"No, in case I'm wrong. I'll sleep on it to-night, Peter. I shall be all right. You go back to your megaliths."

"Not I. I'm seeing you home."

"I'd really, really rather you didn't. Mrs. Barchard's there. I'll be all right."

Jeanie had a great longing to be alone. She withdrew her hand from Peter's, and palely but obstinately smiled at him. He frowned and seemed about to dispute the point. Jeanie was glad when Mrs. Peel, driving her shining black car, overtook them and stopped and insisted on driving her the hundred yards or so on to her cottage.

"I've just been up to see our little saint about my darling daughter. I've decided to go to South Africa in the spring with Eustace. So if Agnes likes to be saddled with somebody else's kid, which, between you and me, she doesn't like at all, but she has to pretend she does—let her, I say! All I insist on is Sally must go to school, and if Agnes is her guardian, which I won't dispute at present, Agnes must pay the school fees! I'm not going to have that snake of a Miss Wills perverting my child's mind," said Myfanwy in maternal and virtuous tones which at any other time might have tickled Jeanie. "So we've settled it that Sally starts going to school next term and spends her holidays at Cleedons. Suits me very well, and poor dear Agnes has to pretend it suits her. The only person it won't suit is dear Miss Wills. Well, here we are."

"Won't you come in and have some tea?"

"Can't, thanks all the same. I've got all the packing to do. Eustace is driving down to Somerset this evening on some wild-goose chase after a house he's thinking of buying, so I've got all his packing to do as well as my own. Do tell me, though—" Myfanwy Peel let down the window of her car to converse with Jeanie as she stood at her gate—"do tell me what you were doing on the roof of that loony's house? I saw you as I went up to Cleedons. What *was* it? Fire-drill?"

"We were looking for old straight tracks," said Jeanie, smiling faintly.

"Straight tracks? I say, you look a bit washed out. Are you all right?"

"Quite, only a little cold."

"Well, I hope you found what you were looking for."

'I found something I wasn't looking for," said Jeanie.

"Like me when I married Franklin," replied Mrs. Peel with a laugh. "Still, that's settled now, for the present. We'll see, when Sally's grown up, if she won't prefer her mother and a bit of fun

and real life to the collection of fossilised remains she'll be living
with here!"

She drove off. Jeanie shut the door.

## Chapter Twenty-Two
### NIGHT FEARS

Those who inhabit timber-framed houses grow used to
unexplained noises in the silence of the night, as the ancient
buildings, like old rheumatic men, crack noisily at the joints and
make their loud comments on every change in the weather. Up in
the loft, rafter shifts upon plate with a faint groaning crack that
sounds like a furtive footstep on the stairs. Tenon moves in
mortice with a loud crack like a pistol-shot. That sudden scurrying
is caused by the rats running between the boards and plaster in
the hidden avenues between the joists of the ceiling.

As a rule, Jeanie did not even need to remind herself of these
things. She scarcely heard the noises of her cottage talking to itself
and its inhabitants; or, when she heard it, heard it as one hears
the friendly noise of the rain or the wind. This evening, a mere fall
of soot down the parlour chimney made her jump up in alarm and
upset the milk-jug. She could not bear sudden noises. Sudden
noises reminded her of shots, and sudden death. And as she
mopped up the milk she saw once again the circle of concerned,
curious eyes which had converged upon her on Cole Harbour roof
just before she fainted.

There was no milk left in the jug, and she wanted another cup
of tea. She picked up the jug and went out with a candle through
the hall to the larder. She could hear the tinkle of metal from
behind the closed kitchen door as she passed. Mrs. Barchard had
not gone yet. Wednesday was her day for cleaning brass, and this
labour, which she loved, usually kept her late. As she went along

the passage, Jeanie realised that the wind had dropped and that everything outside the house seemed silent, magnifying the noises within, as when a storm is impending. Perhaps the threatened snow was about to fall. But there was some movement in the air, for when Jeanie opened too quickly the larder door, a draught through the wire gauze at the window at once blew her candle out. She gave a little, silly sobbing gasp, as if this were a haunted house instead of her own dear home, and she a nervous lodger instead of its happy owner. She knew where the matches were kept in the larder. She put her candlestick down and shut the door and felt about on the shelf under the window.

The sky had certainly become overcast with the falling of darkness. No stars were visible, but a uniform cold grey which, from the pitch darkness of the larder, seemed faintly luminous. No snow had fallen, yet. The square of light from the kitchen window illuminated dry frost-nipped ground. There was a man standing up against the leafless syringa...

Jeanie's gasp this time seemed really to lift a disordered heart a little way in her throat. She stood quite still. She could not see the man now. She would not have seen him before had he not moved. But he was there, standing as still as herself beside the old syringa-bush which made a thick patch of darkness.

No he was not there! Jeanie had seen out of the corner of her eye the flight of an owl, imagined a darkness m the shape of a man and connected the two together. She had her hand on the matches now, but could not take her eyes off the syringa-bush. And as she looked a portion of the blackness moved off across the dark grass, and was a man. The kitchen light fell for a second on the toe of a man's shoe. A black shoe.

Jeanie's first impulse was to flee to the kitchen. Her next, to curse Mrs. Barchard for not pulling the kitchen blind down, for the patch of light thrown by the kitchen window dazzled her eyes.

If it had not been for that, perhaps by now she would have been accustomed to the darkness and have been able to see who it was who was creeping slowly, slowly, in that extraordinary fashion, as though he were doing a balancing feat, along the grass edging at the other side of the path.

The background of dark fruit-bushes and apple-trees obscured all but the movement of a denser darkness. But along a grass verge some fifteen feet from the window, somebody was walking like a man on a tight-rope, putting one foot closely down in front of the other. There was something horrible, it seemed to Jeanie, in the clumsy grotesqueness of the movement. Her foolish heart, as if it were a caged creature that had had enough teasing for to-day, throbbed irritably. The figure disappeared behind an espalier. Softly and suddenly opening the iron-framed casement, Jeanie called:

"Who's there?"

There was no reply, no movement in the darkness. An ice-cold air came in upon Jeanie's hot face. Everything was silent. How foolish that her heart should race so, that all her instincts should silently call for help! Were there no silly boys in the cottages round about? Was not a garden gate open to everybody who chose to trespass? Had not Jeanie before now found on her flower-beds the clumsy footprints of people taking a short cut through her garden from some farm-house below in the valley? What harm could a trespasser in her garden do to her safely behind the barred doors of her cottage?

*Who's there?* indeed, in that foolish, quavering voice! The trespasser was laughing to himself, no doubt, among the apple-trees. But perhaps he was not laughing. Perhaps now, at this moment in that darkness, a rifle or a pistol was pointing at Jeanie's open window, perhaps at this moment a steady determined finger was on the trigger.

Crash! went the casement as Jeanie's hand flung it to. There was a further tinkle, as a little diamond-shaped pane fell out.

"Oh damn!" muttered Jeanie, fastening the catch and fumbling for the matches, crouching, keeping her head down away from the window. She did not light her candle till she was outside the larder again and the door shut. Inside the kitchen, Mrs. Barchard was still singing softly and hoarsely to herself. Jeanie had half a mind to open the kitchen door and reassure herself with the sight of Mrs. Barchard and the steaming kettle and the rows of metal candlesticks and the glowing kitchener. But she was afraid of Mrs. Barchard. She was afraid of everybody. She was afraid of everything.

As she entered the parlour she realised that she had forgotten to bring the milk she had gone to fetch. She could not go back again.

"Mrs. Barchard! Mrs. Barchard!"

That was a foolish urgent voice in which to call a domestic. Mrs. Barchard would think the chimney was on fire or something. But at any rate it brought her quickly to the parlour, still holding a polishing leather in her well-whitened hand.

"Yes, Miss?"

"Oh, Mrs. Barchard! Could you fetch me some more milk? I've just spilt all this."

"Oh dear! Yes, of course." Polishing the damp tray with the corner of her apron, Mrs. Barchard added, for she was nothing if not inquisitive: "I thought I heard you, Miss, going to the larder just now?"

"Yes, I did, but I forgot what I went for."

"You looks a bit pale, Miss."

"I—I imagined I saw a man in the garden just now. It startled me."

Mrs. Barchard's dark eyebrows rose until they almost disappeared into her untidy top-knot of grey hair.

"A man in the garden, Miss? He's up to no good at this time of night! I'll go out with a bicycle lamp if you like and see if he's still there."

"Oh no, don't bother! He was just taking a short cut, I expect; but it startled me."

A short cut. Jeanie saw again in her mind's eye the slow movement of that dark figure in the darkness, balanced on the grass verge as on a high wall, walking like a child who has taken a whim to touch heel to toe and toe to heel all the way from his nursery to Timbuctoo. What sort of a short cut led along the grass verge of her kitchen garden Jeanie could not imagine! But it did not matter. Had she not been in an overwrought state, the antics of a trespassing boy would not have worried her. She made light of the matter, seeing that Mrs. Barchard was disposed to take it with deadly seriousness.

"Well, but you looks real white, Miss. You isn't well, I'm sure. How about a fresh pot of tea made good and strong instead of that weeshy stuff you drinks?"

When she was alone again with her pot of strong tea and her cosy fire, Jeanie tried to settle down happily and enjoy them both. But she found herself continually looking uneasily over her shoulder. Dear little room that she loved, it looked surely as usual. But it did not give her quite the reassurance she had expected. The cottage piano had an odd, dumpy and sullen look, retiring in the corner out of the lamp's rays. There was a folding screen standing beside the piano, and it had a secretive appearance. Under the round gate-leg table there was dense darkness.

Jeanie was still gazing into the fire with her tea going cold beside her when Mrs. Barchard came in, hatted and coated for her homeward journey.

"Oh, Mrs. Barchard, off already?"

"It's past my time, Miss. And it's starting to snow, too, bother it, as if we hadn't had enough slummocky stuff out of the sky this autumn."

"Well, you'll be along in the morning."

"As usual, Miss. Don't you come to the door, you'll catch cold."

A few flakes came in at the door as Jeanie opened it. It was beginning to snow, with small flakes very lightly drifting.

"Nasty stuff!" said Mrs. Barchard, stamping on a wet flake as though it were a noxious insect alighting on the floor.

Jeanie watched her down the path and out of the garden and stood for a moment listening to her brisk footsteps making off down the road. The land, the sky had that peculiar darkness and stillness that come with filling snow. By to-morrow it would perhaps have fallen-snow's peculiar luminousness. The air was very still. There was not a sound among the high-up branches.

It was so still that a crackling rustle in the garden hedge startled Jeanie. She peered out.

"Is anyone there?" she asked quietly.

There was no reply. Weasels and stoats and other nocturnal hunters cannot, after all, be expected to reply to questions in the human language. Jeanie smiled a little at this reflection. But she was careful to bolt and chain her front door, and then did the same for both back doors. Then she gave Petronella the remains of the milk, went round the cottage, making sure of the window fastenings, filled a hot-water bottle, raked out the parlour fire, wound the clock, and taking a book and Petronella under her arm went upstairs to her bed. It was a quarter-past seven. It was one of the advantages of living alone that one could go to bed at strange hours without inviting curious comment.

Jeanie had thought at Cole Harbour that she wanted to be alone. Now, going upstairs with the docile kitten purring sweetly against her neck and her hot-water bottle burning her arm, she was not so sure.

From the sleep into which, after a couple of hours' reading, at last she fell, Jeanie awoke slowly, with an oppressed sensation. Something—what was it?—was the matter. Petronella, in the manner of spoilt kittens, was lying across her neck, and that might account for the oppression. She shifted Petronella, who purred and snuggled down again. The window showed a square of lightness upon the darkness of the room. Was it dawn already?

Shifting Petronella again, more firmly this time, Jeanie pulled out the luminous-faced watch from under her pillow. Dawn, indeed! It was ten minutes past twelve. It was the snow that made that soft sub-luminousness in the window-frame. It would not be dawn for another seven hours, and Jeanie had better go to sleep again as quickly as possible.

"Oh blow you, Petronella! Go away!"

Petronella, offended, got up, yawned, stalked to the edge of the bed and jumped to the floor. The floor was uncarpeted and the joists below unplastered, and Petronella's landing made a surprisingly loud noise for so light a creature. Jeanie was quite startled by it. She was more startled when, from somewhere in the house, from the parlour below it seemed, came an answering sound, a rough sudden sound like the moving of a chair as if somebody else in the house had been startled by Petronella. But there was nobody else in the house.

Was there? Jeanie held her breath and listened. Perhaps that stealthy scraping of a chair-leg was not the first sound that had been made in the parlour. Perhaps there had been others, which had woken Jeanie. Perhaps there *was* somebody in the house!

No. Silence. Of course, there were others in the house beside Jeanie and Petronella. There were mice. There was a bat, very often. And rats, horrible creatures, were frequent visitors from the barns round about. Rats, even mice, were noisy things in a house at dead of night. Let Jeanie go to sleep again and refrain, if possible, from folly. But Jeanie's head would not relax upon her pillow. Stiff-necked, with eyes staring into the darkness, still holding her breath, she listened.

Undoubtedly, there was someone in the house. Someone was making a peculiar prolonged rustling noise in the room below. A stealthy rustling noise, as if someone were crumpling paper and did not wish to be heard doing so.

Just such a noise, in fact, as a mouse might make between the pages of a newspaper. Lie still, Jeanie, and go to sleep!

But it was not easy to lie still, and impossible to go to sleep. Petronella suddenly jumped up on Jeanie's shoulder again, a great deal more quietly than she had descended, and Jeanie could not repress a startled gasp. Petronella settled down upon Jeanie's shoulder with a loud purring that irritated Jeanie, since it filled her straining ears and smothered—so she fancied—sounds that might be going on below.

But why should there be sounds below? There was nothing of value to steal in Yew Tree Cottage. Who would be likely to break in? One might answer that question with another: who was the man Jeanie had seen early in the evening standing outside her cottage near the syringa bush? Oh, lie down, Jeanie, and go to sleep!

But that was, there was no doubt of it, a noise in the parlour downstairs. It was a noise Jeanie could recognise. And it was not the kind of noise that can be ascribed to rats or mice or bats. It was the quiet chink of metal being put down gently on metal.

Very cautiously, as if her lightest movement could be heard by the intruder, Jeanie sat up in bed, hugging her blankets round her. There was somebody in the house. Somebody was below in her parlour, rustling paper and chinking metals together. But what could anyone want in her house at this hour of the night? It could not be a friend, for what friendly motive could there be for such an intrusion? It could not be a mere impersonal thief, for no thief would go to the trouble of breaking into this little cottage. Must it be, then, an enemy?

As her thoughts formed this word, Jeanie's heart started pounding rockily in her chest again. She whimpered a little to herself, in sheer fright at the word. At the same time, she called herself a nervous, fanciful fool, for she had no enemies...

It seemed quite a long time that Jeanie sat up in bed, not moving a muscle, scarcely breathing, all her spirit in her ears. There was no sound. And she began to feel that she would almost welcome a sound. Yet when it came it terrified her. It was the sound of something harsh and rustling being dragged softly over the floor below.

She would of course have to go down and confront the intruder. She would have to go, if only for the reason that she could not sit here in bed with the blankets huddled round her, shivering and listening, much longer. Anything was better than this staring, listening suspense. What was that soft, dragging sound? Was the intruder after all a mere burglar making off with some of her possessions? What could a burglar be moving that would make that peculiar soft dragging noise? His swag, collected in a sack of table-cloth? But a burglar's swag would chink and clatter. It would not be soft. It would not rustle in that ghostly way, like a straw palliasse.

She must go down. In a sort of breathless calm, summoning all her courage, Jeanie slipped silently out of bed. Once off the mat, the floor was very cold. The air was very cold. She groped for her dressing-gown and put it on, wrapping it close around her and tying the girdle with grim fingers as old warriors used to buckle on their sword-belts. She had no weapon. What weapon was there that she could lay her hands on? Switching on her little torch, she looked about her. Nothing. She switched the torch off.

Tiptoeing to the window, she very softly opened it. It was not far to the ground. At any rate she could, if the worst came to the worst, run to it and scream for help.

Scream for help! Foolish Jeanie! She would not need help! She would in a moment or two be laughing at her own fears, when she found the papers that a mouse had been dragging across the floor and trying to pull through his hole in the wainscot to make a cosy nest under the wall-plate. She had her torch in her hand. She would go very quietly out of her room and half-way down the stairs. From half-way down the stairs she could see into the parlour. She had, she remembered, left the parlour door ajar. Half-way down the stairs she would switch on her torch, direct its beams into the parlour and cry: "Who's there?" There would be no reply. Perhaps a little scamper of mice. Then she would descend, light all the candles in the place, search the cottage, find nothing untoward, and return to bed.

She had her torch ready in her left hand and her thumb ready on the knob. With her right she very carefully pushed up the wooden latch of the door. The old wood, polished with use, lifted beautifully without a sound, and quite soundlessly she lowered it. Breath held, she waited a moment, eyes and ears straining through the open door. Had she remembered the window at the back, and how to anyone below in the darkness, she would appear silhouetted against its lesser darkness, she would, perhaps, not have stood her ground so bravely.

The landing was quite dark. With infinite caution Jeanie took two steps upon it. The boards did not creak, they were friendly to her bare feet. She felt a sort of excitement now that was not entirely unpleasurable. She was on her mettle. Anything was

better than lying in her bedroom shivering and listening to
imaginary noises!

As she took another cautious step towards the stair-head,
something dense and firm and living blocked her way. Her scream
of terror was strangled at its beginning. A heavy determined hand
came over her mouth.

## Chapter Twenty-Four
## LADYBIRD, LADYBIRD!

Jeanie had often read, with the mind that accepts and does not
ponder, the oft-used expression "to be paralysed with fright." She
knew now what it meant. Fright did paralyse one, at first. Then,
when the paralysis had died off, how wild, how ill-directed, how
full of panic became one's movements as one plunged and
struggled, trying vainly to make up for that lost moment! Jeanie's
struggles had availed her nothing. Her assailant had been far
stronger than she, and had had the advantage of knowing exactly
what he intended to do, while she was at the disadvantage of not
knowing what plan she was resisting. In a very short space of time
Jeanie had found herself back in her bedroom, and alone again:
but securely bound hand and foot with strong bands of some soft
material that not only tied her hands together but, passing round
her waist, prevented her from even lifting them, and gagged with a
wedge of cloth, securely tied in place, that hurt her tongue and
made it difficult to swallow and added to her general terror the
particular terror that she might suffocate. Lying on the cold
slippery boards of her bedroom floor, in darkness, helplessness
and enforced horrible silence, Jeanie heard her assailant's
stockinged feet going, carelessly now, down the stairs again.

A being larger than life, relentless, silent, animated by some
purpose that was as yet unknown, evil, skilful, resourceful, above

all, strong. For the rest, Jeanie had become aware of a woollen shirt and breeches of some smooth material, of a powerful forearm that seemed hard as iron under the touch of her wildly resisting hand, of a faint smell of paraffin, and of a determined, formidable silence. Not a sound, not a gasp nor a grunt had come from the intruder. No effort had been needed on his part to overcome poor, limp terrified Jeanie.

It was the gag that Jeanie could not endure. To be bound hand and foot was just endurable, but to feel that pressure upon one's throat, that cruel constriction upon one's mouth, to feel one's spirit vocal with cries for help, with cries of pain and fear, and to be unable to utter a sound—that was torture! Jeanie struggled to burst her hands out of the ties that held them, so that her hands could help her mouth. She could not move them one inch. The notion came to her that if she could propel herself across the slippery floor she might find some rough edge, some semi-cutting edge on some piece of furniture against which she could rub her bound hands until the bandage wore through and freed her. She reviewed mentally all the furnishings in her bedroom. There was no such edge.

She had better not agitate herself by any useless movements, but make up her mind to wait, to endure the long night until help came in the morning. She could endure. Her gag was painful, but it would not really suffocate her. Her throat could endure the pain. Her arms and ankles were constricted, but they could endure. Better stay as quietly as might be and count the hours away by Handleston church clock.

The intruder had not harmed her. Evidently, it was not to harm her that he had broken into her cottage. He wanted her out of the way while he got through his business, whatever it might be: but he did not mean to injure her, still less, as she had wildly at first surmised, to kill her.

Perhaps, after all, it was a chance thief, a burglar. Perhaps the news of Jeanie's finding of that half-row of pearls had gone the round of the village, and somebody had conceived the idea of searching for the rest of the string.

Whoever it was, was moving about below with less discretion now, dragging things about, making those rustling noises she had heard before, padding heavily in stockinged feet from parlour to hall and back again He was conducting a very thorough search. But if for the pearls, why in the parlour? The half-string of pearls had been found in the cupboard under the stairs, among the empty bottles and disused andirons and old fittings which Jeanie had removed. Perhaps it was not for pearls the intruder was searching. Perhaps it was for something else. Perhaps there was hidden treasure in the cottage, and someone knew of it.

From below came a little scraping sound, the sound of a match being struck. Jeanie imagined the tall unknown standing below, dark, undelineated, vague, with immense forearms of iron, holding a match to a cigarette, blowing out a little stream of smoke, shaking the match dead. A quite disproportionate resentment and rage surged up in her. How could he, how dared he calmly light a cigarette while she lay here in such undeserved, unnecessary pain and discomfort?

Footsteps padded off. Little rustling crackling noises came next to her strained ears, noises she strove vainly to put a name to. What could be going on down there in the parlour? A faint yet pungent smell had arrived in Jeanie's bedroom through the fireplace or from between the floor-boards. Smoke. Smoke. Something—paper or something—had caught fire. The damned careless fool downstairs had dropped his match, still alight, on paper, and the paper was catching fire while he went off and searched about in the hall. A nice thing if Jeanie's house was to be burnt down while she lay helpless and he prosecuted his illegal search!

This was a furious mental figure of speech. Jeanie did not really believe that her house would be burnt down. The searcher would of course come back and put the fire out as soon as he smelt smoke.

Well, surely the man could smell it now! He could not be far away. Jeanie could hear him, in fact, moving in the passage. The smell was getting more pungent every second. Jeanie drummed with her heels violently on the floor to attract the searcher's attention.

But suddenly she lay still. She recognised the smell of burning paraffin, and the fusty, heavy smell of burning straw. Now what an innocent figure seemed that imagined searcher after treasure! Now Jeanie would have welcomed him, visualising him as a friend and preserver! But he did not exist. There was no searcher after treasure below in the darkness of her house, but a murderer. Robert Molyneux's murderer. Her murderer. Her house was on fire, and the man who had lit the fire would not put the fire out. Nobody would put the fire out in time to save Jeanie.

Chapter Twenty-Five
DEATH IN THE OFFING

There was a sort of ghostly faint radiance outside the window. It was the radiance of fallen snow, snow on the roof reflecting whatever little light there was in the moonless sky. Gazing upwards through the lead-diamonded windows, Jeanie could see the white line of the projecting gable covered with snow. She could see in the dark now, like a cat. All her frightened being seemed living in her senses. In her ears, that strained after every crackling, every rustling, in her nose, which breathed continuously now the oily scent of paraffin and the acrid one of burning straw, so that images kept flitting behind her throbbing eyes of the bonfires she had lit in the garden to burn packing-cases when she first arrived at Yew Tree; in her eyes which stared out upon that snow and remembered last winter in Switzerland and the red glow of the sunset upon the glittering snow-fields. Why at such a moment should she think of that red glow upon the slopes of the Matterhorn? Was it because all her senses combined to tell her that soon there would be a red glow upon these snowy Gloucestershire fields? She thought: But he can't mean to leave me here!

But of course he could. But of course he did. But of course he would. He intended to leave her here in the burning house. He intended her death. He was wiping her out of his way as remorselessly as he had wiped Molyneux—more remorselessly, since murder, like other activities, grows easier with practice. He was watching not far away from her, the creeping and leaping of the flames that were to be her cremation-fires. Perhaps he had gagged her so tightly, not to prevent others hearing but to spare his own guilty ears her outcries. Silent, he might, if his heart misgave him, imagine her already dead.

But why the fire? Why could not Molyneux's murderer quiet her, as he had quieted Molyneux, with a bullet through the brain? What! A second bullet? A second obvious murder? No! Somebody had more sense than that. Somebody was staging an accident with Jeanie's parlour fire. *This old wood, it is like iron in some ways, but it will not stand constant heat. It dries and dries and dries. And one night it starts to smoulder and to smoke. And there is another old house burnt to the ground.* Somebody had said that to Jeanie not long ago. And somebody—several people, probably—would say something like it again at the inquest on her. And the verdict would be accidental death. And the coroner would issue a sapient warning against the danger of coal grates in old timber-built houses. And nobody would ever know that she had been murdered. And nobody would ever know who had murdered Molyneux.

Jeanie writhed upon the floor and dragged at her wrists until it seemed that the stuff that bound them must have cut its way to the burning bones: it was no use. Silently, as in a nightmare, she screamed against the cloth around her face. Her chest seemed bursting, her eyes seemed starting, hot and pulsing, from their sockets. A red cloud seemed to expand and shrink, expand and shrink, before her eyes in time to the thumping of her heart. No writhing of her neck, no twisting of her head against the boards of the floor, would loosen that cruel gag in her mouth.

"Oh help! Oh help!" cried Jeanie, but silently. Her hands plucked at her bonds, her feet ran down the stairs, but all in fancy. She could not stir nor whisper.

There was a crash in the room below. Foolish piercing hope sprang up in Jeanie's heart, stilling her breath to listen. Somebody had arrived to help her. There was another less noisy crash, a busy crackle, a happy rush of rustling sound. No. Nobody had come to help her. Those were the first of many crashes and smashes. Crash! fell the mantelshelf and smash! its ornaments as the flames swept up and burnt away the woodwork. Crash! went the metal tea-things to the floor as the table-legs swept off in a shower of fire, buckled in a heap of cinder. Crash! and smash! would soon go the plaster upon the ceiling below and the plaster on the walls, and the pictures and the screen. Crash the heavy bedroom furniture through the floor as the flames swept upwards to the timber-work of the roof. Then smash and tinkle a few loose tiles and out, flames, to the sky, free, joyful, beautiful, dancing and bowing, rushing up and sinking down, element to element, fire to wind, higher, higher, growing by what they fed on, cracking, exploding, roaring, under the frosty heavens!

Already the skin of Jeanie's face seemed to feel the blistering flames. It burnt. It seemed like bursting, it was so hot with fear and the constriction of the gag. All her blood seemed in her skin.

She lay quite still, suddenly calm, in a sort of unreality of existence, assuring herself that nothing of all this was really happening, that she was dreaming, that all the time, really, she was safe. Such things as these—flames, destruction, hatred, violent death—did not, could not happen to people like her.

"Oh but they did, they could! Molyneux, that harmless, kindly, modest man had been murdered in his safe orchard as Jeanie was being murdered in her safe cottage. Suddenly, with a rush like an enveloping flame in a draught, terror came back to Jeanie. She writhed, she silently shrieked. The heat left her skin, her heart hammered as if it must soon break and fail, her face felt suddenly cold as if a ghost had breathed on it and a wetness that was not of hot sweat but of cold tears ran into her eyes.

There was a crash below. And suddenly there was a dancing in the corner of the room towards which her eyes were staring. A dancing in the shadows, a flickering, a light-hearted soft motion of light on darkness. She could see, fitfully and vaguely now, the leg of her bed and the white coverlet, the gleam of the polished floor. Straining her head back to look over her shoulder, she saw a flame come through the floor at the corner-post, fall back, rise again. That dancing in her darkness was the reflection of those rising flames. The light of the flames danced silently and gaily like fairies upon the walls and floor. But the flames themselves hissed cruelly as they rose. It was foolish to struggle, yet impossible not to struggle. She could see the whole room now, in occasional fitful views. The room with its dark gleaming woodwork and pale bed-clothes rose round her, fell into darkness again, rose round her again. The flames embraced the great corner-post. It was hard, hard with centuries, but it could not resist the flames for long. They hissed continually now, and the air was warm.

All the warm night was full of roaring sound. Roaring, purring sound. What was that screech? a terrified owl, a cat? One screech, no more. And the night was of a roaring, purring, throbbing sound that did not keep time with Jeanie's heart. Not a motor-car. Better not think of motor-cars, and rescuers and life. Better not. That sudden sound was not really the slam of a metal door. This other sound was not really made by feet running up the brick path. The smashing of windows—it was the fire which caused that! A smashed-in window made the same sound, whether smashed by falling timbers or by a man's hand. But voices! Human voices! Strange, lovely and terrifying sound of human voices!

The flames hissed so steadily now in the corner of the room that all Jeanie's strained agonised focusing upon that raucous shouting brought no sense to her ears. Were they stopping to argue, while she lay here in such peril? One raised voice, a man's voice with a queer, loose, hysterical quality, shouted something unintelligible. Another voice, harder and better controlled, replied. There was a scuffle. A crash. A clatter of ironwork on stone.

Silence. Oh God! Silence but for the sound of the fire, the crackling and the hissing. Only a moment's silence. Then footsteps on the stairs. Light, running footsteps taking the stairs two at a time.

"Here! Here!" Jeanie imagined herself shouting. Her head nearly burst with the effort. It would burst soon, did not this gag come off, could not she roll away, somehow, from this fearful, increasing heat. It would swell and swell and burst the gag, and then it would burst itself.

The room sank and rose, sank and rose. As it rose, there rose with it, standing in the doorway, startled, pale, transfixed, wearing a fur-lined overcoat and a scarf hardly whiter than his face, the figure of Eustace Agatos.

## Chapter Twenty-Six

## WARM WINTER'S NIGHT

It was not Eustace Agatos that Jeanie saw. For Eustace Agatos was mortal, a mere man. It was humanity itself that Jeanie saw, the rescuer, a demi-god, a creature larger than life, endowed with all possible human strength and radiance.

Yet when, to the accompaniment of a great many ejaculations and curses over fumbling fingers and a blunt penknife, the demi-god had cut and removed the bonds around Jeanie's ankles and wrists and mouth, and Jeanie had staggered to her feet, all she could find to say with her swollen tongue and tortured throat was:

"You don't need a fur overcoat in this heat..."

The words came out only a hoarse whisper. She giggled feebly. She had a sort of hazy idea that she had said something rather witty. But giggling made her throat hurt.

"Eh?" said Agatos. "Come along. Now come along. Come along quickly. Come along."

All right. Jeanie was coming along. There was no hurry. She was free. Now that her limbs were free she was all right. She could do anything. Get out of the window if necessary. Drop over the well of the stairs. Anything. Come along indeed! A person had to know what it was to be tied up and helpless before he could realise what it meant to have the use of his limbs!

"Now *do* come along! The staircase will be gone in a moment. Come along!"

It was hot. It was terribly, dangerously hot.

"All right, I *am* coming," weakly whispered Jeanie, clinging to the banisters. Good Lord, it was hot! She was in a bath of sweat! "Only my legs are stiff or something."

Stiff! As she spoke they collapsed like boiled bits of macaroni, and half supported by the swearing Agatos, half a willing victim to the force of gravity, Jeanie slithered somehow or other down the stairs.

Downstairs was full of smoke. It got in her eyes, in her throat, it half suffocated her. Agatos cursed and fumbled violently with the chain and bolt she had so thoroughly fastened. With streaming eyes, coughing, supporting herself on the newel-post, Jeanie saw through the open doorway the furnace that was her parlour. Her ears seemed stunned with the roar of the flames. Even out here in the passage the paint was blistering on the panels. Her own skin felt like that, blistering and peeling.

"Hurry up! Do hurry up! It's hot! I can't breathe!"

"Where then is the blasted bolt?"

"Let me!"

With the opening of the door it seemed to Jeanie that the fire whooped joyfully behind her and flung a great arm through the parlour doorway. She did not turn back until her feet were on the beautiful, cold, snowy grass. Then a crash which sounded as though the roof had fallen in made her turn. The roof had not fallen in. But flames were coming through the window of her bedroom. The snow was all melted on the gable-edge. There was light all round, and where there had been night and darkness were strange colours that Jeanie had never seen before. The damson brick of the chimney gleamed a lurid orange m the flames, the yew-tree had flickered out of its night blackness to a brilliant green it never wore by daylight. But oh, its friendly tassels that overhung the roof were black, black and shrivelled and smoking. The tiny crackling of its oily leaflets Jeanie thought she could hear above all the other din.

"Oh, oh, my poor little cottage!" cried Jeanie, with a sudden rush of tears. The tears, washing out smoke and smart and terror, were so consoling that she made no attempt to check them, but stood there in the snow, bare-footed and quite unaware that snow was cold, encouraging her tears by gazing at the ruins of her home. Petronella, indifferent to human sorrow, purred round her ankles.

"That was the joists of the first floor falling down," observed Mr. Agatos beside her. With some satisfaction he added: "It was a good thing you came along when you did. I think there is no staircase now."

His white fleshy face was glistening with sweat and streaked with black dirt, but he looked to Jeanie like an angelic being.

"You had better have my overcoat!"

Jeanie glanced down at her torn dressing-gown, her dirty night-dress, her blackened feet.

"Well, perhaps I'd better. How did you get here?" He guided her arms into the sleeves of his coat and carefully, like a nursemaid, buttoned it across her chest.

"I was on my way home from a house I had been looking at in Somersetshire. I saw the windows lit up with a light that flickered and flickered and did not stay still. I looked in the front window, but the room was all ablaze. I ran round the house and smashed the window of the back room. My good God!" uttered Agatos, breaking off sharply and staring at Jeanie, his hand still on a button-hole, as if something had momentarily stunned his faculties. His mouth was open. His sparse black hair had ceased to mitigate the nakedness of his scalp and stood fluffed on end like a perianth around the disc of his face. "My good God!" he cried again with extreme vehemence, starting away from Jeanie towards the burning cottage and starting back again as the heat drove him off. "That man! That man! Did he get out? My God, I had forgotten him! My God, I should have looked for him!"

"What man? Didn't he get out? What happened? You can't do anything now!"

"If he is still in there, he is a dead man! Oh, but then I have killed him! I heard an iron clattering sound when I pushed him

212 | LET HIM LIE

over! I heard that crash and I heard no more, and I straightway forgot him as I ran upstairs. Suppose he was stunned when I pushed him back into the cupboard under the stairs? I think he fell upon those andirons that are there! If so, he is dead now, that is certain!"

"What happened?"

"I put my hand on his chest and pushed him out of my way. And he staggered back, he lost his balance and fell. I was surprised. And glad too, I can tell you," added Agatos with a pale smile, "because he was much bigger than me, and I did not really see how I was going to get past him."

A question formed itself on Jeanie's lips. She was strangely unwilling to ask it. She knew the answer.

"He was mad, too," pursued Agatos. "Come along, I think we had better go round to my car while we can still get round. This place will soon be too hot to be comfortable. Also you cannot stand about in the snow in bare feet."

"Oh, I can't bear to see the trees all scorched!" uttered Jeanie hoarsely. "I suppose—I suppose the man was—"

"He was mad. He said there was plenty of room in Grim's Grave for everybody!"

"Grim's Grave!"

"Yes. Now come along, my dear, I think I hear a car arriving."

"Grim's Grave!" repeated Jeanie. She had to stand still and think. "Then it *was* because of Grim's Grave that Molyneux was murdered!"

"And I said there is also plenty of room in that cupboard, and in you go! and I pushed him very hard, but I was very surprised and very glad too when in he did go. Ah, there is a car and somebody on a bicycle! We shall soon have all Handleston here! And here comes the fire-engine! Come along, or they will not know you are safe and will be trying to rescue you!"

Jeanie, however, stood still for a moment longer.

"Of course," she muttered to herself with a swollen throat. "It was Barchard…"

"Yes, that was the man, and he is a dangerous lunatic, and now, my dear, do not stand there but come with me."

"And of course the pearls—*she* was in the cupboard! He killed her and put her in the cupboard while he dug her grave."

"*She?*"

"Valentine."

"What are you talking about? Do you know that lady with the bicycle? You had better let her look after you!"

"And now Valentine is in Grim's Grave."

"Are you all right?" asked Mr. Agatos anxiously. "Look, this lady will look after you. I will see to everything. You must get quickly somewhere to bed."

"No, I feel awful," croaked Jeanie. "I'm not all right at all. I—"

"Oh, Miss Halliday, what a dreadful tragedy!" It was Marjorie Dasent speaking: Marjorie Dasent, looking more like a policewoman than ever in her hastily donned blue felt hat and navy overcoat. "I saw the glow from my bedroom window and I came over to see if I could help. Shall I take you over to Cleedons?"

"Barchard!" repeated Jeanie. "It was because he'd murdered Valentine and she was in Grim's Grave! I ought to have guessed! I always did think that story about Hubert Southey couldn't be true! And to think I *liked* Barchard!"

Miss Dasent exchanged with Eustace Agatos such a look as a nurse might give a doctor over the patient's head.

"Let *me* look after her, shall I, Mr.—er—"

"I think," croaked Jeanie, "I'm going to be sick."

Mr. Agatos readily relinquished his charge.

## Chapter Twenty-Seven

## LET HIM LIE

"It was when I saw that white hen," said Jeanie.

She and Peter were leaning against the gate into Cole Harbour meadow, enjoying the still beauty of a golden autumn day in which fear had receded over the horizon and left them both at peace. Idly they watched the comings and goings of two or three labourers who, under the directions of a Home Office archaeologist from Gloucester, were engaged in filling in upon Grim's Grave what the archaeologist insisted on describing as "a secondary interment." Mr. Fone was already there, among the trees, making quite certain that the grave of Miss Vera Drake, alias Valentine Frazer, was duly filled in and grassed over. The Handleston Field Club, not particularly interested in the secondary interment, had hoped to take the obvious opportunity of having a Home Office expert on the scene to investigate the primary burial also, and had made strong representations to Agnes on the subject. They were too late. Even Sir Henry Blundell could do nothing, although Agnes almost wept at having to refuse him. Mr. Fone, it appeared, had offered, two days ago, to buy Cole Harbour meadow from Agnes as soon as the probate of Molyneux's will was through, and had not flinched at her tentative attempt to make him pay dearly for it. Much as she would have liked to please Sir Henry, the advancing shadow of death duties made Agnes realise the necessity of pleasing Mr. Fone. The tumulus was to remain unopened for Mr. Fone's lifetime, anyway. Grim could sleep in peace.

"What white hen? When?"

"When we were on the roof of Mr. Fone's library, the day before yesterday, supposed to be looking for Ancient British trackways. You know the big barn at Cleedons? Well, the doors were open at both sides. You know how those big barns have great high doors in each side, opposite one another, so that a horse and wagon can go through?"

"Yes."

"Well, the big doors were open at both sides, and a wagon loaded with bracken was inside the barn, just as it was the day Mr. Molyneux was killed. And it unloaded its bracken and went off again towards the common. And there were the great barn-doors open, and you could see through them to the orchard. And there was a white hen pecking in the grass."

"I heard you say something about a white hen before you passed out. It seemed to me an odd thing to go all queer over. Nice innocent little Leghorn, there's lots of them about in the yards at Cleedons."

"I know, but this one wasn't in the yard. It was in the orchard. And it reminded me of Sarah's white kitten. The day before Molyneux died, Sarah found her white kitten, the one she was keeping for me, shot dead in the orchard. Nobody bothers much about kittens when they die. Nobody holds inquests on them or tries to find out who killed them. If they had, perhaps Molyneux might have been saved. Because when I saw that white hen, I saw at once that the man who shot Molyneux was the same man who had shot the kitten. And that he'd shot both of them from behind the balustrade of Mr. Fone's library roof. Those barn-doors aren't often open like that—only when hay or litter is being brought in. One doesn't realise how wide and high they are, how plainly one sees the orchard through them. Nor how the ground rises from Cole Harbour to Cleedons, and then is nearly level behind those barns. It wouldn't occur to one, till one saw those doors open, how easy it would be to aim through them. I felt, when I saw that white hen scratching away in the green grass, that if I'd had a gun in my hands I could almost have shot it myself. And there was the white hen, only now it had turned into a white kitten, a poor little white kitten, a wonderful target for a practice shot. And there was the tree Molyneux had been pruning. And I remembered that Barchard had been laying leads on the library roof of Cole Harbour. I remembered the ladder up against the wall, and how anybody might have climbed up there. I felt awful. I thought, it must have been Barchard... Only then I looked at him, and he spoke to me, and it seemed *impossible*. I couldn't see why he should have done such a thing."

Her voice trembled absurdly. She did not enjoy the recollection of that moment of the roof of Cole Harbour.

"Poor Jeanie," said Peter sympathetically, covering her hand with his. He added thoughtfully: "But you were always so keen on the shot having come from the other side of the orchard, from the north-west. What about Mr. Fone's evidence? Was he mistaken when he said Molyneux swung towards the right and turned his face towards Cleedons just before he was killed? I suppose he must have been."

"Not exactly. Molyneux did swing round, but it was after he was killed, not before."

"But Mr. Fone heard the shot."

"Yes. So did we hear the thud of the man cutting down trees in Cole Harbour Wood, if you remember. And the thud seemed to come after the stroke of the axe. Light travels faster than sound. You said so. Don't you remember?"

"Lord, yes!"

"Well, Mr. Fone sat at the window in Black Ellen's Tower watching Molyneux, and willing him to reconsider his plan of opening Grim's Grave. And—how did Mr. Fone put it? Molyneux turned his head in response to this willing. There was a sharp crack, and Molyneux fell to the ground. The inference was that at the moment he was shot, at the moment Mr. Fone heard the crack,

Molyneux was facing east of north, practically towards the Tower, and therefore, since he was shot in the left temple, the shot must have come approximately from the north-west, where the lambing-shed is. But suppose it *wasn't* in response to Mr. Fone's willing that Molyneux turned his head? Suppose it was in response to the impact of the shot? Suppose it was a man already dead who swung round to the right just before every muscle relaxed and he fell out of the tree? The crack of the shot came late to Mr. Fone's ears, you see. And when poor Molyneux was shot, he was actually still facing west, with the back of his head to Black Ellen's Tower. And the shot that killed him came from the south—from the roof of Cole Harbour library."

Jeanie's throat was still tender, and this speech made her voice sink quite hoarsely.

"That balustrade with the flat leads behind makes a perfect screen. You would just creep up there and lie flat on the roof with your rifle pointing between the balusters, and there you would be practically invisible... Oh, but how fearful!" cried Jeanie, "that poor Molyneux should have to die to keep Barchard's sordid secret—not caring, not knowing about it, even, like a—a beetle that gets in the way of a wheel! It seems too horrible, *too* wasteful and silly for words! Couldn't Barchard have moved his wretched Valentine somewhere else? He moved her to Grim's Grave from Yew Tree Cottage in a hurry two years ago. Why couldn't he have moved her out of Grim's Grave again when Molyneux started to talk of opening it?"

"Two years ago, when the—secondary interment was made, the whole tumulus was grown over with saplings, you know. Nobody would have noticed what Barchard or anybody did there. But since Molyneux had those trees cut down you can't even stroll up it without making yourself conspicuous to every passer-by. And since the trees were cut down there've been many more visitors to

Grim's Grave. I don't think he could have risked digging about in it without being found out. And with the official opening of the tumulus looming up in the near future, the man was in a nasty hole."

"Do you think he was mad, Peter?"

"He always seemed sane enough to me. But I should think companionship with William Fone might be rather too strong meat for a man like Barchard to feed on. When it comes to following one's impulses and taking one's instincts as one's guides, and all the rest of the Fone philosophy, what's sauce for the goose isn't sauce for the gander, to put it vulgarly. William Fone's impulses are one thing, and the impulses of a bloke like Barchard quite another! Barchard must have had a nasty moment when you told him about those pearls Agatos found in your cupboard."

"Yes, indeed," said Jeanie. "He hadn't known, you know, that the pearls were genuine. He thought they were an artificial string, the kind of thing anybody might lose without worrying over. I'm sure he knew nothing whatever of Valentine Frazer's connection with Agnes. It would have seemed to him so much more likely that Southey should give Valentine trinkets than that Agnes should. Valentine made her first great mistake when she took that zircon brooch of Agnes's to be real diamonds and told Barchard that Southey had given it her. I suppose she didn't want him to know about Agnes, for fear he'd kill the goose that laid the golden eggs. But she must have been a bit of an ass to risk making a man like Barchard jealous."

"Perhaps she enjoyed risks."

"Perhaps she did, poor creature. But it meant that when she got tired of living in Handleston and wanted to go back to her life in London, Barchard could only think that she and Southey were lovers and that she wanted to follow him. He told me that she'd gone up to London to be an artist's model, and that he'd never believed the village gossip about her and Southey. He was very calm and reasonable about her departure. *Too* calm and reasonable, I see now. It wasn't natural, the unembarrassed cool way he talked about her and Southey. But at the time it took me in. I liked him all the more for being so civilised and reasonable and not being influenced by vulgar talk. Good Heavens, Peter! There I sat in that little parlour with a man who'd done two murders, thinking what a civilised agreeable man he was! And to think what his real feelings must have been about my questions, and about me!"

"He didn't keep them a secret for long, did he?" said Peter grimly. "Oh Jeanie, it makes me feel quite sick with horror when I think of how I let you go home alone that day! Suppose you'd died! What should I have been thinking now?"

His voice trembled. Jeanie returned the hard squeeze of his fingers.

"You'd have been thinking, like everyone else, what an ass I was to tinker with an old fire-place," she essayed light-heartedly. "Do you know, Peter, I believe Mr. Agatos is going to make an offer for my poor little ruin? He rather prefers old cottages burnt down, I believe. It saves him trouble in alterations, and he gets them cheap. I don't believe the idea's ever been out of his head that he'd tempt me out of Yew Tree Cottage sooner or later. In fact, he was responsible for terrifying me out of my life on that awful evening by creeping into my garden and taking the measurements of the kitchen wall to see, he calmly confesses, if there would be room for a garage as well as a study!"

"Infernal cheek!"

"He was just off to look at a cottage in Somerset, if you please, and wanted the measurements for purposes of comparison. Well, I can't really complain of anything Eustace Agatos does or ever did. He saved my life."

There was a little tremor in her voice, and the two of them remained silent a moment.

"Shall we go and see if they've finished ironing out the creases on Mr. Grim's Grave?" suggested Jeanie.

"Old Fone certainly won't let them go until they have! Well he's had his way and averted the curse of the old gods. Though I don't know what could have happened if the grave had been opened much worse than what *has* happened, without opening it! I think old Fone's instincts have played him false for once."

They strolled side by side over the browning grass of the autumn meadow.

"I don't know, Peter. It was talking about opening the mound that made all this happen, didn't it? Well, Mr. Fone might say, if just talking about it caused all this horror, what might not have happened if the matter had gone beyond talking?"

Peter smiled.

"He might say so, certainly. And no doubt he will say so, and a lot more beside. Did I tell you he's invited me to take Barchard's place for a year or two at a very handsome salary?"

"Are you going to?"

Peter hesitated.

"I don't fancy it. I like Fone, but—well, I have a feeling that this place isn't fortunate for me. Sounds silly, I know, but why should Mr. Fone be the only one to go in for impulses and intuitions?"

"I feel just the same. This place isn't fortunate for me, either," said Jeanie, thinking sadly of Agnes, whom she had not seen once since the burning of Yew Tree Cottage. Agnes had her own troubles to reflect on: how should she spare sympathy for Jeanie? If the news of her sister's death had not distressed her, no doubt she found its circumstances distressing enough. The prodigal sister, exhumed two nights ago from her resting-place on the top of Grim's Grave, was having her last, unpremeditated fling at the respectable one. And Agnes was keeping to her room, thinking out, no doubt, the best attitude to take up at Monday's inquest on the remains of Vera Drake, known as Valentine Frazer. Jeanie was sure it would be a graceful attitude. Agnes would not need Jeanie to help her to sustain it.

"I feel just the same, Peter. One can't paint in the country, anyhow. There are too many distractions. I'm going back to London to look for a studio."

"And I'm going back to look for a job, then. When shall we go?"

"As soon as all these inquests are over. Oh Peter, do you realise there are going to be *three* inquests?"

"I do."

They walked up the sloping, rabbit-mined side of the great tumulus. The chill sun of an October afternoon shone red upon the boles of the tall pines, and below in the fields to the south mists were rising as once they had risen over the swampy forests when the tumulus was first raised.

"But no inquest on Mr. Grim," said Peter. "Mr. Grim lies undisturbed."

"Let him lie. I sympathise with Mr. Fone. I used not to, but I do now. There's been too much death and digging and inquests. The thought of digging up Mr. Grim makes me feel quite—quite—"

"It may sound egotistic," said Peter, smiling, "but it makes *me* feel very glad that we're alive."

Jeanie considered a moment.

"Yes, that's what I really meant, Peter. Let's leave Mr. Grim's bones to Mr. Grim, and think about studios, and jobs, and London, and being alive."


THE END

Printed in Great Britain
by Amazon